The Wilson Chronicles

Book 2:

Lightspeed!

Glenn Jackson

Published by:
Light Switch Press
PO Box 272847
Fort Collins, CO 80527

Copyright © 2019 Glenn Jackson
ISBN: 978-1-949563-34-4
Printed in the United States of America

No part of this publication may be reproduced, stored in a retrieval system, or transmitted in any form or by any means – electronic, mechanical, digital photocopy, recording, or any other without the prior permission of the author.

All rights reserved solely by the author. The author guarantees all contents are original and do not infringe upon the legal rights of any other person or work. The views expressed in this book are not necessarily those of the publisher.

Lightspeed!, is a work of fiction. Names, characters, places, and incidents are the products of the author's imagination or are used fictitiously. Any resemblance to actual events, locales, or persons, living or dead, is entirely coincidental.

By Glenn Jackson

A Novel

*The Wilson Chronicles:
Book 1. Unlimited Possibility*

The Siege at Azulon

Leadership Development:

*Growing Leadership, Managing Developmental Chaos
Principled Leadership, A Balancing Act for a Lifetime*

Political Perspective:

Surviving the Radicalization of America

Dedication
To all those who dream of possibilities.

Lightspeed!

4.172.10

The smell. It crawled into your pores. It reeked. Human sweat and piss, mixed with fragrances from scented candles and cooking food. Outside it may be summer, but inside, it was overpowering, dark and damp, life lived in a cave.

Nineteen people gathered in one room in the cave, a small, medieval looking chapel carved out of solid rock. The chapel was illuminated with candles burning in various candelabras, nooks and stands, casting an eerie flickering glow over the alter and hidden faces. Shadows, noises, quiet chanting; it filled the cave, adding to the tension in the room. Eighteen were dressed in dark crimson robes, but there was one dressed in black; Riser, their master. He was adamant they had to stop the usurpers of God from spreading humans to other planets.

"If God intended for humans to live anyplace except this Earth He created, He would have created life on those planets! We have no business trying to alter God's plan! We must stop them. If we do not, God will punish us all with hell and the lake of fire!"

His eyes burned red with anger. He was a powerful voice and dynamic personality. He overwhelmed his servants.

"Humans are meant to be on Earth. Here we must stay until God takes us to Himself. He will decide if we are to live on other planets, not arrogant humans. We must do all that we can to protect humanity from the wrath of God!"

The Servants of Riser, nine men and nine women, were eager to please their Master. Their eyes burned with the passion and zealotry of hate. They would do anything for Riser, even worship the Devil.

"Now go, each of you, to your appointed place. The time is coming, very soon, when we will show these humans how powerful God truly is!"

"Yes, Master!"

The Servants of Riser made their way out of the chapel and down narrow carved tunnels to their rooms, where they changed clothes and departed for their destinations. Riser stood a while longer in the chapel. He had a smile of death for the people that must die in those migration pods; but knew they would be getting what they deserved for their insolent act and defiance of God's plan.

4.173.18

At nearly the same time, Erica was briefing the Federation Council.

"The first three pods are getting close to launch readiness. We will finish construction soon, then move the occupants into their pods to allow them to acclimatize for several months before we send them on their way. The second three will be completed about six months later, and the remaining three will be ready roughly six months after that. In all, we should have all nine pods launched within about two years."

"Simultaneously, we leveraged some of the technology we've learned in the pod construction process for building the asteroid protection system. As you know, we completed the detection system last year, but had not finished the destruction system. Due to some technical knowledge we gained in the pod building process - we learned how to move objects with a tractor beam - we can now reach out and grab an asteroid and move it into a trajectory that drops it into the sun, so it will never come back a second time. This will eliminate threats long-term."

Jeffrey smiled as he watched Erica. He knew he had picked the best person possible for this job. He'd watched her grow over the past four years as his assistant. She demonstrated superb competence in every task, behavior, and leadership characteristic. She was awesome. He watched as she briefed the Federation Council on the progress of their two biggest projects, which had become so intertwined, he had put both of them under her. He was very proud of her. She demonstrated the best of humanity and superb, impactful leadership.

"Because of this progress, I am happy to report that at four point one seventy-three point one eight yesterday, the asteroid protection system became fully operational and is now online to protect us from these threats."

A cheer went up from the assembled council, as they were very happy to learn the asteroid protection system was operational. They congratulated Erica on a job well done. The Russian council member wanted the public to know. "We need to hold a press conference and let the world know we have achieved this goal."

Everyone agreed, and Erica turned to Jeffrey, the Council President, for guidance.

"I agree. Would it be acceptable to the council if we hold a press conference this afternoon here at the Federation to inform the world of this success?"

Everyone agreed with his proposal.

"Very well, Erica, please coordinate a press conference for this afternoon and prepare the talking points for the briefing."

After the meeting adjourned, Jeffrey and Erica left and went back to his office.

"You know, you do a pretty good job for a thirty-one-year-old."

"Thank you, but I do sometimes think you may be giving me more than I can handle."

"Oh really? Can you give me even one example of any task I have given you where you did not completely excel?"

Erica smiled, knowing she had a great boss and mentor. "No, I can't, but that doesn't mean you should keep giving me everything."

"Oh, my dear, if I gave you everything you would have my job."

Erica laughed, knowing she did not want to take on his job. It wasn't so much the work, it was all the conversations he had to have with different national leaders and cultures, trying to get them to all lean in the same direction together, and the decisions he made to move everything forward together. She saw it and knew how hard it was.

"No, you are right. I don't want your job."

Jeffrey smiled, knowing he would eventually do exactly that, give her his job. That was why he kept increasing her involvement in real decision making and operational projects. In a few years it would be time. By then she would be ready. The next task was to have her begin to do even more of the talking with various people he normally dealt with and build a public persona.

"Okay, I'll take it easy on you for now."

Erica completed the talking points and brought them into Jeffrey's office for him to review. He surprised her yet again.

"These are very good. Now remember, the rules are, first, never pass up a chance to keep your mouth shut, and second, always stick to your talking points. If you do that you will be fine."

Erica looked at him wondering what he was talking about. "Why are you telling me this?"

"Because you are doing this press conference."

"What? I have never done a press conference."

Jeffrey smiled. "I know, but after today, you will not be able to say that again. Don't worry, I will be there with you."

At three o'clock, they walked into the press room for the Federation. Jeffrey went to the podium to address the gathered reporters.

"Good afternoon. I'm Jeffrey Wilson, President of the Federation Council and JW Enterprises. The Federation, through the investment of JW Enterprises, has an announcement of significance for the entire human race. I would like to introduce Erica Beckett, the Project Manager for this activity, to provide the briefing."

Erica was very nervous. Her palms sweat, and she knew she was going to flub this. Even so, she had no choice but do it. She took a deep breath and walked up to the podium.

"Thank you, Mr. President. Good afternoon everyone. As you know, we have been working to eliminate the three legs of President Wilson's vision for saving our species, which includes sending out migration pods, discovering faster than lightspeed travel, and protecting us from potential asteroid collisions."

"Today, we are pleased to announce that the asteroid protection system we have been working on for the past several years is fully operational. This means that from this day forward, we, the people of Earth, never have to worry about an asteroid destroying our species. This is the first achievement of our journey to protect our species."

A sense of excitement and wonder filled the room, and several people began talking, trying to ask questions, but she waved them off, saying, "Hold on a moment, then we will have questions."

"In addition to the asteroid protection, we are well underway with the migration pods and will soon be able to launch them fulfilling the second step. We are also investing significant resources researching faster than lightspeed travel, although we don't have an estimate on how long it may take to accomplish this task."

"Again, we have succeeded in accomplishing the elimination of an asteroid event. I will now take your questions."

"Charles Tompkins, Atlanta Constitution; So, you are telling us that we no longer have to worry about an asteroid hitting the Earth. What assurances do we have that this technology will always work and not fail at a critical time?"

"There are two processes occurring simultaneously. First, we are transferring the entire asteroid defense shield over to a consortium of national space agencies who have worked with us since the beginning, for their constant management. This consortium installed the most advanced but proven technology available. Second, they have also established a continuous evaluation and improvement process that will constantly test and evaluate this system. The plan is to update this system as new technology is proven. In short, everything is being done to ensure this system is available at all times."

The questions centered around this critical issue, until one reporter decided to ask a question from an entirely unexpected perspective.

"Sylvia Marcom, Detroit Free Press; We heard that you were the one in charge of this project, and yet you are only an inexperienced young woman with no previous experience in this arena. How can we trust that you truly have this right, and why on Earth would anyone put someone as inexperienced as you in charge of something as important as this project?"

Erica was momentarily dumbfounded and was not sure what the best response would be, but she was saved by Jeffrey.

"Let me respond to this irresponsible and ill-phrased question. You asked your question in such a way as to accuse Ms. Beckett of incompetence, and to accuse me of incompetence to appoint her to manage this project and generate fear that the project does not actually work. The way you asked the question puts in people's minds that this is the situation. Let me be clear, the real issue is not Ms. Beckett's qualifications or the success of the project, but your incompetence at understanding how to properly seek information. Based on how you phrased your question, we will not respond. If you want to take a moment and figure out what it is you actually want to ask, we will wait."

Jeffrey stood at the podium and looked at her, waiting for her to respond. The entire reporter group seemed stunned she had asked these questions; but stood and looked at her and waited to see what she would ask. After a few minutes, Jeffrey spoke.

"I see you cannot figure out how to ask a question. Very well. Does anyone else have a question today?"

"Yes sir, Angela Stewart, New York Times; Can you tell us why you appointed Ms. Beckett to manage this program?"

"Thank you, that is a fair question. I appointed Ms. Beckett to manage this project because I wanted the best possible result. Let me say that Ms. Beckett is the most qualified leader and project manager I have ever met. She is simply stellar. I challenge anyone to provide any information that demonstrates her inability to motivate, coordinate, or succeed at overcoming obstacles in achieving results."

"It is an honor to have her on this team. Everyone on Earth should be proud of the work she has done, because guess what, we can all sleep well tonight knowing our planet will not be hit by an asteroid, so we have avoided one of the three key species extinction events we face. We should be celebrating her, not trying to tear her down."

Jeffrey stepped away from the podium and began clapping. The reporters stopped and applauded Erica as well. She smiled and waved, saying thank you to them all. There were a couple of more questions, but essentially the press conference was over. Once it finished, they returned to Jeffrey's office.

"I'm not sure where that question came from today, but you handled the response wonderfully."

"Thanks, but sometimes you have to take the position that the questioner is the problem, not the question. It was apparent to me the reporter was ill prepared, which basically means someone put her up to it or set her up. I asked Janice to pull her aside and report back on what happened."

Almost on cue, Janice appeared in the doorway. "Jeffrey, I have the reporter in my office. She would like to speak with you personally."

He looked to Stephanie. "Any concern with that?"

"No, we have scanned her, and she appears free of any devices."

"Okay, but I would appreciate it if you were there."

He walked to Janice's office and went in. Sylvia was sitting in a chair in the office and when he entered, she stood up.

"Thank you for seeing me, Mr. Wilson."

"You're welcome, please sit down. I hope you don't mind, but I don't go anywhere without certain people being with me. In this case, Stephanie will remain silent, but will observe."

"That is understandable."

"So, what would you like to discuss?"

"First, I would like to apologize." She began to tear up, and as she spoke, some tears ran down her face. "I was told that you were out to destroy Islam, and that we needed to try and destroy your image."

He looked at Stephanie. "Sylvia, who told you this?"

She suddenly looked scared. You could tell by her expression that she suddenly realized she may have said too much.

"Sylvia, listen. You are safe here. No one is out to get you, no one will use what you say and tell anyone you said it. But we need to know who is behind these ridiculous accusations, so we can adequately prepare a response."

She began to cry. "I'm scared. I know they will hurt me or kill me for telling you this."

Jeffrey got up and walked over and sat beside her. Stephanie went into overdrive watching and being prepared to act, leaning forward on the balls of her feet so far, she was almost falling over. He put his arm around her. Sylvia leaned into him and wept. After a few minutes, she stopped crying and sat up straight.

"Thank you, sir. I am sorry. If I tell you what you want to know, I fear they will kill me."

He got up and went back to his chair. "Let me tell you that we do not agree with you. If we decide to protect you, no one is going to kill you, but we need to know who is driving this agenda."

She sighed, seeming to come to terms with her situation and realizing she truly had no choices. "The publisher of our paper is friends with several individuals who are very close to several Islamic organizations with connections to Middle East radicals, who have expressed a hatred for your actions. They believe you are purposefully working to deny God exists, and especially that you are out to deny the Prophet."

"Sylvia, we do not discuss or involve ourselves in religion. Religion is viewed as a personal issue for each individual, which is even more remote than planetary concerns. We are not concerned with, involved in, or trying in any way to influence or harm any religion. Period. It would appear that the people who believe what you told me think that because we are not actively supporting their religion, we are against it. However, I would challenge you to find a case where we have been either promoting or slandering any religion."

Sylvia looked at him and thought for a moment. "Do you honestly believe they are saying these things because they fear they will lose power if you do not talk about them?"

"Yes, exactly. I believe there are people who perceive they lose power anytime people do not talk about them. It's narcissistic, and I'm sure it has nothing to do with God. Organized religion is often more about human control than God's influence. I'm not saying Islam matches this assessment, but from my perspective, that is what many organized religions seem to show, and the more radical the more so."

"What can I do? I'm afraid to go back to Detroit after the press conference. I know they will be ashamed of me and may punish me for it."

"Have you ever considered a career in the Federation?"

Sylvia was shocked. "What do you mean by 'a career?' What would I do?"

Jeffrey thought a moment. "We always need people who are pro-species versus pro-one aspect of humanity. We are trying to save our species. We do not care about a person's religious belief or anything else, as long as it does not cause them to be biased or discriminate against their fellow human beings. Be Islamic if you want, but that does not mean you can discriminate against Jews or Christians, you may end up working side by side or even living in the same room. We are all in this together."

Sylva thought about it. "I have a degree in speech and communications. Is there a place for me?"

"Yes. I know we can find a place for you where you can thrive as part of our team."

Sylvia cried again. "Mr. Wilson, would it be acceptable if I hugged you?"

Jeffrey stood up and gave her a big hug. Afterwards, he told her to wait in the office for a moment, then went and discussed the situation with Erica. They decided to offer her a position in the Federation Communications Directorate. They both walked down to the office where she was waiting.

"Sylvia, this is…"

"Oh, I know who you are. Ms. Beckett, I am so sorry for the question today. I hope you can forgive me for putting you on the spot in such a negative way."

"I can, if you can agree to be a member of our team."

They offered her the position and she accepted. Jeffrey had Stephanie assign a team to monitor and evaluate her behavior over the next several months, but there was never a time when they found anything that demonstrated a less than committed and joyful person. She thrived in an environment where there was no fear, which was exactly what the Federation was working to achieve, and the type of environment Jeffrey wanted for everyone.

Jeffrey thought about what they had learned and talked with Erica and Stephanie about who to inform. They decided to pass the information to the Federal Bureau of Investigation quietly, so as not to involve Sylvia.

"There's no reason to bring her into the FBI's process at this time. I believe she told us everything she knows, which is not very much."

"I agree. I think she's a pawn being used to cause confusion and misunderstanding. The way you handled the question she asked today actually reversed her intent, and I also agree they would probably harm her if she returned to Detroit."

"Yes, and we can keep an eye on her to make sure our thought process is correct."

"Very well, we agree. Oh, by the way, don't forget, I'm leaving to go to Destin and meet Heather for a short vacation. We should only be gone a few days."

"Oh sure, that's what you always say. Last time you said a few days and we didn't see you for a full week."

"Jealous?"

Erica laughed. "Yes! I never get to just go away and be lost for a week."

"Well, maybe one day you will have my job. Then you can take off for a week and leave your hard working, dedicated, competent personal assistant to manage everything for you."

"I can't wait! By the way, what time do you want to leave this afternoon? I would like to be at Khloe's school play at seven."

"I think everything is on order, so I'm ready when you are."

"I'm ready as well. That should get us home by three thirty and give me plenty of time."

4.178.20

Heather was in her element as the President and Chief Executive Officer of the Sally Wilson Children's Philanthropy, an organization dedicated to helping children around the world have a better life through educational, medical, and nutritional improvements. The philanthropy was three years old, and they initiated the fund with two hundred and fifty billion dollars, making it the largest philanthropy in the world. Tamara, the Chief Operating Officer, was exceptionally proud of the name of the philanthropy, as it recognized her mother and the work she had done helping children.

Together they had already overseen projects on every continent, and today they had been in Libreville, Gabon, dedicating a new children's teaching hospital. The goal was to produce more qualified nurses specializing in children's issues, so the people could begin to help themselves more than depend on others for help.

As they settled into their seats for the long overnight flight home, Heather and Tamara discussed the day's events.

"I thought those little boys performing that dance during the opening ceremony was the cutest ever! It made my heart melt."

"Yes, and then the singing for the dedication; it was so beautiful, colorful and rhythmic. I loved the entire event."

"That was a great project, Heather. I believe it's going to have a significant impact on the health of a lot of people for many generations to come."

"I agree. This is the type of project I want us to focus more of our attention on, projects that provide an ongoing service helping people take charge of their own destiny, not just a quick drop of funds into a non-repetitive program."

"I bet dad would love to hear about this one."

"Well, let's give him a call."

Jeffrey had just picked up Erica and they were on their way out of the Federation heading home. "Hi, gorgeous."

"Hi, dear, where are you and how is your day?"

"Erica and I are heading home. It's been a long week and I am looking forward to seeing you tomorrow. How was the dedication?"

"It was wonderful. We built an extension to the main hospital that will teach two hundred new nurses a year. We also completed dormitories and other facilities, including that highspeed internet wireless project you had funded for their university. All in all, Tamara and I believe this project will significantly improve the quality of life for a lot of children in Gabon and surrounding countries for generations to come."

"Awesome! I am glad to hear it and that you two enjoyed yourselves. Change of subject. Tell me, are you ready for that vacation yet?"

"Yes I am. It's been quite a long stretch since we took some time off; but you haven't said where we're going."

"We are going to the beach to relax and then ride jet-skis."

"Right now, that sounds like a wonderful idea; and I assume that means we are returning to Destin?"

"Yes, we are. As a matter of fact, I will fly down to Florida and be there when you arrive tomorrow, so I will see you at the airbase. Say hi to Tamara and let her know I am bringing Steve and the grandchildren, so they can have a relaxed vacation as well. In the meantime, be safe. I love you!"

"Wonderful. I can't wait to crawl back into your arms. I love you! Say hi to Erica!"

Heather loved the beach. Now she had someone to fully share it with. She loved when they found the time to go lay in the sun, play in the water, and just be together at the beach. She thought, this is the most satisfying part of life, getting to do what I love doing with someone who loves me and loves doing these same things with me. She couldn't wait to see Jeffrey and spend some time together in Destin.

4.179.14

Jeffrey arrived at Eglin Air Force Base at two thirty in the afternoon. Heather arrived at three. She had taken the Boeing 747 on the overseas travel, while he had flown in their Boeing 757. He walked over to her plane, and as soon as the steps were in place he almost ran up the steps to get inside to see her. Heather was still in the bedroom in the front of the plane when he entered the room, and when she saw him they rushed into each other's arms, enjoying the touch and a very long kiss.

"Welcome home, dear, I missed you."

"I missed you. We have to stop being apart for so long. What was it a full week this time?"

"I think so, but it felt more like a month!"

They left the plane and walked down the stairs together holding hands, overjoyed to be back together again.

They had both changed into their swimsuits before getting off their planes, so the destination was not the hotel, but the beach. They drove straight through Destin, across the bridge over to the military beach. They preferred it there because it was quiet and secure. They grabbed chairs and towels and their cooler and walked out and found a spot. Stephanie had security personnel stationed around the area, and a couple of boats in the gulf off shore to keep everyone away.

Then they spread their very large towel on the white sand beach and laid down together, kissed, and laughed and talked about their life together.

"Everyone seems to be doing pretty good. I have to tell you, Erica is really coming along. I really believe she will be ready to take this on in a few years."

"That's great! Then Tamara can take over the philanthropy and we can just be retired together! I sure hope we find a way to spend a lot of time at the beach once we retire."

He laughed, "Count on it."

Occasionally they would get up and walk down the beach, holding hands and looking for any unique sea shells, then go splash in the water, body surf, or just hold each other and enjoy the waves together. These two were still lovebirds. They felt as if they were still newlyweds and acted the same.

"You know, dear, I have to tell you something."

"Oh? What's that?"

"I have just discovered that I can be who I am, a strong, competent woman, and you are not threatened by it and love me for it. It is such a wonderful and empowering feeling, knowing I can lead a huge organization without the fear of losing your love."

"I believe the most important and empowering thing in life is to be loved for who you are. You love me that way and I do my best to love you the same way."

Later, they went to the Emerald Grande to their suite, showered, then lingered with a glass of wine. Eventually, they got dressed and went to the Harbor Docks restaurant for dinner. They loved this restaurant.

The destination is one of a kind, surrounded by old wood and ocean decorations. The bar is filled with bottles and glass, lots of old aged wood, and some tables in the front area. Walking down from there is a larger space, open all the way through from the bar, with tables that look over the harbor. Even further down are some more tables. This was their favorite place to eat, and whenever they were in town it was reserved for them.

When they entered, Gloria, the hostess, called the owner, who came out and escorted them down to their table. It was the perfect location with the perfect view, and away from all the activities of the main restaurant. The owner, Louis, always provided them with the best wine in the house, a recommendation from Sierra, chilled to the perfect temperature. Gloria brought them their menu and bread.

Tonight, Heather ordered a seared Ahi tuna, while Jeffrey ordered fresh grouper. With veggies and desert, they enjoyed several hours at the restaurant, talking, laughing, and watching the sun set over the harbor. Once they finished, they walked back along the harbor walk to the hotel, holding hands, enjoying the sights, smells and sounds of the harbor. They ended up sitting on their balcony enjoying the evening breeze and a glass of wine.

Finally, they went inside. Heather walked into the bathroom to change, and Jeffrey followed her. He walked up behind her, and gently moved her hair, softly blowing onto her neck, moving from right to left, giving her goosebumps. She arched her body, pushing herself into him. He put his arms around her, and gently squeezed as he kissed her neck. She sighed with delight as he began to unbutton her blouse, one button at a time, until he reached the lowest one, when he turned her around to face him and kissed her as he removed her remaining clothes.

She began undressing him in the same slow manner. She reached the last button and slowly kissed his chest and stomach as she began undoing his belt and pants. After a few moments he reached down and pulled her back up for another long kiss. He then guided her back into the bedroom where he sat her on the bed, then gently pushed her back to lay down, while he laid on the bed beside her and they continued to touch and kiss.

Heather kissed him deeply, her hair gently falling across his face, as they moved together to a release of their pent-up passion. Finally, their energy spent, they laid together, enjoying more long kisses and touch, until they eventually found their way to a wonderful night's sleep in each other's arms.

5.147.19

Riser was happy. He had taken steps necessary to end the un-Godly attempt to leave this Earth and spread humanity to the stars. The Mujahideen devils had helped his servants with access. They were sure to succeed. He hated these Islamists. He hated that they denied the true Lord. But he had put aside his hatred for them to accomplish this greater work for God. He knew the Lord would approve. The best part, no one would ever know what happened.

He smiled thinking about how he had organized this group. He had begun in college to actively work at getting people to understand the ungodliness of leaving the Earth.

"I believe whole heartedly that humans are the divine creation of God, beginning in the Garden of Eden. God has established a place for us and through a vision, He revealed to me that He is angry that humans are trying to abandon this Earth He made for us, in search of another home. He is angry because we humans do not believe His creation is good enough."

It was not hard finding people who held a similar view. They were angry at so many things; religion, politicians, unfairness, the list was long. They were Antifa, ecological protesters; they were terrorists who had not yet terrorized. He brought them together into a group and taught them how to hate these things with energy, all the while binding them to him and to each other, using all the tools at his disposal, including sex, starvation, deprivation, and behavior rewards. He shaped them into perfectly behaved vassals for his plan. Now, they were in place, and he had confidence they would be loyal to the plan and succeed.

Would they ever figure out who did this or why? He smiled, knowing that should the plan go as imagined, the only thing anyone would ever find were corpses in the pods. Yes, this was an excellent way to stop this migration, by not showing any attempt to stop them until it was too late.

5.164.09

The following June, Erica invited Jeffrey and Heather to tour a migration pod.

"I want you to see the program first hand. Besides, you will love the ride up. We have drastically improved spaceflight from what it used to be. We have implemented some very new technologies that include reduced weight materials, enhanced thrust, and improved aerodynamics, that enables the flight to be more like being in an airplane."

They entered a large swept wing craft in a hangar at the Federation and taxied out for departure. The initial thrust was conventional jet engines, carrying them up to fifty thousand feet and five hundred miles per hour. Then thrust boosters kicked in to accelerate and activate hypersonic engines, enabling an altitude increase to one hundred thousand feet and a speed increase to seven thousand miles per hour. At that point, pure rocket boosters kicked in elevating the craft out of the atmosphere into orbit at a speed over seventeen thousand miles per hour, as it climbed on course to match speed and altitude with the pod industrial complex orbiting at forty thousand miles above the Earth.

Erica smiled watching them get adjusted in their seats. As they began the climb, she said, "Look through the windows and watch."

The view was simply glorious. They watched the sky become a deeper shade of blue then turn black and the stars emerge in such clarity, it was an adventure all by itself.

"Oh my God, this is spectacular."

"Look, you can see the northern lights!"

They watched as the Earth shrank so you could easily see the curvature of the planet. Once they reached orbital height, the Earth was a beautiful ball of near blue.

As they approached the industrial complex the shear magnitude of the project finally set in.

"The complex has nine pods around a large core. Each pod is two miles long and half a mile in diameter. Three of the pods are complete, three are nearly complete, and three are less than a year away from completion."

The scale was staggering. They could not have made this happen without the huge investment in research and technology from JW Enterprises. These pods represented over a trillion dollars of investment. As they approached the core, they began to realize its size.

Erica explained, "The core is three miles across and built in several levels. Each level connects to the pods separately, providing a means of access to each pod for multiple functions to speed the construction and loading processes."

"The sheer amount of material involved, the engineering, it's staggering. At one time, there was a rocket lifting off from the Earth every fifteen minutes with just raw material. Nothing was wasted. Boosters landed and were reused. All other parts of the rockets were used in some fashion, even melted down and reformed. Once the heavy lifting phase was complete there were still craft launching with cargo every ten minutes from somewhere. These delivery and construction phases lasted several years before the pods began taking shape."

"Today there are only people traveling back and forth. Once the construction is complete the complex is to be transformed into a platform for building and maintaining starships. Raw material will be shipped in from the asteroid belt, Mars, and other extraterrestrial sites. There will be some limited use of Earth resources, but long term that is not the solution."

Upon arrival they were met by the core site manager, Derek. "Welcome to the complex!"

"Thank you, Derek. Looks like quite a large operation running here."

"Yes, sir. We have three thousand people currently working to get the pods complete."

"Erica, didn't you say that three of these pods would launch soon?"

"Yes, there are three prepared for launch with their crew on board. We intend to move them out into a deeper orbit this week. Following that are three that are nearly complete, and we expect to bring their crew up starting next week so they can begin acclimatization projects. Then the last three should be ready within a few months. Same process, so we should have all pods launched in less than a year from now."

"Can we go into a completed pod?"

"Absolutely, that is the main reason I wanted you to make this journey. Derek, would you please take us to pod one?"

"Yes, ma'am. Please put on these boots before we go. Erica has worn these boots often, but for the two of you, they help you maintain proper contact with the surface. We have a nice rotation, but the gravity is still not the same as Earth. You use your boots to make sure you have good contact with the surface before you take your next step. It feels awkward at first, but you get used to it. By the way, your bodies will hurt tomorrow, because this does use your muscles in a very different way."

They took a few steps and both Jeffrey and Heather started laughing. "Oh my, this is really weird! I can tell this will hurt. I can already feel muscles I didn't know I had!"

Once they had walked a short distance, a transport rover picked them up and took them directly to pod one. Stephanie did not like the apparent lack of security on the station but made sure her team was prepared as needed.

They could see the exterior of the pod as they made their way inside and it looked like a sleek shiny surface. Inside, the walls were quite thick. Once they passed through the various airlock controls they entered into a very large central open area, where they could feel some humidity.

"All the major structural integrity is provided by the external wall, with only a few large beams used in the cross-section. There is one large central pipe running the length of the ship providing stability and connectivity. It also provides the moisture you feel. Otherwise it is a huge open space. There are several farms being set up and you can see people in those areas."

"Right now, they are getting themselves, their livestock and other animals and plants, on a regular solar cycle. In about an hour the lighting will begin to dim until it is almost dark. In ten hours, the light will return and stay on for fourteen hours, then repeat. Humidity is controlled, and moisture released as necessary to create clouds and rain, as pressure is shifted slightly. All in all, they are now living in their new environment. They also participate in all environmental control and system issues. There are classrooms, a hospital, research laboratories; we have provided everything we believe is necessary, but they will have to do the time. So far, they seem to appreciate it. They also have observation decks where they can see the galaxy around them."

"Once they uncouple from the factory and move out to their pre-launch position, they will initiate their own rotation for the pod. The rotation will be enough to generate eight tenths of the pull of Earth's gravity, so it will not be as hard on their bodies as standard gravity. However, this will allow them to uncover all the fields around the interior of the pods and begin working all the areas within. Eventually you will be able to stand here and see various fields growing all over the interior. It should be quite a sight."

"Well, it looks like a big space. However, I am sure after a while it would feel small."

Heather held Jeffrey's hand. "Yes. God bless them. I could not do this."

The return to Earth was more intense, as burning through the atmosphere was still a bumpy experience. Jeffrey couldn't wait until they had an ability to manipulate gravity, so they could simply travel at a slow speed directly up or down without the need for such drastic speeds or burning re-entries.

Until then, he knew this was the last time he would ever do this. At sixty-two, he just wouldn't do this anymore. Let the young people ride this crazy elevator. The landing was smooth, much better than dropping into the ocean.

Once they landed, they went home. Sitting around the fire on the patio was a favorite pastime for them. On this evening Heather, Jeffrey, Erica, and Tamara were enjoying the moment and a glass of wine, while Stephanie observed.

"It was amazing! My gosh, I never realized how beautiful the Earth was until I saw it from space."

"Yes, and how fragile. It was something I thought about the first trip out, that you had visualized the fragility of our planet and our species, Jeffrey, and began the hard work of doing something about it. Now every time I make that journey, I think about our species spreading to the stars and it is so powerful of a feeling and thought. We truly are spreading out into the galaxy. No more science fiction, this is the real thing."

"Erica, how many times have you made the journey to the construction site?"

"Oh, probably thirty times. I try not to spend too much time there, because I'm not an expert at the processes underway; but I still try to be there often enough to make sure they know who they work for and evaluate overall performance trends and spending. Stephanie has traveled with me several times, so she has good space legs as well."

"Have you met any of the people who are going to make the trip in a pod?"

"Yes. Most of them seem eager and willing to experience the adventure, although there are some who seem almost zealous about it. I almost envy them, because they will have a finite world in which to live, play, and experience the intimacies of life. They will not have all the distractions we have. I don't know, it's interesting."

"Well I for one do not envy them. I am not sure I could live in a spaceship traveling through space for possibly the rest of my life. I am just glad there are people, pioneers, who want to take the chance to make a fresh start, either for themselves or their children, on a new planet."

5.327.09

"Our master was right. These Islamists are smart, even if they are servants of death."

"Our master is always right. Now, the next step is to become one with the sheep being led to slaughter."

This group of the servants of Riser were intermingled with the pioneers of pod one, two and three. They knew there was a second and third group, following the same path, for the remaining pods. Their calling was to be first.

"Regina, we must convince these barbarians that we are dedicated to the survival of our species. We must convince them that we are the best choice and fit the mold they seek perfectly."

"Yes, Samuel, we will. It cannot be to hard to convince these Philistines that we are genuine."

After several weeks of final testing, they were selected for pod three and began the journey to the pod. Their first stop was to the Federation airfield, a place they loathed, where all the evil of the world resided, to catch a craft to the orbiting space station, SB1. As the plane lifted off and began acceleration, they saw the wonder of the changes outside the window and were amazed.

"Oh my God. Our master would love to see this. It is the image of our God's work, His creation."

"Yes, it is beautiful. Why would anyone want to leave this perfection for some unknown place?"

"I can see why our master believes as he does. It reinforces that we should not go."

Once the craft docked, they were housed with the other pod three pioneers. They would be with these people for a very long time, and worked hard at fitting in. They volunteered for any additional chore. They were model pioneers.

Eventually, they were brought into the pod. They marveled at its size.

"Oh my God. Look at this!"

"Don't feel too much in awe Regina. Remember, our task is to stop these people from violating the will of God."

"I know, Samuel. But look at the machine these people have built. It is wonderful. It is a shame they did not use this energy and effort to improve the Earth itself, making it an even better home for God's children."

"You are right. Again, our master is right in knowing these usurpers must be stopped."

6.028.14

Erica, Tamara and Stephanie had decided to celebrate Heather and Jeffrey's fifth wedding anniversary. They were so appreciative of how far their family and team had come overcoming the challenges of the past few years, and what an integral role Heather had played.

"Seriously, it seems like yesterday we celebrated the way they embraced the change in their life."

"Especially the way Heather established her role as a friend and supporter to all of us. She never has used her position with Jeffrey to change anything."

"I know, she has never acted like she was important, even after they started the philanthropy. She is just such a good person, and everyone loves her."

"Yes, and she is so supportive of the wives with children in the team and really makes sure that everyone has plenty of time to spend with their family."

Erica chuckled, then said, "I often think that I was so right years ago when I told Jeffrey he needed a girlfriend to help his schedule be more like ours. To me, that is exactly how our lives have been since these two married. Busy? Absolutely. But it is a more relaxed and comforting family style process."

"Yes, dad needed this and I am so happy for him. That is why I am so joyous to be able to show them how much they mean to all of us."

"So, you have reserved the entire Emerald Grande Hotel for the weekend?"

"Seriously, Erica, this is a very cool idea, because it's their favorite place for a getaway, and where they honeymooned. It's perfect. This also gets everyone in one place together, which is awesome."

"Thanks, and yes, I did that last year, so we would have no issues with space. Now we are six months away, and I don't want anything to interfere with this celebration."

"You are the best. I know you're arranging all of this, but you have to let us help. What can we do?"

"Well, we have to start working on final coordination. You can be a huge help in helping me coordinate getting everyone there without either of them finding out about it."

Tamara thought for a moment. "That will not be easy. I know I can make excuses why we are not home, and I am sure some others can as well; but if everyone is gone, it may look bad."

"Yes. I already talked with Jeffrey and let him know that when they go to the beach next time my kids want to go. I am hoping that he will invite several of us on the trip, so he will not suspect that we are in on a plot of a surprise."

"Okay. What about the setting, food, and the rest?"

"I talked with the event coordinator at the hotel and we will have a large room with an open bar for the initial surprise. My biggest concern is getting everyone in the room unseen. We need to get those people that are already at the hotel into the room before Jeffrey and Heather arrive at the hotel. For those of us who travel with them to Destin, my idea is that once we arrive, everyone goes to their rooms. Then, as soon as Stephanie says Jeffrey and Heather are in their suite we have to get everyone to the room for the surprise. Stephanie will wait for word from me, then remind them they have dinner reservations, so they don't linger too long."

"Once Erica says the word, I will escort them downstairs to the room for the surprise. Once the initial surprise is over, we will all go outside to have dinner."

"I talked with the head chef and he is planning a delicious steak and seafood meal for the evening. It all sounds divine."

"Have you thought about fireworks?"

"No, I didn't think of that."

"Well, we've all seen their fireworks display, and if we could get them to do one that night after dinner, it would be awesome."

"Perfect, how about if you work on that?"

"Okay, is there anything else I need to do?"

"I think the biggest need is to focus on making sure they take the trip on the right day and getting in the room for the surprise."

It was not too difficult for Tamara to talk them into taking a quick trip for their anniversary to Destin. Jeffrey asked Erica to coordinate plans for them and reminded her that since they were going to a beach, she should bring her family. He also said she should offer the traveling staff the opportunity to go, if she could get hotel space. That made getting people there much easier.

6.171.18

On the day of their anniversary, everyone moved quickly to get into place. Stephanie escorted Jeffrey and Heather downstairs, but Jeffrey wanted to know why they were taking an unfamiliar path.

"We've never come this way Stephanie. Where does this lead?"

"No problem, this is simply an alternative path we have worked on for vehicle access. I prefer to have alternatives and not use the same path each time."

Then Stephanie opened the door to the room where everyone was waiting and stepped aside quickly.

"Happy Anniversary!! Surprise!!"

The entire family, blood-related and otherwise, were cheering at the surprise they had managed to pull off. Heather and Jeffrey had no idea this party was planned. He looked over at Erica and she just smiled back.

They were elated! Heather said, "Thank you everyone! Thank you so very much, we are thrilled you remembered our fifth anniversary."

"Yes, let me say how happy we are and how surprised we are that even you, Erica, could pull this off without us having the slightest hint it was happening."

Erica beamed! She was so glad this had worked out the way she planned, and yes, it had been really hard to coordinate this without either of them knowing it was happening. "You are both welcome. We all wanted to show you our appreciation for all that you do to take care of us and help us enjoy the best lives we could ever have. Thank you and Happy Anniversary!" Everyone cheered!

Jeffrey and Heather made the rounds and personally thanked everyone for attending. A while later, they joined in the feast that had been prepared by the head chef at the tables set up outdoors overlooking the harbor. It was a magical event, that culminated with a dazzling display of fireworks right in front of them in the channel.

It was the perfect way to end a perfect day and a perfect five years of marriage. They eventually made their way back to their room and enjoyed a last glass of wine to celebrate, while sitting on their private balcony, looking out at the lights reflecting on the water, enjoying the light salty breeze. They held hands and kissed, still newlyweds.

Their time together was magical, and they always took full advantage of it. It was not too long before they went inside. Heather was very prepared this time, having changed out of her clothes earlier. As soon as they were inside, she turned facing Jeffrey and dropped her robe, revealing her full, perfect body to him.

Jeffrey smiled, saying, "My God, dear, how do you always look even more delicious than the time before?" With that he walked to her, reached out and held her close as they kissed deeply. Heather's hands were busy undressing Jeffrey, which was not difficult since he only had on a tee-shirt and shorts. Very soon they were both naked, enjoying the curves and touch of each other's body.

Heather was leaning against the kitchen counter as he slowly kissed her neck, giving her a rush of excitement. He gently kissed and touched her until she moaned gently. They walked together into the bedroom to enjoy the touch and rhythm of their bodies, then held each other, until they finally drifted off to a wonderful sleep.

6.172.06

At six fifteen the next morning, there was loud knocking at the door and Jeffrey got up to go see what the noise was. He looked through the peep hole and saw Erica and Stephanie outside. He had on his robe, so opened the door.

Before he could say anything, Erica said, "Jeffrey, there was a massive explosion in the Z-wing research laboratory. We don't know what happened, but we do know there are casualties. We don't know how many casualties or the severity of injuries, but it looks bad."

"Ok, prep the jet and let's get home ASAP."

Erica and Stephanie nodded and moved to get things coordinated.

Jeffrey told Heather what had happened, and they took a quick shower and got dressed for the flight. They ate quickly, just toast and coffee, and packed their clothes into bags for the trip. As soon as they were ready, someone arrived to take their luggage. They were escorted by Stephanie and other agent's downstairs and climbed into a suburban for transport. Erica joined them.

"Additional reports seem to indicate they were working on the X-drive. There were at least twenty people in the lab. So far, they have found six alive while the search continues."

"Dammit. Why is it so hard to manage this technology? That is the third explosion for this project. I almost feel we can't continue if it means people keep dying."

Heather reached over and held his hand. "Jeffrey, I know this event upsets you, but if we are to achieve the dream of faster than light travel, we have to keep pushing the envelope. These scientists know the risks and they go forward willingly."

"Heather is right. You have even said we have to take risks if we are to be successful. Nothing comes without cost."

Jeffrey had been gazing out the window as they drove across the bridge on the way to Eglin Air Force Base to board their jet. He hated that people died for progress. He hated that he was the main cause of the push for that progress. He truly hated having to tell parents, spouses and children that their loved one would not be coming home but had died for the betterment of humankind.

"Yes, I know we must, but I don't have to like it."

"None of us like it."

They arrived at the base and boarded their private Boeing 747 and departed. They arrived at Federation Headquarters at eleven in the morning. Jeffrey was glad they had built these long runways, so they could land directly here without having to fly in a helicopter from Offutt Air Force Base. He didn't actually like flying, and especially hated turbulence. At least in his jet it was almost always smooth.

Admiral Chen met him when he landed. "Welcome back, Mr. President. It is good to have you here."

"Thank you, Admiral. What is the status on the explosion?"

"There were eleven killed and nine injured. All of the injured were in a protected room, so only have minor injuries."

"What were they trying to do?"

"The injured staff said that the group felt they had reached a point where they could effectively surpass the Special Relativity effect and could generate the necessary force to exceed the barrier. That did not turn out to be the case. The ensuing explosion was contained within the lab, but it was very powerful. Everything in the lab was destroyed."

Jeffrey thought for a moment. "Ok, well, let's get it repaired as soon as possible. This research into faster than light is dangerous but necessary. Also, take a look and see if we can improve the space for the people there. If nine survived, we should be able to build safety facilities so that everyone can. See what you can do."

"Yes sir."

Jeffrey really hated to be called sir, but he understood that in his current role, temporary he hoped, as President of the Federation Council, he had to follow protocol. There were now three thousand marines and one thousand support members of the military organization of the federation, plus about five hundred new recruits in the Academy. Mostly the active military practiced a lot; but they did have operational control of space beyond Earth high orbit, which essentially provided every planet with a five-hundred-mile buffer around their planet.

The Federation meetings he had hosted over the years had approved these rules and would wait until there were ten planets in the federation before they were readdressed. To date there was only Earth and Mars and it was working out fine.

He went to the hospital and met the team members who had survived, thanking them for their work in this dangerous but necessary research. He then went to the damaged lab, once it was safe to do so, and saw that it was, indeed, destroyed. Finally, he went to the Federation Council to his office to coordinate the transfer and burial of those who had not made it. He wrote a personal letter to each of the deceased' loved ones. This was by far the hardest part of his job.

Once he had completed this task, they left for Omaha. They did not live at the Academy or Federation Headquarters. They still lived at home. He tried to get out to the Federation a few times a week, but his job as the President of JW Enterprises still involved more business than federation work.

"Erica, what areas are we currently researching in the Z-wing?"

Erica looked at her tablet. "We are working the X-drive, astrogation, computerization, thrusters, enhanced aerodynamics, nuclear and ion drives, materials and communications. In the W wing we are working on enhanced weaponry, including laser, plasma, photon, energy, magnetics, and hypersonic."

"Isn't it interesting that we have an entire wing of research on weapons where we have not had a single accident, yet here in the Z-wing, where we are working on peaceful applications, we have had three major accidents?"

Erica had been thinking about this. It did not make any sense except for one thing. "Yes, but all the accidents have been in the area of the X-drive. There does appear to be something inherently dangerous about this that we are missing."

Jeffrey agreed, although he too did not understand it. "Make me an appointment tomorrow with Admiral Chen. I want to have this discussion with him to see if we can make any sense of it."

"Will do."

6.173.09

The next day Admiral Chen came to Jeffrey's office.

"Good morning, Admiral, please come in."

"Thank you, sir."

"Please, have a seat, I just wanted to speak with you for a few minutes about my concerns regarding the X-drive research."

"Oh?"

"Yes. It puzzles me that we have so many accidents in this area, yet we do not have this type of issue in any other area. Is there any explanation for this?"

The Admiral leaned forward and spoke carefully. "I am glad you see this problem as I do, sir. The accident rate in the X-drive area is very high. My team has discussed this issue many times and have taken steps to try and mitigate the problems, as well as evaluate all the staff to detect if there is any foul play at work. However, after all these reviews, it appears the problem is limited to the nature of the forces the scientists are working on. They simply seem to be beyond our ability to tame, at least at this time. We keep working on it, but it is not easily solved."

Erica asked, "Admiral, are there no steps we can take to more carefully plan and execute the research so when we get to a danger point we can stop and make sure people are safe, before taking that step?"

The Admiral did not like Erica. He viewed her as a young upstart with no possible reason, talent, experience, or skill to be here. But he always treated her gently, because he knew she was a favorite pet of the President, and he did not want to be in his bad graces.

"That is a good question. We tried to do this on this occasion, but when the team reached the point where safety was necessary, there was no time. The process simply spiraled out of control before safety could be achieved."

Jeffrey continued to look at the Admiral. "Very well. I know you are trying to accomplish something that is beyond anything we have ever tried before. Please let me know as soon as you can of any additional resources you may need to complete this project."

"Thank you, Mr. President."

The Admiral left. Erica looked at Jeffrey. He waited a moment, to ensure the Admiral had truly departed, before he spoke.

"I think the Admiral knows more than he is saying."

"Yes, I agree. I will ask Stephanie to have someone keep an eye on him."

"Very well. In addition, we cannot rule out sabotage or terrorism. We know there are many people who want us to fail, especially those radical Islamists. This could affect every activity we have. For example, the last thing we need is a successful attack on one of our pods. We need to make sure there is no chance of a terror cell infiltrating our operation."

"Agreed. We have had a separate security service intelligence unit working on this project since inception, same as the asteroid defense. I will talk with them about our concern and have them double efforts to ensure we do not have a concern. In addition, I think we should ask Stephanie to open that case with the FBI regarding Sylvia's situation. While she has been pristine, we do not know if we have any other individuals who may have infiltrated our organization. Perhaps we can run a scan of our database against any known or suspected contacts the FBI has been able to identity in the past two years."

"Yes, do that. Let me know what you find. We are a much bigger organization today than we were a few years ago and we depend on so many people to get this vital work accomplished. Let's also put together some simple talking points and quietly begin discussing this issue with our leadership team."

6.221.09

In August, pods one, two and three launched. The launch was broadcast live on all media channels, with a camera from pod one showing the Earth, and how it began to get a little bit smaller. Since they were powered by ion engines, the acceleration was small, but it would continue for a very long time, getting them up to a very high rate of speed within several years. The live feed remained on for several weeks to allow for the change to become very noticeable.

Jeffrey had set up a huge screen in the main ballroom of the Embassy Suites in Omaha and invited all the leaders of every country around the world. Stephanie was in charge of security and made sure everything from the airports to the hotel was locked down. All the hotels where dignitaries were staying were under very tight security restrictions. She did not want anything to go wrong with this visit. Once everyone was gathered in the ballroom, Jeffrey took the stage and made a short speech.

"Good Afternoon! A couple of years ago we achieved the first step in assuring our species survival by having an asteroid shield established. We have caught and destroyed about seven asteroids that could have had serious if not species ending impact to us since that time, so it was a timely effort."

"Today we move to step two. We are launching the first three of nine interstellar migration pods. These pods contain several hundred people each, with the capacity to grow up to some thousands. Each pod contains all the seeds we know of, and multiple members of some domestic animals. We did not include our wild animal friends, but we could, if the planet was right, perhaps send some other types of animals to these planets as well."

"The brave men and women, pioneers, who are on these pods are our best hope for the survival of our species. They carry with them the hope that we can grow and survive and be part of the larger Galaxy. Today, we take the first step to become an interstellar species."

"So, without any further ado, we will launch these ships."

At that time the large screen showed the view of Earth from pod one. The speaker was Derek from the construction facility. "Mr. President, we are ready for launch."

"Okay, everyone please join with me and count down from ten, nine, eight, seven, six, five, four, three, two, one, launch!"

The view shifted to pod one, more importantly, to the ion engines. They began, and you could see a red glow coming from the engines. Each pod had over fifty engines and as the camera pulled back, you could see all three pods engines glowing. The view then shifted to a view from pod one showing the Earth.

Jeffrey was celebrated around the globe for accomplishing the second leg of his vision to save the species. These pods were insurance that even if something bad happened to mother Earth, there were humans traveling to the stars who could establish our species on different worlds.

6.222.17

At about this time, Gabriella, Gabby to her friends, of which she really only had one, received some incredibly good news. She was accepted!! She didn't know if she could get into the Federation, but she had tried, and now she had made it! All she ever wanted to do was go to the stars.

She was twenty-two years old when she completed her double master's in computational physics and nuclear physics from the Massachusetts Institute of Technology. Over the past two years she had worked harder than she had ever worked in her life and had recently graduated with her PhD in Nuclear Physics, specializing in superconductivity and molecular physics. All of that was wonderful, but today, she was accepted to the Federation!!

"Sheryl, I was accepted!"

Her friend Sheryl was totally elated for her. "Awesome!! Congratulations Dr. Anderson!" They hugged and danced around the floor. "Gabby, that is so wonderful! When do you have to report?"

"It says I have to show up this Thursday. I am to travel to the airport in Omaha and there will be a shuttle provided to transport me to the Federation. Looks like I made the cut! I am so happy!!"

They hugged a few more minutes, then Sheryl said, "Your parents would be so proud of you."

"I know. I wish they had been here to share it with." Her parents had died many years ago when her dad crashed his private plane flying in turbulent weather conditions delivering supplies to a remote village in Alaska. She missed them terribly.

"You just go out there and make me proud, and I know your mom and dad will be watching. They will be very proud of their little girl."

"Thanks Sheryl. You are the best friend anyone could ever hope for. I love you."

"I love you."

Gabby knew this would be a challenge and an opportunity. She had always wanted to prove herself. She wasn't sure anymore why she felt that drive, and even who she needed to prove herself too. But regardless of the cause of the motivation, she was going to do this and succeed!

6.224.13

On Thursday, she arrived at the Omaha airport. The shuttle turned out to be a very large helicopter, which transported her and the other fifteen personnel that arrived with her. She was by a window, and as they approached she could see the complex. It was massive! Two huge runways and buildings that looked like sculptured sky scrapers. It looked like something out of science fiction! It was beautiful!

"Everyone, if you would please follow me, we will get you to your assigned teams quickly. Through this door and into the reception area. Very well, let's see, we have marines; line up over here please. We have medical officers, you can wait over there, that's fine. I believe you three are pilots, so please remain in that area. That leaves our newest scientist, you can remain where you are. Let me contact your teams and we will get you sorted out."

After about half an hour the marines left with a sturdy looking Sergeant. The two medical officers left with a doctor; and the three pilots left with a Commander.

Gabby stood in the middle of a very large room by herself. After a few minutes, she wondered if she had come to the right place. Finally, a door opened.

Jeffrey, Heather, and Erica were escorted into the reception room by the research department head, with Stephanie and her security team escorting them all. The young lady waiting in the room appeared to be almost frightened by the group. Jeffrey walked straight up to her and introduced himself.

"Hi, I am Jeffrey Wilson, President of the Federation Council and JW Enterprises, which is funding this research project. I would like to welcome you to the Federation."

Gabby shook his hand. "Thank you, sir. I recognized you when you walked in the room. My name is Gabriella Anderson." She looked at Heather and smiled. "I recognized you from *Andromeda Reigns!* That was an awesome movie and the motivation for me to go into physics. Thank you so very much!"

Heather smiled. "Thank you, Gabriella for remembering. I appreciate that. It means the work in my past life actually accomplished something."

"Oh yes. I am a huge fan."

Jeffrey enjoyed the conversation. "Well done, Dr. Anderson."

"Oh please, call me Gabby."

They all laughed. "Very well, Gabby, welcome to the Federation. I am sure you are wondering why we came here to greet you."

"That thought has crossed my mind."

"Sadly, we are here because the field you are in is dangerous. A few months ago, there was an accident in the Z-wing area where we are working on faster than lightspeed travel. Several of our scientists were killed, and several more were injured. It is my duty to inform you, that if you continue on the journey you are on, you could end up working in such a lab. Because of that, I am meeting every research scientist and offering them the opportunity to turn around and walk away with no penalties. The choice is yours."

Gabby thought for a moment, but she knew what she wanted. "I am not afraid, sir. I know it is dangerous. I am prepared for that and will do my very best to avoid injury and death while pushing the envelope further out until we do achieve the goal we need – travel at faster than the speed of light."

"Are you sure?"

"Yes, I am certain. I do thank you, though, for providing me this opportunity. Both opportunities really, to withdraw or to be on the cutting edge of research."

"Very well. I wish you all the best, Gabby. Please be safe and let me know if there is anything I can do to make your life more comfortable."

He left with everyone except the department head, who escorted her out to join his team.

6.247.11

A few weeks later, Jeffrey thought it was time to make some additional changes in Erica's growth path. They were sitting in his office.

"Erica, now that your time is not needed for the asteroid project and since the pod project seems to be moving on a routine schedule, I want you to focus more of your time and energy on the research and development we are doing here in the Federation. Especially Z-wing. There is something not right about that X-drive project, but I can't put my finger on it. Perhaps once you spend some time focused on it you can help uncover the safety issues we have and correct them."

Erica did not look forward to this. Admiral Chen had personal control of the Z-wing labs, and she knew he basically hated her. She was not sure she could bring value to the project if he was still there.

"Thanks for the vote of confidence, but I am not sure it is a good idea, as long as Admiral Chen is in charge of Z-wing. You know he holds me in special regards."

He chuckled, and said, "Yes, I do. Which is why I believe placing you in direct supervision of him will possibly break the logjam to improvement. If he has a good idea of what needs to be done, he will want to implement that as soon as he can to get you out of his hair. If he does not, then he may get irritated enough to actually work at a solution. In any event, he has been in charge of those labs for a while now, and we have gained a lot of valuable knowledge and sales based on the discoveries that have been made, so I think we still need him in that position."

"Okay, well, Derek can handle the work on the remaining pods with minimal supervision. I also think he would be good as the manager of the overhaul we will give the site once the last pods are launched. We will need to accomplish a lot of retooling. Going from building two-mile-long pods to three hundred-yard starships will be a significant amount of work."

"Have you thought of a name for the site?"

"I was thinking about Star Base 1, referred to simply as SB1."

"I like that. It would fit, as that will be the primary place we build and launch the very first starships. Have you thought any more about the idea of leasing space to commercial projects on SB1? It would certainly simplify a lot of processes and generate some revenue."

"I have. I think after the pods have departed we should put together a team, including our staff, Federation staff, and commercial companies interested in the action, and have some conversations about this idea. Do you envision giving SB1 to the Federation for their use?"

"Getting people together is a good idea, and you could probably start that sooner rather than later. As to giving SB1 to the Federation, no. JW Enterprises built SB1, and we will continue to own it. We will provide our services to the Federation for a price, but the commercial companies should be the ones actually building starships for the Federation. We could probably either lease or sell parts of SB1 to commercial companies and pull back out of that operation over time, but certainly not give it away."

"Alright. I suppose I can find a few minutes here and there to put together a working group."

"You are the best delegator I know, so I am sure you have already thought of who you will delegate this project to. It is yet another positive trait you possess, Erica. You don't get overwhelmed, you follow the big items and effectively delegate the minutia to others. I have seen it over and over. You are a great leader."

"Thank you, Jeffrey. It is one of the characteristics I have seen in you and I have tried to emulate it."

"Well, thank you. I suppose we have been learning from each other over the years. By the way, can you put together a comprehensive list of all the research projects we are currently running? I would like to review those with the council next week."

"Of course."

"One last thing. Stephanie, would you come in please? Okay, I am not afraid for your life; however, I want you to do me a favor. I want you to prioritize time for you to take personal fitness and combat training from Stephanie."

"Really? What on Earth for?"

"For situations where your self-confidence is important. You may be placed in positions where people feel they can intimidate you. I want you to have all the confidence possible that you need not fear anyone. Oh, that does not mean to get cocky or arrogant; instead, it is designed to give you the confidence in your abilities to defend yourself in any personal conflict. It's important."

Stephanie smiled, and said, "We can start in the morning. We will use the gym in the compound and each morning at five we will devote an hour to both. Within a few months we should have you in a good place."

"Five o'clock in the morning? Oh my gosh, I never get up that early."

"Starting tomorrow you will need to get up at four thirty to be at the gym by five."

Jeffrey laughed at her expression. "Seriously, Erica. I would not request this if it was not important."

"I know. It's just I had never expected to do this."

"Well, if I was any younger, I would absolutely insist on learning this for myself. I think everyone should do this. I'm going to have Tamara participate as well. If you want, you can get Janice and Michelle to participate. That way you can all moan and groan together. I don't expect any of you to keep up with Stephanie, but I sure expect you to try."

6.272.10

Heather occasionally had moments of weakness. It usually centered around the same subject. It wasn't that she dwelled on it, just that it sometimes crossed her mind. "One thing I do regret, Jeffrey, is that I never had children. I always wanted to have children, just never put myself in the position to go through with it or have the time."

Jeffrey knew this subject was hard for her. They had talked about it several times in the past few years. It did not get any easier for her. He could sense there was a deep fissure in her life that she had wanted to fill.

"I know that I could have and still could adopt, and there is nothing wrong with adoption, it's just that I wanted one of my own, created inside of me, my very own flesh and blood."

"I would love to make babies with you, dear."

She teared up. "I know, me too with you. I just know we are too old now. No, it is not in the cards anymore; I am too old to carry a baby safely. Maybe in our next life."

He smiled. Should he tell her what he was working on, or keep it secret? She was fifty-three and he was sixty-three. He would wait a few more years to see where the research managed to go before he mentioned it.

"Yes, because we will have another life. We missed the whole young and immature part together, so we should get that part at least!"

She smiled. "You always can make me smile, even when I am trying to be depressed."

"Oh, was that depressed? Sorry, I missed that. I thought you were practicing for a part in a movie on the Hallmark Channel."

"That is probably the one channel I have never been invited to be on."

"That makes no sense, because you are the most beautiful, most sensuous and deliciously talented woman anywhere, and it would only help their ratings."

They laughed a while, then she kissed him. "I love you."

"I love you."

6.283.07

"Good morning Erica, and how is your day going on this fine fall morning?"

They were on their way to work as usual, traveling in their suburban convoy. They nearly always rode to and from work together, so they had private time to catch up and keep their work coordinated.

"Oh, I am fine. Khloe is ten, and apparently, she has decided to become an actress like Heather. She watched *Andromeda Reigns* for the tenth-time last night."

"Oh my, well that is an interesting choice. Although I am sure she will go through many variations of what to be before she makes her final decision."

"Yes, but as long as she is happy, I really don't care what she decides."

"Good point. By the way, how is the physical training coming along?"

Erica rolled her eyes. "Seriously, I believe this is both the hardest thing I have ever done, and the most rewarding thing. It hurt at first, but today it feels good to be able to physically accomplish things I never dreamed I could do. I did a running reverse jump kick this morning. Really? I never thought I could learn these types of moves, much less be good at them. Stephanie is incredible. She pushes us hard, but she supports us. Everyone is enjoying it, especially Tamara. I think she needed this kind of a challenge."

"That is wonderful to hear. I am glad you are all doing this. I just wish I was younger, so I could learn it too. Well, Erica, this morning I wanted to discuss something very important with you. That being that I intend to retire in four years."

"What? I thought you would continue until you were at least seventy." This was very surprising for her and a little intimidating. She had not known this new world without Jeffrey in it. What would she do when he retired? She would probably have to quit, as she was certain she could never work as closely with anyone else as she had with him. Thankfully her salary and bonuses had provided a very nice nest egg, so she did not have any financial concerns.

"No, I will make it ten years leading this organization, then I retire. The big news is that I intend to name you as my replacement, if you will take it."

She was dumbfounded. It was probably the first time Jeffrey had seen her speechless. He chuckled. "What? No words?"

She laughed. "I have to give you credit, you do know how to bring in some huge surprises. I think this is even bigger than when you first offered me this job six years ago." She leaned back in her seat. "Why would you choose me, Jeffrey? I am only thirty-three years old." She was very surprised and a little worried about what this decision would entail. This was big.

"That's easy. You know everything and everyone, you are completely competent, smart, self-deprecating, loved by the team, share the long-term vision and strategy, love life and want to make it better for everyone; in short, you are the very best person to lead this operation into the future."

Erica smiled. "Thank you, Jeffrey. I really appreciate that. But still, I am not experienced in other things in life. My college stopped when I started working for you, so I don't even have a post-graduate degree. I will be challenged. I mean, look at Admiral Chen. He does not respect me at all."

"I know you will be challenged. I also know you will defeat anyone who challenges you, or you will win them over to your perspective. You are that powerful, even though you don't know it yet. You also have one other asset, which is that the entire team will support you, because they love you and respect the work you do. You have earned their respect."

She took a moment and gazed out the window. He waited, letting her think about it. "If I do this, when will you make the announcement?"

"I would prefer to wait until one year from the retirement date. That provides plenty of time but gives you three years to further prepare yourself. For example, you talked about a degree. I can't think of anything any business school could teach you that you don't know already. I'm certain you could test out a doctorate. However, perhaps you should contact the school of your choice and see what they think? I bet you would be accepted and provided expedited service, so you could finish your education before you become the next owner of JW Enterprises."

She nodded. "Alright, I will do it, if you believe it is the best thing for the company."

"I do, and so does Heather, who is the only other person to know of this decision. You will also be my choice to become the next President of the Federation Council, because I believe until we attain the X-drive and get those ten or more planets on the council, the owner of JW Enterprises should be the President of the Council. I will work this angle over the next few years and by the time I retire, it will be accepted."

"I do agree with that in principle. I just never thought of myself in that position."

"It is a new thought. However, you can do this. One other thing; I think you should consider right now that you will only serve as President of JW for ten years. That means you will need to think about who to groom so that when you get to four years out from retirement, ten years from now, you have someone you trust, as much as I trust you, to take over the reins."

"You do think long term, don't you?"

He laughed. "Yes, I suffer from strategic thought. You know Erica, I love you like my daughter. I only want what is best for you, but I also want what is best for our company and our species. I say our company, because it would not be what it is today without you being there helping to build it. But this is not a reward for your work, this is both a challenge for you and the right thing to do. I am completely satisfied and comfortable with this decision."

"I love you too, Jeffrey. Thank you. I will accept your challenge and be ready when the time comes."

6.285.20

Simon was a nerd. He had always been a nerd. Everyone he knew believed he truly was **the** nerd the word was named after. Even when he completed his double masters in quantum mechanics and mathematics from Georgia Tech, people still thought of him as a nerd.

He joined the Marines as a way to try and break out of that shell, because he did not feel like a nerd. It helped. After a couple of years, he was muscular, tanned, and could actually carry on a conversation without sounding too nerdish. He applied for the Federation Marines as his time in the United States Marine Corps drew to a close. He was very happy when he was accepted. He would be an officer, working in research.

Upon his arrival at the Federation he was transferred to a Marine research unit, where he reported to the major in charge of several smaller research teams. His team was working on vacuum flight dynamics and surface operation integration. His initial task was to learn how to operate a craft in space and to provide recommendations on structure, engines, controls, navigation, guidance, etc., everything about operations in space close to planets and in the vacuum of space close to other craft. This was all brand new, but they knew eventually they would need tactical craft in deep space.

He worked as a lead flight commander because of his exceptional skill at maneuver in three-dimensional space. Mostly he practiced close-in tactical integration in low gravity. He spent quite a lot of time on the moon, or in orbit around the moon. They developed surface integration areas on the back side of the moon to avoid creating changes to the image of the man on the moon the Earth population was familiar with.

He really enjoyed his job, but at times he found it to be boring. He wanted to go at hyper speed, but usually he was in a cargo hold going nowhere. Still, he felt it was a step up. At least he was in space and not still a ground pounder standing guard over a piece of dirt.

His parents and siblings thought he was crazy, and they did not respect his decision to join the Federation. They believed the Federation was made up of people they couldn't trust. That meant that now he was someone they could not trust.

His family were basic simple folks in Georgia and he loved them, but sometimes they just did not think about anything beyond the here and now or their front yard. He did. He thought about the 'there and future,' which he believed was in space at the speed of light.

6.323.08

In November, Jeffrey, Heather, and Erica flew to London to attend the annual finance dinner hosted by the Chancellor of the Exchequer, which would be held in the Savoy hotel again this year. They arrived several days in advance, as Jeffrey wanted to visit with the friends they had made of the Royal Family and have plenty of time to visit and see some history.

Heather had invited Maria and her family to join them on this vacation, as well as Alexandra and her family. She missed her friends and tried to see them as often as she could. One of the side journeys on this trip was an excursion to Scotland. One place Heather had always wanted to visit was Loch Ness. She had been fascinated by 'Nessie' years earlier and wanted to see the loch. They took a tour guided by a local historian and Nessie expert, a natural born Scotsman. Afterward, they went to Edinburgh for some celebrations and a concert in their honor. It was a wonderful affair, with the bag-pipes, clans dressed in kilts of many colors, Rod Stewart's classics and romantic songs, and some delicious ale.

They had a grand time, staying out late and enjoying the culture. They spent the night and had a late morning start the next day. They flew back to London and took refuge in the Savoy until dinner that evening. Alexandra and Brad were looking forward to the dinner and the speech, as Jeffrey was again to deliver the keynote address, and they would sit with Heather. Maria and her family went sight-seeing. In the quiet hours of the afternoon, Jeffrey discovered he was having some trouble gathering his thoughts.

"Erica, it has been six years since I addressed this group. We have come a long way since then. What do you think we should focus on with this address?"

One of the things Erica loved about Jeffrey was his easy way to include her in everything he did. By asking the question the way he did he made it sound like she had something to do with everything that had happened since that day six years ago. She truly only felt she had been an assistant to Jeffrey, but looking back, she could finally begin to see that he had been grooming her for many years to take on more responsibility.

"I think this might be a good time to report on everything that has happened since you were last here and the progress we have made. You might also want to discuss our work at lightspeed travel, mentioning that it is very difficult and dangerous to push this envelope as fast as we are trying to push it."

"Yes, I think that is about right. Heather, anything you would like in this speech?"

"I think Erica mentioned the key things that you should cover."

"Okay, let me think a little while and finish the notes for this speech."

With that, he walked back to the desk and began writing his notes. Heather came over and gave him a kiss, explaining that they were going for a massage, pedicure and manicure. They wanted to feel relaxed and look their best for the dinner.

The food was once again delightful. Tonight, they served a delicious Chicken Cordon Bleu with a rich creamy sauce and perfectly roasted sliced red potatoes with asparagus spears. Jeffrey had to admit, he had never had a meal at the Savoy that was less than excellent. When it was time, the Chancellor introduced him.

"Ladies and gentlemen, we had the honor of having Mr. Wilson speak with us six years ago. While he has been fairly busy for the past several years, he has finally agreed to come back and provide us with an update. I hope we learn some valuable information tonight on how far his project has come, and his plans for the future. So, without any further ado, I give you Mr. Jeffrey Wilson."

The audience applauded for Jeffrey's appearance. "Thank you, thank you, please, take a seat."

"Thank you, Chancellor for the opportunity to come back here for a second time. Perhaps my first appearance wasn't too dull, since you have brought me back. Thank you all for coming out this evening. I know the weather outside seems to have changed for the worse, so hopefully you can all make it home tonight without getting too wet."

"I would like to address several items this evening. First, I want to tell you a little about the changes in my personal life; second, take a few moments to have a conversation about how we are doing; and third, spend a little time talking about where we are going."

"To begin, from a personal perspective, the past six years have been wonderful. As you know, Heather and I celebrated our fifth wedding anniversary recently."

"Happy Anniversary, Congratulations, Well Done!!" calls came from the audience.

"Thank you, we appreciate your kindness and well wishes. Something you may not know, is that Heather was here, during that first speech. We had not met, but we saw each other and eventually we found each other. Over the past five years we have been able to find plenty of time to continue to grow closer, even with our busy schedules."

"As you know, Heather runs the Children's Development Philanthropy Fund, the largest philanthropy in the world, and she is very busy managing projects across the globe designed specifically to help those children who have the least, have a good life."

The room applauded and stood giving her an ovation for the work she does. Heather stood for a moment to acknowledge the applause.

"Thank you for that recognition on Heather's behalf. We continue to be blessed as we work to improve the lives and future of all."

"The second item is how we are doing. There are a couple of prongs to this, including the Academy, the Federation, investments in projects around the globe, and the business of JW Enterprises."

"To begin with, the Academy is thriving. We only take, for now, five hundred new students each year. This smaller number allows us to hone our processes to provide the highest level of academic, physical, and emotional development we can manage. These cadets grow through a three-year system until they graduate and enter service with the Federation. To date we have only graduated two classes, but we are expecting to graduate a full class each year going forward. Once we reach a point where the need exists, we can expand the class size upwards to as many as two thousand a year. We have built that capacity and will use it when it is needed."

"The Federation project is also going very well. As you know, this project is built with the exclusive purpose of helping to manage extraterrestrial government relationships. We created a constitution that was ratified by the United Nations, cementing our role. A key aspect of this constitution - we do not get involved in terrestrial governance."

"Today there are two planets in the Federation Council as full voting members, Earth and Mars. These two do not pay any dues, as the cost of the Federation is paid for by JW Enterprises until there are ten planets on the council. At that time these ten planets must decide how to fund the cost of the Federation."

"We have also funded nine migration pods. Three have launched, and we hope to launch three more in a couple of months, with the remaining three in about nine months. These pods fulfill the second leg of our species existence. Today, if we are foolish enough to destroy ourselves or if a threat we have not yet imagined occurs and our planet is destroyed, our species is traveling into space in different directions, providing a means for the survival of our species."

"Also, we are, as many of you know, investing two trillion dollars around the globe on infrastructure projects. To date the return on this investment is wonderful, as people are able to have better infrastructure in roads, bridges, ports, and electrical grids than ever before. We are raising the education level and already see a decline in poverty. These investments are reshaping how we live on this planet. We have also discovered that the financial return on these investments is that the base fund has grown, which means we can continue with this project development model for many years to come."

"Lastly, the business of JW Enterprises is very strong. We began with a little over six trillion dollars. We have invested nearly five trillion, meeting the requirements of the initial contract. Yet the net worth of the company today is about seven trillion dollars and growing."

"It appears then, that the entire process we began six years ago has worked. People are getting better, we have safety from asteroids, we have launched migration pods, we are seeing improvement in infrastructure globally, the global economic engine is running smoothly, and the company is thriving. If that is a measurement of success, I believe we have done very well."

The audience stood and gave a resounding ovation for all the achievements made by Jeffrey and his vision.

"Thank you. The next area of discussion is the more interesting, where are we going? This area is largely dependent on the results of the massive research and development investments we are making. If we surmise that we do not discover faster than light travel, we will essentially be where we are; investing in making life here on Earth better and safer, while perhaps building additional migration pods so we can at least continue to strive to expand from this one planet."

"The reason we need faster than light travel is easy to grasp. We estimate the first pod will take twenty years to reach the first possible planet, that is a twenty-year journey one way. Then, if it is not habitable, they will need to do it all over again for an additional thirty-year journey to their secondary target. This is grueling and cumbersome, much less a hell of a lot to ask of people for the sake of spreading our species around. We need faster than lightspeed travel, so we can get to other planets in days or weeks, maybe months, but certainly not years. This continues to be a major area of research."

"In addition, the lightspeed travel project is by far the most dangerous project we have undertaken. We have had several accidents thus far, in which unfortunately, we have lost several members of our team. Yet we continue, improving safety procedures as we learn, because we have no choice but to crack this nut and deliver a means to travel at such a speed as to make fast interstellar travel possible. While the current situation in itself is not necessarily a bad future; it isn't the one I want. So, let's postulate that we do have success with our research."

"Additionally, we are researching in a host of other directions. We are researching everything from human DNA and longevity, to materials, advanced computing, system integration, time travel, and of course, lightspeed travel. Because of this multi-faceted research approach, we hope to be able to leverage each small gain in knowledge in multiple areas."

"Perhaps we will discover how we can live longer. That would be good and would reduce the need to have so many children so quickly, modifying the pressure on the ecosystem. Perhaps we do discover travel faster than the speed of light. That would enable us to begin exploring and settling the near galaxy and both assure the survival of our species and provide new experiences, investments, trade, and a host of other positive outcomes."

"Assuming we do make new discoveries, JW Enterprises will be at the forefront of providing these services or systems across the globe and across the galaxy. We need to make sure that nothing we discover is ever held by a clique or group, or even a single planet, because when we spread our capacity and knowledge across the spectrum of our people, we all thrive. That is what we learned as we built the asteroid defense system and is a process we must ensure continues to happen."

He paused for a moment, then continued, "As you can tell, my comments do not foreshadow a super government out of the Federation. I see the Federation as a peace keeper and fair play monitor for relations between planets, while being strong enough to repel any who may want to harm us. Rest assured, I am confident we are not alone in this galaxy. It would make no sense for that to be the case. I believe, wholeheartedly, that at some point in time we will indeed meet others. The question is whether or not they will be friendly. It is for this reason we must always invest in a strong interstellar defense, the Federation."

"I am very confident in the future. I see so many positives we can accomplish when we put our minds to it and set aside our differences. I know there are some countries who do not feel they are a full part of this effort, and we have been working to isolate and modify their behavior for several years and will continue to do so, until they too, join us on this great adventure."

"Ladies and gentlemen, I believe we are entering a new era for our species, an era where we explore and become the masters of our fate, and finally put to rest our age-old ties to bias, discrimination and prejudice based on the color of our skin, our nationality, our religion, or our gender. Thank you for listening to me this evening, good night."

The audience provided a rousing standing ovation that lasted until Jeffrey and his entourage had departed the event.

6.333.21

On pod one, Charlotte and Henry, two unassuming pioneers, were working alongside their fellow travelers.

"Henry, we can tend the goats and become friends with everyone."

"I know. That way they will never suspect our true motives."

They were responsible for tending to the small herd of goats. They would get their milk, process for drinking and for cheese, feed them and generally herd them around. As part of their daily routine, they walked past the supplies along several hallways. They knew that for their plan to work they had to be accepted as complete members of the society developing in the pod.

They volunteered to work any extra shifts. They took on any task necessary. They helped build new fences for new fields. They helped work the earth to prepare for planting. They did everything they could to show everyone they were part of the team.

At night, they would go to their quiet cabin and take out the scroll they had made with the symbols of their beliefs and a picture of Riser. They would pray to him to watch over them and pray for guidance as they worked to ready themselves for their mission.

6.334.09

Erica had three resumes for possible personal assistants. She did not have the luxury that Jeffrey had when he hired her, an employee of his he was already familiar with, for this job. She was going to have to find an outsider and blend them in. The human resource team had worked tirelessly searching for candidates for this position. She had been very vocal in the areas she wanted them to find, and the personality types she was not interested in. The end result was three candidates.

Candidate one was Bartholomew Johnson. He was twenty-seven, currently working in a financial firm on Wall Street. He had an MBA and very good references. He came from a small family in Vermont.

Candidate two was Cecily McGowan. She was twenty-nine, currently working in a legal defense fund in Los Angeles. She had her jurisprudence degree and had excellent references. She came from a large family from upstate New York.

Candidate three was Arabella Roberts. She was twenty-four, currently working for JW Enterprises in the marketing department. She had degrees in design and business and had very good references. She was in school working on a Doctorate in International Relations. She had no family except her brother, who was a minister. She came from a small town in Nebraska.

Erica read the resumes, then read each of the cover letters, then read their responses to the questions she had asked. She picked them all up and walked over to see Jeffrey.

"Jeffrey, when you hired me to work for you the first time, I did not meet the minimum qualifications for the job, yet you hired me. Do you remember why?"

"Yes, actually, I do. I read your responses to the questions we asked and there was something about the way you responded, not necessarily the actual content of your responses, that caught my attention. There was a quality I felt, more than read. Why?"

"Here, read these three and decide which one you would hire. Don't tell me, then let me tell you what I am thinking."

In a few minutes, he had completed.

"Okay, there are three perspectives captured in those letters. The first one, Bartholomew, sounds slightly stuffy or superior. The tone doesn't sit well with me. The second, Cecily, sounds nervous and unsure. It is almost as if it is filled with drama. The third one, Arabella, sounds confident, not arrogant; pleasant, not overly intruding; intelligent, but friendly about it. In short, were I to hire from this information, Arabella would be my choice. Thoughts?"

"I couldn't agree more. Is this for your personal assistant?"

"Yes."

"Then, if I were you, I would interview Arabella soon. She gives me a sense of belonging; yet needs support. I agree, there is a quality in the voice of the letter. You had that same voice in your responses. Also, one thing to consider; you may want to take some time to think about your original requirements and make sure you are actually looking for someone to complement you, not be like you."

"Okay, I think I will take some time to think about that, but if it still seems to be the right choice, I will interview her and see what happens. Thanks, Jeffrey."

6.337.10

Erica took almost three days to ponder Jeffrey's comments, but eventually she believed her character and personality requirements were the right ones. A few days later Erica interviewed Arabella. She was actually nervous about the interview. She thought about asking Jeffrey to participate, but then thought no, this was going to be her decision, right or wrong, hers alone. At ten o'clock, Stephanie escorted Arabella to Erica's office.

"Hi Arabella, I am Erica Beckett. Nice to meet you. Please, have a seat."

"Thank you, Erica. It is incredible to meet you."

"Can I get you anything before we begin?"

"No, I am fine, thank you."

"Okay. Well, tell me about yourself."

"Thank you, well, I was raised in a small town, Silver Creek, Nebraska. My parents were the best, but they passed when I was in high school, about seven years ago. My brother is a minister and between us both working various jobs, we managed to support ourselves until I finished high school. Afterwards, I came to Omaha for work and began taking college classes with student loans, eventually finishing a double marketing and business degree. Today I work in the marketing department for JW Enterprises."

"I am sorry to hear about your parents."

"Thank you. It was a hard thing, finishing high school and getting married without mom or dad there. It still hurts."

"I cannot say I know how it feels, because I don't. My relationship with my parents went downhill after I graduated high school and does not exist today, but I did not lose them, they pushed me away. I wonder which is worse? Anyway, what else can you share about your personal life?"

Arabella had never expected this type of personal conversation or anyone to ask these types of questions. "Marcus and I married two years ago and I'm currently pregnant, with a due date in five months."

"Why do you believe I should hire you as my personal assistant?"

"Because I am dependable, resilient, competent, and I care. I can't promise you I will be spectacular or wonderful, but I can promise you I will work my heart out making sure I get it right, so you don't miss anything important to you. I will give you all I have. I just need a break."

Erica could see in her eyes the same desperation she had felt when she interviewed with Jeffrey. She recognized that, even with Jeffrey's warning, she may be finding someone who was like her. She did not know if this was good. She decided to do something drastic. "Come with me."

She got up and led Arabella down the hall to Jeffrey's office. Jeffrey did not know this was going to happen. She entered his office and introduced Arabella.

"Jeffrey, would you please ask Arabella a couple of questions to verify my assessment?"

"Certainly. Hi Arabella, Jeffrey Wilson."

Arabella was startled. She had never expected to meet Jeffrey Wilson! Oh my god, he was the richest human in the history of the world and the President of JW Enterprises and the Federation Council. She was momentarily at a loss for words. She quickly caught herself to speak.

"Good Morning, Mr. Wilson."

"Arabella, you obviously want this position with Erica or we wouldn't be here. So, tell me, what do you see as the biggest opportunities and concerns with the position?"

"Mr. Wilson, I believe this is a fantastic opportunity to be a part of history. As I understand it, today we are on the cutting edge of exploring the galaxy, healing our species, and helping create a new world. I would love to be a part of that, and I cannot think of a better place to be than as the personal assistant to someone who is so close to the decisions and choices being made to make it happen."

"As to concerns, I am confidently concerned about being able to provide the support this position requires in the near term. I am pregnant and will be out soon to deliver my first child. That will hinder my learning and set me back from being able to provide one hundred percent commitment to the job, until that is, I return to work. Otherwise, I am just excited to be here and hope I can convince you I am worth the investment."

Jeffrey looked at Erica and nodded his head. Erica looked at Arabella. "When can you start?"

"Seriously? I mean are you really serious?" Arabella was ecstatic!

"Yes, I am serious. I would like you to start tomorrow morning at nine o'clock sharp. Be here and we will get started."

"Welcome aboard, Arabella. I look forward to getting to know you."

"Thank you so much. Oh my gosh! Okay, tomorrow morning. You will not regret this decision Ms. Beckett or Mr. Wilson. I promise."

After she left, Erica and Jeffrey had a very good chuckle.

"I have to say, that was you when I hired you."

"You know, I remember feeling exactly how she feels. Well, I hope she works out and believe she will."

6.354.17

Heather was so excited to get back home from London. She had discovered something about herself over the past few years; she simply loved Christmas! The past five years had changed her entire perspective on the season, both the reason for the season, and the joy of the holiday spirit. She went overboard with lights, trees, snowmen, and every kind of decoration. This year was no exception. On the weekend after Thanksgiving, she began working feverishly to transform not only their house, but the entire President's compound, into a winter wonderland. All the trees had lights, so it looked like a forest of Christmas trees!

She had worked with Erica, Tamara, Michelle and Janice to make sure all their houses were completely decorated, inside and out. All of the children loved living in a winter wonderland. There were snowmen, reindeer, Santa and his elves everywhere. The center of the compound had the loveliest nativity scene anyone had ever seen. It was beautiful and showed the baby Jesus surrounded by all the key players in the Bible. Across the street from this scene was the biggest Christmas Tree ever, well-lit and sparkling.

"I do believe you have outdone yourself this year." Jeffrey and Heather were walking through the trees, taking their time enjoying the moment, drinking hot chocolate. "This Christmas tree forest is seriously the coolest thing I have ever seen."

"Thank you, dear. I have discovered that I just love Christmas. I have to thank you for enabling me to be so free to feel again. Your boundless unconditional love has changed my life."

They stopped and set their chocolate down, then stood and kissed and snuggled for a while. Eventually they picked up their chocolate and continued the walk.

"Any big surprises for Christmas Eve this year?"

Heather's eyes sparkled. "Yes, I have hired a Santa, sled and reindeer, to go from house to house and deliver the gifts we bought for all the kids."

"My goodness, the kids will be delighted with that. What about you? What do you want for Christmas this year?"

Heather had thought about that very subject a lot. She honestly could not think of any 'thing' she wanted. However, she did have desires. "I really don't want anything. I would love to have children, Jeffrey. I so love seeing the all these children in our compound, but truly, if I could ever have a dream come true, it would be to have my own."

Jeffrey held her and kissed her cheek. "I know."

They continued to walk until they made it home. By then Heather had let the pain go and they soon found that the parents had all brought their children over to sing for them. They sat on the couch while all the children sang Christmas carols.

They provided everyone with the most delicious hot cocoa and marshmallows, and simply enjoyed the evening. The oldest children put on a play and helped decorate their tree with even more ornaments. It was a family filled fun event, a wonderful evening, reflecting the joy of Christmas and the closeness of this large family.

7.014.09

Erica had been thinking about the conversation with Jeffrey regarding her education. She did some research and decided to contact the London Business School about their PhD in Strategy and Entrepreneurship. She didn't have any specific contact information and did not want to call out of the blue and get transferred from person to person, so she contacted the Chancellor of the Exchequer for her help in finding the right person to talk to and was provided contact information.

"Hello, this is Sharon, how may I help you?"

"Hi Sharon, my name is Erica Beckett. Chancellor Darlington provided me your contact information. I am wondering about the possibility of participating in your PhD program for Strategy and Entrepreneurship. I have a fairly busy schedule, so am hoping to find a way to work a unique schedule with you."

"Did you say Erica Beckett? As in the Erica Beckett that works for Mr. Jeffrey Wilson?"

"Yes, that is me."

"It is an honor to speak with you, Ms. Beckett. We would be delighted to work with you. Can you tell me what education you have attained so far?"

Erica knew this was the crucial issue. "I only managed to complete a Bachelor's in Business Management, that was about six years ago."

"So truly, what we need to do is create a plan to take you through the MBA as well. How much time do you desire to spend on this program?"

"I need to wrap it up within two years. I was hoping to use current experience to obtain some credits, life experience, then work at the necessary courses and dissertation."

"Yes. Well, let me talk with the leadership of the school; however, I can assure you we will work with you to both get you the program you need and help you acquire the learning you desire. Would it be okay if I called you back?"

Erica provided her contact information and asked her to not share it with anyone.

7.017.10

Simon had been at the Federation for a few months and often found time to participate in a passion of his – Space Tetramax. It was a multi-dimensional space strategy game. He was a level six player. There were only five level six players and one level seven player in the world. He had never met any of them, as they had game names, but he challenged them in the games. He had played the level seven player, Dinatrex, several times and he could never win. He at least could defeat the other level six players, sometimes. But Dinatrex was just brutal.

Today there was a competition at the Federation for anyone who wanted to participate in the game and he had registered to play. He was shocked to learn all the other level six players and Dinatrex were also registered. That meant all the top players in the world were here at the Federation! He was stoked to find out who they were. The players would all be in the main simulation room for the game, and it would be projected onto monitors throughout the Federation.

When he entered the simulation room there were only five other people in the room. That meant that between them, they represented all the level six and seven players in the world. He looked around at the competition, trying to decide who Dinatrex could be. He recognized two of the marines, but the other three he had never seen before. One of them was a Cadet and the other two were support officers. There were two males and three females. He had no idea who Dinatrex could be.

After a few minutes, the judge of the game, a Marine Colonel, entered the room and began introductions. "Good afternoon, everyone. If you do not know it by now, let me say that you here represent all the level six and seven players in the world. It's a reflection of the attraction and standards of the Federation and the Academy, that you would all chose to be here."

"First off, let me introduce the players. At level six: Fourslayer, Marine Captain Simon Jackson; Tigress, Captain Delores Thompson; Pitchfork, Marine Captain Igor Rikoyovich; Mummer, Marine Lieutenant Kim Su Han; and Dreamweaver, Cadet Steven McIntosh. Finally, I am proud to introduce the only level seven player in the world, Lieutenant Gabriella Anderson, known in the game as Dinatrex."

They looked around at each other and nodded politely. Gabby knew they were all gunning for her, which was fine. You did not get to level seven by worrying about what other people thought.

Each contestant would play every other contestant. Whoever had the most victories would win, unless there was a tie, then a playoff would take place. Simon hoped he could do well against the other level six players, but he really wanted to do his best against that young Dinatrex lady. Each of the contestants were assigned a virtual reality station. Once they were all in position the competition began.

Simon played Pitchfork first, and it took nearly an hour, but he won. He then played Mummer, and after a two-hour game, he lost. Next, he played Dreamweaver, and thinking he was tired, he won in only thirty minutes. Next came Tigress. This was a tough game that lasted nearly three hours. They fought back and forth in a nearly even match, but he did eventually pull out a win. Okay, he thought, I am three and one, not bad. Now to play Dinatrex.

Gabby had played each of the other level six contestants and defeated each of them in an average of thirty minutes. She was simply a dynamic force in this game. It was as if she knew the parameters so well that she was the dimensions themselves. No one could get past her, she was dominating. When Simon was ready for his game, she was well rested. It only took fifteen minutes for her to defeat him.

Simon took off his goggles and looked at her. "Really? Fifteen minutes?"

Gabby laughed. "Yes, well, I think you may have been tired from the long game you just finished. Better luck next time."

Simon just shook his head. "I don't think it matters whether I am tired or not. You are just brutal in your ability to manipulate the dimensions within that matrix."

"Thank you, but I don't consider it to be brutal, just efficient."

Simon reached out to her. "Hi, my name is Simon. Glad to finally meet you."

She shook his hand, saying, "I'm Gabby, glad to meet you Simon."

"While you probably are not hungry after such easy games, I am famished. Would you like to get a bite to eat?"

"I would love to, but I can't. My shift starts in thirty minutes, so I need to get back."

"Not a problem, how about a rain check?"

Gabby liked his smile, so gave him her number. "Okay, here's my number, give me a call sometime and we can have that bite to eat. Bye!"

"Good bye." Simon liked her demeanor. She was not arrogant in her skills. She seemed like a normal person, even if she was killer in that game. Pretty cool.

7.037.11

"The migration pods should achieve travel at close to sixty-five thousand miles per second, their terminal velocity. Pods one, two, and three are well underway. Pods four, five, and six launched last week with no issues."

"Thanks, Erica. I just hope they are moving along well and that the inhabitants are doing okay. I still cannot imagine getting into a pod and traveling for such a long time in one. In all the psychological testing we accomplished finding these pioneers, claustrophobia was one of the worst conditions to overcome. With my level of claustrophobia, I just couldn't do it."

Heather added, "I agree. Me either."

"Erica, do you remember when we began building all of this and the effort to launch so much material into orbit? It still amazes me that we were able to pull off the major task of building SB1 to use as construction station, much less get these pods built."

"Oh yes, I remember that too well. Talk about stress! The stress of getting so much done so quickly, of moving so much material, I mean, this facility has worked around the clock for several years, first to build itself, then these pods. It was an incredible achievement."

"Yes, and the amount of raw material we provided to the pods themselves for their journey, by itself, that was a herculean feat to get up there."

"And after all that was accomplished, we still depend on the inhabitants to spend the greater part of their journey constructing the fields and farms necessary to grow their food for survival. I hope our decision to provide enough food for only a year was the right one."

"I know, me too. But these pioneers knew the requirement going in, and growing their own food was up to them. What is the latest on communication with them?"

"We receive a monthly data burst from them; but the latest reception from the first pods are getting weak. As they continue to accelerate, we expect their communication to degrade. We don't know if we will receive data from pod one, two and three for very much longer. In any case, they are on their own now. Once they are at full speed and leaving the solar system, even if we did transmit to them, they probably wouldn't receive the transmission."

"When is the first pod expected to reach their destination?"

"We estimate pod one should arrive in the vicinity of Wolf 1061 in eighteen to twenty years, accounting for mid-course thrust reversal for slowdown. We programmed the pod to accomplish this automatically. As long as no one in the pod tampers with the program, we expect it to occur as scheduled."

"That's not too bad, only twenty years total travel time."

"Yes, but what if they get there and determine the planet cannot sustain life?"

"They would then need to set a new course for their secondary destination which is another thirty-seven years out."

"I can't imagine that. I mean, how would you feel if you arrived, after a very long journey, and discovered you needed to lock up and travel another thirty-seven years? How terrible would that be?"

"I can't imagine it either. But these brave souls were talked with over and over about these very real possibilities, and still they wanted to be part of the first wave. I am proud of them and scared for them. If only we could crack this faster than lightspeed travel. It would alleviate so much misery."

7.054.12

Simon was very excited to finally be having lunch with Gabby. They had managed to talk on the phone a few times, but this was the first time they found a time when they could both get away from their duties together. He was mesmerized as he watched her walk across the quadrangle in front of the cafeteria. She was shorter than he was, and her hair was tied up in a bun, so her hat could fit over it; but it looked red, surrounding a pure white face. She had a beautiful smile that could melt butter at a hundred yards. He smiled.

Gabby saw Simon watching her walk over to him. She blushed under his gaze and took a better look at him. He was a little taller than she was, but he was chiseled. He had such solid yet warm features. His smile was one of those infectious types that just made you feel good. She thought she liked him.

"Hi Gabby!"

"Hi Simon, looks like a lovely day to sit outside for lunch."

"Yep, I saved this table for us. Do you want to order from the table or go through the line?"

"Let's order from the table, so we can spend our time talking, instead of in line waiting."

They took a look at the available items and placed their order.

"So, what have you been up to?"

"Well, I recently returned from a short expedition out beyond the Moon. We are working on some tactical applications for deep space warfare. It's interesting, or not. Kind of not what I thought I would be doing, but oh well."

"Oh? It sounds terribly dangerous."

"Yes, it is, if you make the wrong decision. Otherwise it's easier than Tetramax. What about you? What have you been up to?"

"Well, I recently shifted from the propulsion development team to the lightspeed navigation team. We are trying to understand how we can navigate and steer a craft moving at greater than the speed of light."

Simon was very excited about this. "Does that mean they have achieved the speed?"

"No, there is a team still working on that. The last time they got close an explosion killed the chief scientist, so they are working from a different perspective. It seems the hardest thing for them to get past is the Special Relativity effect, when the energy needed to push past the speed of light is greater than the combined energy of the object to so travel. It is a dilemma."

Their food had arrived, and they ate while they talked. In only a few minutes they talked about what they were doing, where they came from, why they were here, and even their dreams.

"I really want to go into space."

"Me too. I can't wait to zoom out to some new planets."

"Yes! Can you imagine starting a new life on a new planet? I think that would be so exciting!"

Simon was surprised and happy at her eagerness, because that is exactly how he felt. They continued talking for a little while, then had to go back to work. They agreed to find another time to meet in their busy schedules.

7.062.09

Heather was visiting the Federation with Jeffrey when she decided to go get a coffee. She walked through the corridors and open spaces until she came to a lovely little garden with a Tim Horton coffee shop close by. Abby's security team gave her plenty of space, while remaining observant and prepared to act on a moment's notice. Abby walked with her and they discussed the various settings in the structure. Once she got her coffee, she found a bench in the garden to relax and be at peace. Abby stayed some little ways away, giving her some private space.

Gabby often walked the corridors of the Federation complex and had found this same garden before. It was now her favorite place to get some thinking time. After she got her coffee she walked over to the garden and was looking for a quiet space when she saw Heather. She walked over and said hi.

"Hi Mrs. President Wilson. Isn't this a lovely garden?"

Heather was surprised by her, but quickly responded. "Hi yourself. I believe your name is Gabby, correct?"

"Oh, I am sorry, ma'am. Hi, yes, I am Lieutenant Gabriella Anderson, but people call me Gabby."

"Then hello, Gabby. My friends and family call me Heather, so why don't you call me that as well?"

"Thank you, Heather. I apologize for intruding, but when I saw you, I immediately thought of Diedre, your character in *Andromeda Reigns*. I just love that movie."

"Thank you again, Gabby. That was several years and a lifetime ago. I'm glad you enjoyed the movie."

"No, you don't understand," she said, as she sat on the bench beside Heather. "The role you played, being the mentor to Andromeda, it was so fulfilling. I mean, you were there for her when she needed you. You understood what she needed and gave her such support and love. It was beautiful."

"I have to admit, you are the first person to talk about my role in that way. I too felt the role had impact. Mostly the role attracted me because I was able to be someone I did not have in my own life, a strong female figure. Tell me, what are you up to today?"

"Well, I am working in the research area of Z-wing. My research is fairly tame, working on astrogation and navigation of a craft traveling at lightspeed. Mostly we are speculating and running a lot of theoretical designs. We won't truly know what it is like to travel at lightspeed until we do it. This research should at least give us some ideas on what to think about when it happens."

"Interesting. I know Jeffrey often talks about the need to finally crack this lightspeed travel nut. Are you enjoying your time in the Federation?"

"Yes. I have met some really wonderful people and the overall attitude and positivity of the place is awesome. I mean look at where we are sitting. I don't know of any other campus or organization that can provide such lovely unexpected small touches as the Federation. It keeps it interesting, real, and alive."

"Yes, I agree with you. Well, Gabby, I must be off. I only had a few minutes to get away and now back to meetings. It was very nice to meet you again."

"Thank you, Heather. It was a dream to meet you. Have a wonderful day!"

Heather walked away, and Abby was quickly at her side. "I did not perceive you were irritated with that interruption, Heather, so did not interfere."

"You did the right thing, Abby. She is a nice girl and it is good to visit with different people sometimes."

Gabby was in heaven. She had visited with Diedre! Well, Heather, but still, she was so wonderful. She wished she could grow up to be like her, a confident, successful, lovely lady. Well, no need to expect that, as it was out of the question for a red haired, pale complexioned girl from North Dakota. Still, one can dream.

7.117.09

In April, Gabby and Simon had their first 'date' at the Henry Doorly Zoo and Aquarium in Omaha. They took off on a Saturday morning and rode an excursion bus to the zoo. It was a beautiful day, lots of sunshine and the temperatures were in the middle seventies, Fahrenheit. They took in the desert, the rain forest, and totally enjoyed the aquarium. But the best part was just being together.

"So, you are from Georgia?"

"Yes, ma'am. I grew up in a tiny little town called Hahira. It is a really nice town, but it is just too small for my dreams to take place. I went to high school at the county high school, and then went off to Georgia Tech in Atlanta. That was more my size."

"What is your family like?"

"My mom was a teacher, and my dad was a fireman. I say was, because they are both retired now. I'm the baby of the family and was born when they were in their forties. I have three brothers and three sisters. Goodness knows how mom and dad survived all of us, but they did. How about you?"

"I was an only child. My parents were killed in a plane crash several years ago. So, I have no family."

Simon had never met anyone his age who did not have family. "I am so sorry to hear that, Gabby."

"Thank you, but you know, I have my dreams and the Federation. Oh, did I tell you I got promoted? I am now Captain Anderson."

"Hey congratulations! I suppose that means you will get some new, choice assignment."

"Well, I don't know about that. You know, I keep hoping I can get on the X-drive team, but they keep those guys really separate from the rest of us."

"Why do you think?"

Gabby had tried a couple of times to get transferred over to that team. Each time they had said she would need to wait until she was approached. It seemed strange, but they did not want people on the team who tried to get on the team, only the ones they wanted to be on the team. It was odd.

"I really don't know. I have tried a couple of times, but they say to wait, so I will wait."

"Where did you go to college?"

"Oh, I went to the Massachusetts Institute of Technology, and graduated with a double master's in computational physics and nuclear physics. Then I completed my PhD in Nuclear Physics, specializing in superconductors and molecular physics. I think my parents would have been very proud of that accomplishment."

"Wow, you really are a super brain. No wonder you kick everyone's butt at Tetramax!"

Gabby laughed, feeling that even the way Simon said that, he still didn't think she was weird or something. "Thank you, I try."

"I heard they took a sample of nearly every species in those migration pods. Imagine being in one of those pods with a herd of elephants!"

"No thanks. That is why I think solving the lightspeed issue is so important. I do not want to travel for forty years just to get to one planet that might not be habitable. I want to get there in four days, or better yet, four hours, then go somewhere else, over and over. Until I find that right planet with just the right sky. Then I think I just want to settle down, raise a family, and enjoy living."

Simon nodded his head. "Yep, that sounds like the dream. Speaking of dreams, can we see each other again? I mean, I really like you and that would be really cool."

Gabby blushed. "Yes, I would like that, Simon. I would like that a lot."

As they walked back to the bus for the return trip to the Federation, Gabby took Simon's hand and they held hands for the entire trip back.

7.190.10

"What have you heard?"

"We have heard that the FBI and other agencies have identified your voice talking to that idiot Islamist."

"Damn those people. Now they are looking for me. Thank God we successfully got my servants to the station, so they could board the pods. Now, whatever happens, we are assured a place in heaven."

"Yes, master."

"Take all who remain and depart the site immediately. Do not tell me your plans, do something I know nothing about. If God wills I survive, you can contact me. I will make my way back to the site and eliminate certain information. One thing though, I do not intend to be captured alive." He thought for a moment, then added, "One more thing. If I do not survive, keep the faithful safe. This will not be the end. You may find you are called to lead this holy war. Be strong!"

"Yes, Master."

He left his apartment by a different route than he had ever taken, found the vehicle he had prepositioned for this type event, and began a long circuitous route to the cave. He threw his old phone into a creek mile's from anywhere.

He planned to get to the cave complex as soon as he could, but most importantly, he could not be captured before he got there. There were still three pods left to go. He needed to protect his servants and their mission. He intended to go out in a way to protect their identity.

7.193.14

Erica had some good news she wanted to share with Jeffrey after the financial meeting she had attended the previous week. It was the mid-year report for January – June, and it looked good. She walked into Jeffrey's office and sat down in the chair facing him. Jeffrey was never surprised when she did that, as she was nearly always a fixture in his space. He just looked up and waited.

"Jeffrey, I have some very good news. When we started out JW Enterprises we had six and a half trillion dollars. In the past several years we have spent nearly five and a half trillion dollars, and yet we are now worth seven and a half trillion dollars and growing. It looks like the return on investment is continuing to pay off."

Jeffrey smiled. "Yes, and with the copyright of all the discoveries at the Federation, we continue to earn royalties everywhere. Once we discover faster than light travel we could enter the business of building ships, but we can still charge huge royalties for the drive itself, even if we do not build the ships. It will probably be something you need to think about, as I suspect that will happen during your watch."

"Yes, I hope we do achieve faster than light soon. Won't that be an incredible thing? Travel at faster than the speed of light. Awesome."

"Yes. By the way, did you hear we diverted another potentially species destroying asteroid last night?"

"Oh yes, I was going to mention that to you. Jeffrey, without your vision and energy, our entire species would already be destroyed. I don't think many people thank you enough for what you have done."

"That's okay, because the fact is it worked because you built it. The asteroids are under control, we have migration pods outward bound, and now, it is getting closer to the time for me to retire. Two more years and I announce. How is your preparation coming along?"

Erica thought about all the things they had accomplished, and all the plans that Jeffrey had spurred. This was an area that concerned her. "Jeffrey, all of the ideas we have implemented over the past seven years have been yours. Yes, I worked with you to pull them off, but you are the idea generator, not me. What will I do if I find myself leading the team but unable to come up with an original idea?"

"You do exactly what I did at your age. Ponder. Think. Listen. Read. Think more. Ask. Get a team together and brainstorm. Struggle for an idea. Listen to your heart. All of these things generate ideas. However, you are at the same place as me – you see the species and the spread of humanity through the galaxy as a larger issue, not from the perspective of being a person scared and looking for escape, but from the perspective of someone who grasps the intricacies involved in shaping the larger picture."

"I hope you are right."

"As I always say, hope is not a strategy. Hard work, hard thought, these will get you there. If nothing else, think about how you want the world and the galaxy to be for your own grandchildren and make it so. That always worked for me. But you are going to have even more opportunities and challenges than I faced. You are going to face the reality of managing our business and the Federation through the acquisition of travel at lightspeed."

"I know. I have spent a lot of time thinking about all that can both go wrong and be successful. If we fail to manage the initial deployment of the star drive, we will have chaos as people simply head out in multiple directions. It isn't that we need to know where everyone is going, but we do need to have a means to respond with force should they encounter something they can't handle. I have been really trying to understand how we can provide that balancing act."

"It is an interesting dilemma. It would seem to me the first step, once we acquire a star drive, is to build a Federation starship for every two or three built and launched commercially. At least in the beginning, you will want to expand your capacity quickly, but not too much. After we stop chairing the Federation

Council it will be up to politicians, and from my observation, they are not really to be trusted that far."

"Yes, I believe having an overcapacity of military power may cause some to want to control expansion. I would rather we build a few private starships that happen to have the same firepower or greater as a Federation cruiser and keep them traveling with our own commercial starships, instead of depend on too many or too few Federation cruisers."

"Yes, you have some interesting decisions to make. Oh, by the way, we need to take a look at the current benefits of our medical research efforts. I think there are some early products we can market. That way people see that we are using the research to provide some specific relief for the problem of aging and early death."

"I agree, that is an area we have not worked very much. How about if I put together a team and begin working on some marketing ideas?"

"Perfect. Also, we should plan on immediately pushing this technology off planet once it is successful and setting up on a different planet. They can do what they want here on Earth, but we need to make sure we provide all our services elsewhere in the Galaxy as well."

"Good thought. I have also thought about transferring all of our knowledge to a library off planet as well."

"Now that is a good idea. Maybe we can set these up in Jeffreyville on planet Erica."

They both burst out laughing, just as Heather entered the room.

"What is so funny?"

Jeffrey got up and kissed her. "Nothing dear, just two silly people being silly. How is your day?"

"Oh, it is fine, but I am ready to go home."

"I agree. Hey Stephanie, let's travel."

"Okay, but it will be a little while. I sent the transports to fuel and wash. How about in an hour?"

"Sounds good."

"Well, if we have an hour, I will go back and finish up a grant for a project in Beirut I was working on."

"Okay. Hopefully it doesn't take much longer than that as I am really ready to go home as well."

7.199.05

It was very early in the morning, just before the first light of day breaks the horizon, when the special operations team entered the cave. They had worked hard the past three days identifying and removing improvised explosive devises, trip wires, razor wire, bobby traps; it was an exhaustive process. They were certain they were being observed; but had no choice but to keep moving.

High above three very special satellites were observing visible, infrared, and many other spectrums to detect activity. Nothing so far. In addition, there were several drones with various weapons circling at about ten thousand feet, ready if they were needed for a strike.

The area around this cave had been sanitized and was under control and observation of several hundred members of the US Army special forces. This was a dicey operation, and it was very close to Roscoe, New York. They had evacuated most of the town, not knowing what they would find.

Intelligence had connected two people talking. One was an American, the other was a Libyan. The Libyan was identified as a known, highly sought-after leader of one of the most notorious Islamic terrorist organizations. They had only caught his voice pattern twice before, both before significant strikes that cost a lot of lives. The American was an unknown entity.

They had worked backwards and eventually discovered his identity as the Riser in a radical Christian cult. More time was needed, but they eventually tracked him down and he fled to this cave. They knew he was here, they had followed him, thinking it would be an easy capture. That was three days ago, and they were only now getting to the cave entrance.

From what they had learned, Riser and his group believed humanity was supreme and the Earth was the seat upon which God sits. They had issued a couple of limited manifestos in the past, but nothing had been heard from them in almost three years.

The team lead paused and listened. Nothing. They looked with night vision and without and saw nothing. Even when it was light, it would be dark in here. They saw no wires, felt no vestiges of civilization. They could tell the path was used, but that was all. The lead scout took a step. The explosion could be felt in town. It had decimated everyone and everything within two hundred feet. The cave entrance was destroyed and collapsed.

It took most of the day to recover bodies, the ones they could find, and tend to the injured. IR scans showed air had pushed out in three places when the explosion occurred, so three teams were assembled and sent to each vent site to see if there was a way in. Another team was sent to the collapsed entrance. They brought in heavy equipment and dug out the rocks enough to see the cave, and went in. If this guy went to this much trouble to secure this cave there must be something pretty damn important inside.

One of the teams at a ventilation area found a body. It was identified as Riser. Apparently, the blast had pushed him through the rocks and popped him out the hole. There was not much to identify, but somehow his face had remained intact. With this information, they began crawling into the shaft. The other two teams at ventilation shafts also began crawling inside.

It took quite a while, but eventually all four teams entered the cave and met at a central space. From this space were several corridors chiseled into the rock into various rooms. It looked like they were sleeping quarters and other personal space. They found food, water, and finally, a room with information.

"General, you need to get in here."

"What did you find?"

"You need to see this for yourself."

The Lieutenant told his Sergeant to gather the men and make damn sure no one entered this room except the General. After about half an hour, the General arrived.

"What have you got?"

The Lieutenant led him into the dim room, and then pulled a cloth over the entrance behind them. The General looked at him with raised eyebrows.

The Lieutenant then turned up the light, so he could see the room clearly. He looked at the charts and pictures and felt the blood drain from his face.

"Good work, Lieutenant. Gather all this information and secure it. No one is to see it. Load it into the smallest number of containers you can and bring them to the field headquarters. Do this quickly."

The General left and went back to his field headquarters. He called for a large Chinook helicopter for transport. Then he called General Nelson and arranged a meeting. The Lieutenant and Chinook arrived at the same time, so he loaded everything, including the Lieutenant and his team, and departed.

"Yes, General?"

"Stephanie, as the head of security you need to know something we discovered today."

"And that is?"

"Please come with me and we will both see the information together. General Anders will be here in a moment. He is arriving from a site in New York where they found some pictures and charts that provide information on a possible intrusion into our pod process."

"Very well. Abby, you are in charge."

They went to one of the hangars on the airfield where the Chinook was parked. General Anders had already deplaned and was waiting. General Nelson explained who Stephanie was, and he then informed her of the information he was providing. Stephanie had the containers taken to an office located in close proximity to her normal office. There, she brought in two other agents and they opened the containers.

Oh my God, she thought. "I have to get this to Jeffrey, but first, I need Erica to confirm this information."

"Erica, sorry to interrupt, but you need to come and see what we have discovered."

Once in the room, Erica began to review the information. "Oh my God, this is real. We have to tell Jeffrey."

Jeffrey was in his office when Erica, Stephanie and General Nelson walked in.

"Jeffrey, we have discovered some unsettling information. A group, headed by a terrorist named Riser, is planning to destroy the pods."

"How can that be, they are already underway. No one can get to them now."

"You misunderstand. This group, the Servants of Riser, have people on each pod. They plan to destroy the food supply inside each pod so everyone, including themselves, dies. That way no humans can get to another planet. They believe we are forbidden by God to even try to do this."

"How sure of you that this is real and actually taking place?"

General Nelson replied, "We have all the intelligence special ops managed to get, at the cost of twenty-five lives. They killed the leader, or he killed himself, possibly accidentally, but the data they collected is unequivocal."

"How far out are the pods now?"

Erica looked at her tablet and searched for the information they needed. "Pods one, two and three are close to the orbit of Saturn; pods four, five, and six are past the orbit of Mars. No one can get to them now, they are beyond our ability to catch them."

"Are we still in contact with them?"

"No, we lost contact with pod five last week, the last one we were able to communicate with."

"Alright. We still have three pods up there we have not launched. I assume we know who these saboteurs are?"

"No. We have some photos, but they may be of some who have already departed. We do not know who is on which pod. The intelligence we managed to get our hands on was damaged in the explosion getting into the cave where they operated from."

"Suggestions?"

Erica said, "The travelers are already in their pods. Whoever these saboteurs are, they are in place and may already have done damage to the systems. I can have Derek run full diagnostics on all ship systems to see if there is anything that has changed."

"Yes, and General Nelson can move troops to SB1 in preparation for any type of engagement. I can take a few of my agents and circulate with the people in the pods on a pretense of inspecting environmental systems before they get final launch approval."

"Very good. I suggest we get up there as quickly as we can. General, notify the Captain of the Endeavour as well, we should have them standing by in case they are needed. In the meantime, we do not know who is doing it or how this sabotage project is being managed. Since it is the food supply, I would suggest we seriously focus on that area. Let's go."

When they arrived on SB1 Derek met them. "President Wilson, good to see you. We have completed all the diagnostics Erica requested and everything is nominal. There have been no changes to any system."

"Very good. General Nelson, please deploy your team for fast reaction to all three pods. I don't know if these individuals are armed, but we should be ready for a very fast entry to each pod should the need arise."

"Yes, sir."

"Stephanie, your task is the most important and potentially dangerous. Be safe, keep in touch."

"We will."

Stephanie motioned for her team to move. She would lead the team into Pod Seven. Abby would lead the team into Pod Eight. Rodney would lead the team into Pod Nine. They all went in their different directions. Each team was composed of five agents, enough to react, not too many to cause undue concern.

Stephanie led her team into the pod and once inside, could feel the humidity. She looked and saw where the travelers were beginning to plant crops and acclimatize to the environment. They spread out, there was a lot of ground to cover.

Jeffrey and Erica were discussing the food supply with Derek. "So how would you destroy the food supply? What is the easiest and most effective way?"

"Well, it couldn't be the seed. We received the seeds in triple sealed vacuum containers that are not opened until needed. Each container is connected to the system, so when a container is opened we know it. None of them have been opened."

"Okay, so what next, could the soil be contaminated?"

"No, we ran a lot of tests on the soil all over the pod. We tested for chemicals, makeup of the soil, everything we could think of. From what we can tell the soil is safe. And, if you wanted to destroy the food supply it would be hard to do so by trying to contaminate thousands of acres of soil."

"Okay. What about the water?"

"No, we constantly monitor the water supply, it is scrubbed and sanitized. If there was a problem with the water, it would affect more than the food supply."

"Well then, I don't get it, what is left?"

Erica said, "Fertilizer."

Derek seemed momentarily startled. "You may be on to something. We only inspected the fertilizer when it was brought on board, but it can be accessed at any time without anyone knowing it. All someone would need to do is drop some contaminants into a fertilizer container and it would be a poison. We would need to inspect all the fertilizer containers. That will take some time."

Jeffrey was listening to the conversation, then said, "Not necessarily. We should assume the saboteurs will wait until the pods are well on their way, like the others, before they do anything. They may have already put the contaminants in the fertilizer, but they would have selected fertilizer that was well behind the fertilizer to be used for the first several months to a year. After all, they don't want anyone to be able to escape or be able to survive. If they wait, they can accomplish this unnoticed."

"You are right, we should look at containers for six months or a year out. That at least narrows it down. I will get a team on it."

"Wait, we have staff inside looking for these culprits. We don't want to tip our hand just yet. After all, we can delay the launch if we need to."

Suddenly alarms began going off all over the station. "That is an air leak and explosion alarm. Stay here!" Derek left the room and closed the airtight door.

He ran across the station in the direction of the fire vehicle responding to the explosion, towards Pod Nine. In the distance he could see flames and smoke, and occasionally, an explosion. He grabbed an oxygen mask and kept running.

General Nelson was behind a mobile evacuation vehicle, Derek went to him and asked what had happened.

"We believe the agents inside actually found the saboteurs and a confrontation ensued. The saboteurs exited the pod and saw us then opened fire. They had grenades and automatic weapons. They ran in the direction of pod Seven, but we cut them off. Right now, they are held up over in that storage area. We are trying to limit our actions so as not to cause a hull breach, but I fear these two will cause it just to end the missions."

Rodney and his team had only begun to investigate the people in the pod when he came across someone holding a gun. Before he could react, he was shot, point blank. That began the firefight inside. Two other agents were killed as the two saboteurs made their way out.

Stephanie heard what had happened. She decided they needed to change tactics. She ordered the marines who were waiting outside to enter the pod and instructed Abby to do the same. They then gathered everyone together and searched them. No one had a weapon, but there were some oddities. She ordered the marines to hold everyone in one place until she returned, then exited the pod and had Abby join her to see what had happened at pod nine.

"General Nelson, what is your status?"

"Stephanie, we have taken casualties. There are two of them, heavily armed, holed up over in that supply area across the bay. Every time we move, they fire. I don't know how they see us."

"Okay. I ordered your marines into pod seven and eight to hold everyone in place. We need to get these two sorted out fast. Abby, you go right, I'll go left. Cover us."

With that Stephanie and Abby leapt over the vehicle and ran in a zig zag pattern to the right and left of the supply area. As soon as they started to run they were fired upon, but the marines fired back and helped suppress the fire, giving them enough time to make it. Once there, they both took different routes through, around, and behind the area. The two saboteurs were obviously very dangerous. If they had defeated her agents and defied the marines, they were skilled. She and Abby were the best she had. If they could not take these two down, then it would not end well.

Abby froze and listened. There was a lot of noise, but slowly she segmented it into compartments, so the noise became quiet. This allowed her to hear anything that was not part of that chaos. She listened intently, then heard a breath. It was close. She didn't move. She knew there was nothing behind her and resisted the temptation to turn around. Almost as soon as she did this, she noticed, out of the corner of her left eye, a slight movement. It was miniscule, but it was different than the surroundings. She waited. The motion continued, and she could tell it was someone moving very gently in the aisle next to her. She still waited. Suddenly, the individual stepped into the aisle she was in looking the other way. She realized this was a female. She did not hesitate; but aimed and shot her in the upper right shoulder, causing her to drop her weapon and spin around. She had another gun in her left hand and fired, hitting Abby in her left arm, but Abby was already pulling the trigger, firing, hitting her in the chest, blowing her heart out and killing her.

Stephanie heard the shots and hoped it was not Abby. She also froze. She was waiting for some motion when the wall of supplies to her left started to fall on her. She ducked to avoid the worst of it, then heard shots. She felt one slice through her left side, but knew it was superficial. She slid out from under the mass of cans and boxes and found a large male standing watching her with his gun aimed at her. Her gun had been knocked out of her hand. She waited for the shot. Instead, he lowered his gun. Then he set it down, and grinning, walked towards her. Stephanie launched herself at this madman with all she had. She hit him full on, but he somehow grabbed and flipped her over his shoulder to land on the floor behind him. He quickly spun around and moved at her aggressively raising his arms to hit her. She had a can of something in her hand and threw it at his groin as hard as she could. He bent to deflect it, giving her time to get to her feet.

She crouched there, prepared for defense as he approached again. He did not hesitate, but strong armed his way past her defense. He was brutal. He hit her multiple times and grabbed her by the neck. She kneed him in the groin as hard as she could, and in the slight moment his strength was not in his arms, she twisted free, grabbing one arm and throwing herself on the elbow joint, breaking it.

He did not make a sound; instead, he reached around behind his back with his good arm and pulled out a gun, and as he was bringing it around to point at her, a loud shot went off. His head exploded from one side. Abby had pushed her way through the supplies and found them, saw what was happening, and ended it.

General Nelson and the marines had heard the shots and waited. After a moment, as he was going to order his team to attack, Stephanie and Abby came walking out of the supply area. They were both bleeding from their injuries. "Medic!"

Jeffrey and Erica had made their way to the same location, but at a much slower pace than Derek. Jeffrey said, "You are one hell of a fighter, Stephanie, and you Abby. Amazon's, I think."

Stephanie smiled, but did not say anything.

"Alright, we have eliminated two perpetrators. However, we still have four in the other two pods and we still have not discovered how they were going to destroy the food supply. Stephanie, you had the marines gather everyone together and watch them, correct?"

"Yes, but I do not know if they managed to get everyone, or just the ones who would cooperate."

"General, work with Derek, identify every individual in every pod. Bring them outside. Make sure your marines are prepared for what just happened at pod nine. Once we identify everyone and have them isolated outside of the pods, then we need to get back in there and search the fertilizer supplies. Let's go."

They found the first two saboteurs in their sleeping quarters. Apparently, they decided to take their own lives rather than face capture or the wrath of the Riser. They found the second two when they fired on the marines searching the far side of the pod. The difference is that these marines were not caught by surprise. They returned fire killing them both.

Once the saboteurs were eliminated, the search of the fertilizer stores began. They ended up searching each entire pod. They discovered poison in multiple bags in various parts of the pods. To be safe, they delayed departure of the pods for a week, and removed all fertilizer and replaced it with new, just to make sure there were no containers they missed. Once this was complete, the pod departure was back on track.

"Now, we have these three pods under control, but how do we notify the other six pods?"

"We could transmit a massive energy signal to them. It might get through to them. If we do it repeatedly for a few days, hopefully they will catch it at least once."

"Okay, put together a short transmission with what they need to know and do it. Let me know if you hear anything in return. Otherwise, we can only pray they discover the truth and take care of it themselves."

7.211.09

They had managed to keep the sabotage of the pods secret from the world media. No one knew about the disaster that may be happening on board the other six pods. He couldn't sleep when he thought about it. It must be terrifying, regardless of what was happening, to be on one of those pods.

Jeffrey suffered from claustrophobia and simply could not imagine being inside a pod traveling through space. Then to have the food supply being killed off. Well, there was nothing they could do until they developed lightspeed travel. But those pods would be the first destination once they managed that feat.

Today was the last launch. Jeffrey had decided to fly to SB1 one last time, to be there when the last three pods were launched. He hated the re-entry getting back on the ground, but this was too important not to do it in person. The pods had already been moved out into deep space and would initiate their ion engines after he gave a few comments. His words were transmitted in the clear for all the world to hear.

"First, congratulations to the entire team who managed to design, build, and launch nine interstellar migration pods in such a short time. It seems the past seven years have been a blur of activity, so many things have happened. We are safe from asteroids, we have improved the quality of life for people around the globe, and now, we launch the last of our migration pods."

"I know the pioneers on these three pods are eager to get moving, so let's get started. As usual, everyone please join with me for a countdown to launch starting with ten, nine, eight, seven, six, five, four, three, two, one, launch!"

The control room initiated the ion engines for the pods. Slowly, they began to accelerate away from Earth. This was the culmination of a lot of work.

Now to look to the future. Jeffrey had them cut the live feed, so he could talk to Derek.

"Derek, congratulations to you and your entire team. You have performed admirably."

"Thank you, President Wilson. We appreciate your vision and support."

"You are welcome. Now as to vision. I believe Erica informed you that we will begin re-tooling SB1 towards the goal of building starships. I would like to offer you the job as director of SB1, if you want it."

"Yes sir! I would love the opportunity to transform this facility into a viable facility for the future. We were created for one future and that era is done. Getting ready for the next one will be a huge challenge, but a wonderful experience."

"Very well. Please drop down to our offices in Omaha so we can have some conversations and finalize this change."

7.256.14

Gabby and Simon had spent a lot of time together over the past several months, growing closer every day. They still had not had time to go on a true 'date,' except the zoo. But they did take in movies and have dinner together at the Federation.

They spent a lot of time in quiet conversation and shared their dreams of the future. They shared stories of growing up, families, college. They discovered they liked the same types of food, music, and art. They found themselves in each other; but were too nervous about speaking about their feelings to actually say anything. Other people could see they were growing in love with each other, but they held out stepping over that line.

They were both very positive that a star drive would be invented. They were also equally positive they wanted to be part of the team that made the discovery.

Gabby had not really talked about her parents to anyone except Sheryl before. But she found herself talking about them to Simon. "My dad was larger than life to me. I loved him dearly, but I also know that he had always wanted a son. I did everything I could to fill that role, but he never really seemed satisfied with my accomplishments. I graduated as the valedictorian from high school, and I believe he would have been genuinely happy that I had reached the top of the class. At least, I've always wanted to believe that. It's probably what's driven me to be the very best I could be in college. It still irritates me that he went off and got himself and mom killed in his plane."

Gabby had tears rolling down her cheek and Simon held her hand while she talked.

"Still, I wish he was here to give me a hug and congratulate me on this next step. I will tell you this, if I ever have children, my husband and I will love them for who they are, not hold back love and approval until they do something that impresses us or because they aren't the sex we had wanted."

"I totally miss my mom. When she died, I didn't believe I could go forward in life. I felt that the most important part of me had died as well. I thought, 'Who will I giggle with?', 'Who will I talk to about boys?', 'Who will help me pick out a wedding dress or be there when I have children?' God, I miss my mom so much. I miss all the conversations, the quiet times just being together. My mom was my true rock. I miss her every day."

Simon continued to hold her as she cried. It wasn't too long that she wiped her tears, and asked, "Simon, why don't you ever go home to see your parents?"

"Well, it's complicated. But the simple answer is that they don't trust the Federation or anything I am doing. I think if I was dead they would probably not be upset."

"Oh Simon, I had no idea it was that deep. I am so sorry."

"Yes, well, thank you, but I have come to terms with it."

"I don't know how you can do that. I lost my parents and miss them terribly. I think it is so sad your parents don't love you unconditionally."

"Well, they don't. I am not sure they understand what love is. I mean, to love someone is to care more about them than you care about yourself and to always do that at all times, isn't it?"

"Yes, it is. I want that kind of love in my life. I haven't felt that since my parents died."

"I know you will find that, Gabby. I just know it."

"I know you will too."

8.169.14

"Viper 31, Eagle 41, you need to take a hard look at your trajectory, over."

Simon was the pilot of Viper 31. "Roger, Eagle 41, looks like the aft rotational stabilizers have failed, not sure I can stabilize, over."

"Endeavour con, Eagle 41, we have a potential problem with Viper 31. His trajectory is shifting for possible impact with the hard deck, sector Delta Three, over."

"Roger, Eagle 41. Break. Viper 31, status."

"Viper 31 is experiencing rotational degradation, unable to initiate effective stabilization, appears rear stabilizer thrusters have failed, trying to hold it as steady as possible, but its slipping."

"Roger, Viper 31." The watch officer turned to the commander on duty, "Sir, we have an imminent surface impact with Viper 31, stabilizer out."

"Launch search and rescue, let's get as close as we can." He reached over and selected the connection to Federation HQ. "This is Endeavour, we have an imminent impact for Viper 31, Moon surface sector Delta Three."

Simon was very engaged in trying to stay alive. He could tell he was losing altitude, and his attitude was slipping, but the uncontrollable rotation was his biggest concern. Essentially, if he could not stabilize, he would simply tumble over and hit the surface. Not a good solution. He shifted his brain into hyperdrive, testing various actions, results, feeling the ship.

"Prepare to abandon ship." He informed his crew of the possibility of a crash. There were fifteen go troops in the craft. They were practicing low level surface integration tactics in low gravity. Each marine had a suit that could protect them, but not if they were damaged in a crash.

"Endeavour, Viper 31, abandoning craft, over."

"Roger, Viper 31, Endeavour copies."

"SAR 14 departing Endeavour for Delta Three, ETA three minutes."

The craft was beginning to spin, Simon knew if the troops did not get out now it would be too late. "Eject, Eject, Eject." The marines pulled the main hull breach handle and they were in space, descending towards the surface, now only a hundred yards below. While the speed was slow, their mass would still cause a slow-motion collision of bone crushing proportions. They had prepared for this, but never from this height or this speed. It would be a tough landing.

Simon remained with the craft. He anticipated bailing out in about five seconds, but felt the craft demonstrate a slow recovery. His mind worked quickly. "Endeavour, Viper 31, the reduced mass within the craft has slowed the rotation and is allowing me to regain some control. I will try and hold it together to impact. Estimate fifteen seconds."

Endeavour could not respond. What could they say? He was the commander of the craft. It was his decision. The only response, "Roger."

He watched as the craft slowly righted, then just before impact tilted dramatically to the left. He thought he had it, but he must have over-compensated. He hit the surface with the left side of the craft first, felt it break up and roll quickly to the right. The craft rolled over and over, finally coming to a stop after traveling 200 yards.

Heather had just left Jeffrey's office when General Nelson knocked, then entered the office. He stopped. "Mr. President, we've had a training accident on the moon. It appears one of our craft experienced equipment failure. The marines on board abandoned the craft, but they were at one hundred yards elevation traveling at ten yards per second. Of the fifteen, only seven survived. The pilot of the craft is alive but in critical condition. All survivors are on board the Endeavour and enroute to orbit for transfer of the injured to the Federation medical center."

Erica watched as Jeffrey bowed his head a moment. "Thank you, General. Please keep me advised of changes and when they return."

"Yes sir." He turned and left.

Erica said, "I think this is the only reason I do not want your job, Jeffrey. Every time someone dies, you have to deal with it. I don't know if I can do that."

Jeffrey turned to her. "Erica, you are the most empathetic person I know. You will show these men and women a higher sense of empathy than I ever could. When you meet the survivors, you will encourage them and thank them for their service. When you meet the families of those who fall, you will be able to comfort them and help them to live with the knowledge their loved one gave the ultimate sacrifice for a noble cause. I know you can do this. If for even one second, I thought you could not, I would never have offered you to take this job."

Erica was in tears as he spoke. He got up and walked over to her and held her, letting her cry. He knew she could do this. It was never easy, but she was strong enough to be a great leader. She just had to believe in herself.

8.170.13

Gabby was working in the lab when the call came in.
"Captain Anderson?"
"Yes."
"Please report to the Central hospital, reception desk."
"Yes, sir. Can you tell me what for?"
"No, you will need to find out at the hospital."

Gabby had no idea what could be going on as she traveled to the hospital. When she arrived at the hospital, there were quite a few people gathered in the lobby. She made her way to the reception desk and reported in. The nurse said to follow her. They walked around the counter and into the office area behind reception. Gabby was surprised to find the President of the Federation Council, his wife, Heather and some other lady there. She entered, and the nurse closed the door behind her.

"Please have a seat." Jeffrey did not know how strong the connection was between Gabby and Simon, but knew she needed to know what happened.

"Please sir, can you tell me what is going on?"

"Yes. There was an accident yesterday in a training activity on the moon. Several marines were killed. The pilot of the craft they were in survived, but he is in critical condition."

"Simon?"

"Yes."

Gabby started crying. Heather and Erica both went and sat beside her and held her while she cried. "How bad is he?"

"From what I am told, he has broken several bones, injured several organs, and has a possible concussion. We don't know more than that. We will know soon if it is as bad as it sounds or not. He is being worked on right now, just down the hall. We are waiting, and will wait with you, if that is okay with you."

She tried to stop crying. "Yes, please, thank you."

"It is hard not to expect the worse. We always do that to ourselves. It helps to manage our expectations and feelings. But he is in the best hospital in the world getting the best support possible. If he can fight through, he will be okay."

Gabby looked at Heather and smiled a little. "You sound like Diedre again. I believed you in the movie and it turned out to be what you said. I believe you now." She leaned her head over onto Heather's chest and closed her eyes. They stayed that way for a while.

Eventually, there was a knock at the door. Dr. Nielsen entered and had a smile on his face. "Mr. President, I have some very good news. Captain Jackson did not break his back or suffer any irreparable nerve damage. He also did not suffer a brain injury. He does have seven broken bones on top of three broken ribs, and he did injure his liver. But again, none of these are irreparable, so he will be fine, albeit he will be in some pain for quite a while and the recovery period could be as much as a year."

Gabby jumped up and gave him a big hug. "Thank you! Can I see him?"

The others laughed at her reaction. Dr. Nielsen said she could, in a little while, and excused himself to continue working with patients.

Jeffrey was curious. "Gabby, I didn't know you and Simon were this close. I thought you were only just getting to know each other."

Gabby smiled. "Yes, but he is the first person to ever look at me like a real person and not a zombie. He is not threatened by my brain. I almost feel that…"

Heather interjected "…he likes you for who you are, not who he wants you to be."

"Yes!"

"I completely understand. That is how Jeffrey makes me feel and one of the things I fell in love with first about him."

Gabby looked at Heather, and asked her, "Would you mind if I visited you again sometime?"

"Of course not, please stop by anytime."

"Well, where would I go? I have not been off the Federation grounds except to the zoo once."

Erica said, "Gabby, here is my number. When you are ready to visit Heather, you give me a call and I will arrange for you to get to wherever she is, okay?"

"Perfect."

They visited for a while, then Gabby left to go see Simon.

8.193.09

Heather loved what she did. She had seen so many wonderful projects over the years doing this work. It always gave her such satisfaction when children were able to be safe, smile, and thrive. She loved her work, and she loved Jeffrey for letting her do it. She paid attention to what he was doing and was heavily involved in it, but this was her passion. He set her up and stepped aside and let her go. It was just wonderful.

About a month after Simon's crash, she was working from her Omaha office, just down the hall from Jeffrey's. Unexpectedly, Erica stopped in.

"Hi Heather, how goes your day?"

"Hi, very well. I didn't expect to see you, is there something going on?"

"No, just letting you know that Gabby called this morning and wanted to visit with you, so I am stopping by to see what you want to do?"

Heather smiled at the thought of Gabby. Something about that girl was so near to her, but she couldn't quite put it together. "Well, I am in the office all day today, so anytime would be fine."

"Alright then, I will bring her in."

"Thanks!"

A little over an hour later, Erica appeared at the door. She had Gabby with her and they were smiling and laughing about something. "Okay, Heather, here you go. Let me know when you are finished, and I will get Gabby a ride back to the Federation."

"Thank you, Erica. Hi, Gabby, come in."

"Hi. I am embarrassed being here, but I just felt I needed to see you."

Heather closed her door and escorted her over to the couch and chairs she had for visiting with people. Gabby sat on the couch while Heather took a chair. "Well, I am glad to see you. So, tell, me, what can I do for you?"

Gabby just looked at her for a moment. "Mrs. Wilson, you are sure it is alright if I call you Heather? Should I call you something else?"

"No, Heather is fine."

"Thank you. Where to begin? Please be patient with me while I go through this. I am feeling very emotional right now and don't know who to turn to."

"It's okay, just take your time."

"Thank you. You don't know this, but my mother and father were killed in a plane crash thirteen years ago. I have no siblings, aunts, uncles; I am by myself. I try hard not to feel sorry for myself, but there are times when I just wish I had someone I could really talk to about life, love, loss, all the important things in life. It is one of the reasons I loved your movie so much, because you were that person for Andromeda. You were so empathetic, yet vulnerable yourself. I just loved your character."

"Thank you, Gabby. I enjoyed playing the role. We have something in common you and me. Neither of us has any family. My family, biologically, is me. My mom and dad died in a car crash when I was five, and my aunt died from cancer when I was twenty-one. I am all that I have. Until that is, I met Jeffrey. He made me his family and gave me a very big loving family."

"I hope to one day be part of a family like that. I know Simon and I are getting close and he comes from a very big family. But right now, I don't have a mom or someone I can talk to about how I feel. It makes me sad and all I want to do is cry, but I don't know how to deal with it sometimes." She started to cry, and Heather went over to the couch and sat beside her and wrapped her arm around her and just held her.

After a while, she stopped crying. "Thank you. I am so sorry for bringing this to you."

"Shhhh. Don't be sorry for having emotions. Be thankful you are courageous enough to reach out for someone."

"Thank you. It's just, sometimes it really feels lonely, you know? Not to have someone you can go to that you trust completely, someone who will listen and not judge, someone who will love you unconditionally. I really miss that."

"I know exactly how you feel. Tell me, when do you have to be back at the Academy?"

"I have a shift at midnight tonight."

"Wait here, I will be right back." She got up and walked down the hall past Stephanie and Abby into Jeffrey's office. Jeffrey and Erica were discussing some budgeting issues. "Can I talk with you two?"

"Of course."

"Okay, Gabby is in my office. We were just talking, and I discovered we have something in common. She does not have any family at all, like me. However, she is doing something I never had the courage to do, she is reaching out for emotional support. She has a shift tonight at midnight. Can we get her out of her shift?"

"Of course, we can, but why?"

"I love you unconditionally, Jeffrey, but right now, I feel I need to be something for this girl I have never been with anyone. I need to be her emotional support, her pillar of strength, her resource."

"Her mother, you mean." Jeffrey said this with a smile, and Heather noticed that Erica was also smiling.

"Why are you two smiling?"

"Because this is the first time, in all the years that I have known you, that you have come out fighting for someone like this. It is wonderful."

Heather blushed. "Well, it is emotional."

Erica walked over and gave her a hug. "I know, and you are a beautiful strong woman reaching out to help a lovely young lady learn to be a woman."

"Thank you."

"Okay then, I will call and have her placed on leave for a few days. What is your plan?"

"I don't know. I thought maybe see if she wants to come home with us tonight and have dinner, maybe sit and drink some wine in front of the fire? Just visit, talk, relate. It may not lead to anything, but I feel I must do this, or I will regret it immensely."

"Done. Erica, would you please inform Stephanie of our new plan? Oh, and are you and Steve free tonight?"

"I will. No, we have a play to go to tonight. Khloe is playing Snow White in her school play."

"Oh, I am so sorry we will not be able to make it."

"Not to worry. However, if I was you, I would see if Tamara could join you as she is free, while Steven is on an overnight trip to his mother's house with their children."

"Ah. Good call, I will invite her over."

"Thank you. I really appreciate your support."

"No problem, dear. We are all on your side."

Erica added, "By the way, if you want some real bonding time, you may want to take her shopping. I know she did not bring a bag along and does not expect an overnight stay, but if you do what you are talking about doing, then chances are she will be spending the night and she will need some clothes, among other things."

Heather nodded. "Good idea, thank you."

When she walked back into her office, Gabby looked very nervous. "I am so sorry, you probably want me to leave, so I will just go if that is okay."

Heather smiled at her. "Gabby, not only do I not want you to go, but I just talked with the President of the Federation Council and he informed me that you are on vacation for a few days."

"What?"

"Yes, and since you are on vacation, I was hoping you would agree to go shopping with me and then come over to our house this evening for dinner. It will be something simple, Jeffrey will probably insist on cooking. It will give us some time to visit. What do you say?"

Gabby hugged her. "Thank you so much."

Heather held her for a few minutes, then they got moving to leave the office.

"Hi Dad."

"Hi dear. Are you free for dinner tonight?"

"Yes, of course. Steven took the kids to his moms for a slumber party, so I am available."

"Great. I think dinner at about seven. But that is only part of why I called you."

"Oh, what's up?"

"You know that Heather has never been a mom. She misses that role and has a gap in her heart that cannot be filled. You obviously know what I mean more than I do. I can understand it psychologically, but not emotionally."

"Yes, I know what you mean. If I had not had my kids I know there would be a great big empty space. I think for Heather it is a large gap as well, although you have managed to help her keep it manageable."

"Thank you. There is movement in that front, I think."

"Oh? What do you mean?"

"I don't think you met Gabby. She is a Captain in the Federation doing research. She is actually a genius, with an IQ of 190. She only completed a double masters at MIT by the time she was twenty-two and a doctorate by twenty-four."

"Wow. She sounds like a genius."

"Yes, well, Heather and I met her on the first day she arrived at the Federation a few years back. I have seen her a couple of times since. When that ship crashed on the moon a while ago, Gabby was listed as the point of contact for the pilot of the craft. He survived, and we went to see him. We also met Gabby at that time. In the conversation she mentioned she loved the role Heather had played in her last movie, when she was a mentor to the heroine. She even asked if it would be okay if she visited with her sometime. Well, that time, apparently, was today."

"She stopped in to visit Heather and in a very moving manner, she and Heather have connected emotionally. I think Heather sees in Gabby the daughter she never had. Gabby is twenty-six. Her parents were killed in a plane crash thirteen years ago and she has no other relatives of any kind. I know that really pulled at Heather's heart strings. Also, I have had Gabby investigated. She is everything she says."

"Okay, so how does this tie into me?"

"Tonight, Gabby will be joining us for dinner. It will give you a chance to get to know her, but I wanted to let you know that we may both be second fiddle tonight, if these two really do strike a chord together and create a strong bonding relationship."

"Thanks dad. I actually hope this does happen. Heather and I have a great relationship, but it is a strong friendship, not a mother-daughter relationship. I knew mom too long to ever let someone take that place."

"Yes, I understand. I just wanted you to know."

"Thanks again, see you tonight. This should be fun."

Heather and Gabby had a great time shopping. The first thing they did was go to a clothing store and purchase her some comfortable clothes for Gabby to wear for the day. That way she could get out of the uniform she was in and relax. Then they shopped for some real clothes. Gabby had never purchased clothes that cost this much, she was a pauper by comparison. The clothes Heather bought her were perfect in both fit and style.

"Heather, Oh, my god, I cannot believe you are buying me these clothes. You have to stop this!"

Heather was having a wonderful time. "Well if you are going to come over to our house tonight and have dinner, chances are you will be spending the night. In that case, you need clothes for tomorrow, plus shoes, lingerie, and toiletries. So yes, we are going to buy you everything you may need."

"Can I hug you?"

Heather took her in her arms and held her, saying, "Anytime. I will be here for you."

Gabby felt she had found home again. She missed her parents terribly, but now, for the first time since that tragedy, she felt she could breathe and let some of the emotion go.

Heather looked at her hands. "Gabby, have you ever had a manicure or a pedicure?"

"Oh no, those are way too expensive for me. I just keep them clean and groomed."

"Well, my dear, that ends today."

They found a spa and spent a couple of hours getting the prettiest fingernails and toes Gabby had ever seen. She was so thrilled. She insisted on getting a pair of sandals to wear so her toes could be seen. Heather loved every minute of it and laughed harder than she had in a long time.

At dinner that night, Jeffrey had asked his chef to help him with the crab stuffed filet mignon and whiskey peppercorn sauce. It was either that or cook chicken cordon bleu. He loved cooking, but he was getting a little tired of the chore of it all. Between his chef and sommelier selecting the wine, it turned out to be perfect.

"Honestly, Mr. President, I have never had food as good as this."

Jeffrey put down his glass and leaned in her direction. "Let us get something settled between us." Heather and Tamara both chuckled, knowing what was coming. Gabby heard this and suddenly thought she had made a mistake and was scared. "My name is Jeffrey. I know I fill a role as the President of the Federation Council. I know I am a lot older than you. I know there is every reason for you to call me Mr. President or Mr. Wilson. But when you are here in this inner sanctum with us, my name is Jeffrey. She is Heather, she is Tamara, and I am Jeffrey. And that lady over there who is always around, is Stephanie. Okay?"

"Yes sir, I mean, Jeffrey."

"Good. It will take you some time to get used to it, but you will. Now, if you two ladies will go sit by the fire and smile at your lovely fingers and toes while my daughter and I clean up the dishes, that would be just about perfect."

"Gabby bring the wine." Heather stopped and kissed Jeffrey. "Thank you, my love. I love you totally."

"Yes," he whispered, "and I can't wait to get you in bed tonight."

She wiggled with anticipation and kissed him again, then went over to where Gabby had sat down on the couch.

Tamara just laughed. She had been around these two enough to know they showed their love and appreciation for each other in private all the time. "Okay, let's clean dishes."

At nine, Tamara bid everyone farewell and went home. At ten, Jeffrey bid them goodnight and went to bed. But Heather and Gabby stayed up for quite a while in quiet conversation.

"Yes, my mom was the cook in our house as well. She did a wonderful job, well, nothing like what we had tonight, but it was always good."

"I remember that my mom really couldn't cook very well. My aunt Ruth, however, was excellent. Still, I would agree the meals I have now are better than anything I have ever had before, and Jeffrey does like to work in the kitchen."

"What is the last thing you remember about your mom?"

"I remember she gave me a big hug when they left to go the store. I was at my friend's house next door when she stopped over to say they were going to the store and would be back in a little while. She gave me a big hug and told me she loved me. I can still remember how she smelled and how her long hair was free in the breeze."

"I bet you will always remember your mom just like that."

"Yes, I believe so. How about you?"

"I was thirteen and the school year was about to begin when my parents decided they were going on this month-long support trip for our church. They were going to deliver needed supplies to some remote villages in Alaska. When they were getting ready to go, my dad gave me a hug, said he loved me and went out the door."

"My mom though, she truly stopped and sat on a bar stool by the island in the kitchen. She pulled me over to her and held me for a long time, whispering she loved me and would always be with me. I don't know if she had a premonition or not, but we hugged each other for quite a while before she walked me over to my best friend Sheryl's house next door. I also remember how she felt and how she smelled. I will never forget that."

"We do have a lot in common, dear."

"Yes. I think the thing I most feel about you, is that I can trust you. I know it is too soon to know someone and tell them you love them, but I feel that way."

Heather held her in her arms, saying, "I know how you feel. I believe I love you as well."

They hugged for a while, the Gabby asked, "Will you help me understand men?"

Heather had to laugh at this unexpected question. "I will try, but until I met Jeffrey, I seemed to always meet the wrong men."

"I read about your romance with Jeffrey and how you met. That must have been exciting."

Heather smiled remembering. "Yes, it was. But tell me, how did you and Simon meet?"

Gabby also smiled. "We met in a game."

"A game?"

"Yes. There is this game, called Space Tetramax. There are only five level six players in the world and one level seven player. We had a contest at the Federation and everyone was surprised to learn that all of these players were at the Federation, well one is a Cadet at the Academy. Simon is a level six player and I am the only level seven player. Needless to say, I defeated everyone else. He was flummoxed, as it only took me fifteen minutes to beat him. He asked me to lunch and we have been seeing each other as often as we can since then, but our schedules are different. We did have a date at the zoo, which was marvelous. You remember he was on the moon for training and got hurt."

"Yes. So, you are the world's only level seven player? You really are a super genius."

"Yeah, but the thing is, Simon doesn't make me feel like a weirdo by being so smart. He just goes with it and lets me be me. Just like you do."

"I learned a long time ago the hard way, that the most important thing in life is to be loved for who you are while you are being yourself. Anything else is just stupidity."

"Heather, thank you so very much for letting me in. I have not felt this free, relaxed, and unstressed, since before my parents died. It is just so nice to be able to finally let some things go, like the energy of the pain, and have fun."

"You are very welcome, dear. I know the energy it takes to hold onto pain. It really is harder than people think. Being without a family is hard. But it makes finding family wonderful."

The two ladies stood up and gave each other a very long hug. Heather walked Gabby down to the guest room and said goodnight. Then she went back and crawled into her bed and snuggled up to Jeffrey for a very good night's sleep.

Gabby went into her room and carefully hung up what were, to her, very expensive clothes. She went into the bathroom and could not believe the opulence of it all and the space! She stopped and looked at herself in the mirror. She leaned in and looked directly into her eyes. She said, "Thank you, Lord, for finally giving me hope." Then she went out and climbed into the softest sheets she had ever felt, and went to sleep, getting one of the best nights rest she had ever gotten.

9.011.10

Jeffrey had worked for several months to get the council to this point. Even though it was January and snowy and cold outside, he felt good and believed now was the time.

"I would ask the council to consider that all funding for the Federation, including hardware, infrastructure, facilities, you name it; everything, is provided by JW Enterprises. In short, there is nothing this Federation and Academy have that was not paid for by me. Now we have discussed and agreed to the stipulation that the Federation Council would remain in its current form until ten planets joined, at which time the funding model would be changed so JW Enterprises is not the sole financial supporter of the Federation. Furthermore, the Federation also agrees it will arrange a means to repay, at fair market value, the investments made by JW Enterprises to establish and support the Federation."

"However, my point is this, until such time as we reach that benchmark, I believe the President of JW Enterprises should remain the President of the Federation Council and retain veto power over decisions made by the council."

Jeffrey had maneuvered the agenda for the past several months, raising different aspects of this argument. Today was the culmination of the argument. Erica was very pleased with how he had presented it. She looked around the room while he was talking. There were only two chairs in the inner council occupied, that of the Earth and Mars. The remaining chairs were empty. In a second row, chairs were taken by the fourteen states who were actively working to create this reality for the future. Looking at their faces, Erica was assured they were on board.

"I agree you have provided all the funding, support, guidance and the vision we have needed to move this project forward. As the representative from Mars, I fully support the direction you have laid out."

"As the representative of the people of Earth, let me be the first to make the motion to approve the recommendation of the President on the sustainment of the Presidency to the President of JW Enterprises, up until such time as we reach ten planets sitting in this council."

"I second that!"

"All those in favor, say aye."

"Aye!"

"Those opposed?"

No one opposed the measure and it was passed unanimously.

When Erica walked past Jeffrey, she reached down and squeezed his shoulder. He looked up and winked at her.

9.258.16

Heather was feeling mellow. "Jeffrey, I am perplexed."

He dropped what he was doing to focus on Heather. "How so, dear?"

"You know I always wanted a baby of my own, right?"

"Yes."

"Well, how is it that this girl, Gabby, can seem to fill that spot in my heart, yet not be biologically my child?"

"Well, maybe she fits within your needs. In some way, she fits and fills your emotional need."

"I think you may be right. Dear, can we just go to Destin today and play in the water?"

"Of course. I don't have anything pressing, we can leave this morning, if you want."

"I do, and can we take Gabby with us?"

"Well, I don't see why not. But dear, will I be a third wheel for this trip?"

She laughed, saying, "Never. It's just that I would like to do something with her like a mother/father/daughter weekend."

"Okay, let's go."

Jeffrey informed Erica and Stephanie of the plans, and they made the necessary coordination.

Gabby was ecstatic to be going with them on a vacation. Once they were ready, they boarded the plane at the air base and departed. Gabby had never gotten to sit in the front of the plane, so totally enjoyed the experience.

When they landed, they went straight to the beach. Whereas Heather and Jeffrey usually laid on a blanket together, they had beach chairs and umbrellas for them all. Gabby was trying to figure out how to body surf. Heather sat on the beach, watching Jeffrey try to explain to Gabby how to get it right.

"Okay, look, it's a timing thing. First, let's find a spot where the water is not too deep, so you can jump and grab the wave. Now, you have to imagine you are a surfboard. A surfboard does not ride the top of the wave, but the front of the wave. So, you have to launch yourself right on the front of the wave, and then hold your body rigid, so the water pushes you forward, but does not fall over you. Watch me."

He then waited for a wave, and right as the wave was getting to him, he jumped. It was perfect timing, and he rode the wave almost the entire distance to the shore.

"Okay, you do it!"

Gabby watched the waves. She waited until she thought a good one arrived, then jumped and forced herself to feel like a board. She rode the wave all the way to Jeffrey!

"Wow!! That was awesome!"

"I know, right? It feels so good to catch a wave perfectly. Great job, Gabby. That was fantastic."

"Heather, did you see that?"

"Yes, dear. That was wonderful!"

Gabby insisted on trying to catch additional waves, and drug Jeffrey with her. After a while, they went back to the umbrellas, sat in the shade and drank some water.

"I am having the best time of my life. I cannot thank you enough."

"Gabby, I have a question for you, and I want you to think about the answer before you say anything. Let me also qualify this by saying we do not mean to cause you any harm or disrespect your parents in any way. That being said, Gabby Anderson, would you consider the idea of allowing us to adopt you as our daughter?"

Gabby burst out in tears. Heather quickly moved from her chair to hold her and comfort her, saying, "Oh Gabby, I am so sorry if I offended you."

Gabby sobbed, but managed to say, "No, Heather, mom, you don't understand, I am so happy, I love you so much!"

"Oh, my dear, I love you."

They hugged for a while, then Gabby said, "Mom, can you please excuse me." Then she went over to Jeffrey, and said, "Is it true you would be my dad?"

"Yes, dear. With all my heart, yes."

She immediately hugged him, and said, "I love you."

"I love you, Gabby."

After some time, they left the beach and went to their suite, changed and went to dinner.

"A toast. To the newest member of the Wilson family!"

They clinked glasses, and Gabby knew she had found her home, her parents, and her future.

Later that night, after Gabby had gone to bed, Heather and Jeffrey talked.

"Well, dear, you out did yourself today."

Heather smiled, saying, "Maybe. But guess what, we have a new daughter!"

Jeffrey hugged her, saying, "Yes, a new, young daughter. I think she will challenge you. But I must say, I believe this is the best thing we have done together. I love you."

"I love you dear. And I agree, this is one of the best things I have ever done. I am so excited! I can't wait for tomorrow!"

Jeffrey just laughed with her, knowing that his wife was happier than he could remember, which only meant his life was going to be even more wonderful.

9.303.12

"Winter is coming. I can feel my bones hurting as the temperatures fall. It's only November, but my bones, where they were broken, can feel it."

"Well, you have not completed healing yet."

"True, but I have been in physical therapy for over a year and feel like I should be almost done. But still, for some reason, there are times when I experience such pain and just can't function at one hundred percent."

"That must be infuriating more than anything."

"Yes, it really is. Plus, my ribs still bother me. Anytime someone makes me laugh it still hurts."

"What are they doing in physical therapy now?"

"Well, today they were working on my range of motion and pushing the limits. But the thing is, I believe I am nearly ready to leave the hospital, but then what? I'm not ready to go back on duty, at least not do anything more than manage a desk, not for a long time, maybe nine more months anyway."

"I guess we will have to wait and see how you feel once your therapy is complete. In the meantime, I have to go. See you tomorrow?"

"Definitely, bye."

When he got back to his room he laid down to take a nap. These exercise sessions were always really tough. He laid there, but he just could not get to sleep. His mind kept going back to the crash and whether he could have done anything differently. He hated what happened, but he always came to the same conclusion, he did not know the problem of mass relating to the crafts configuration until after the marines had ejected. He only found out about the problem when the rotational stabilizers failed. He did everything he could. It was not his fault. Still, it haunted him.

9.304.08

The next day he reported for duty. "Captain Jackson reporting sir."

Major Fitzpatrick, his new superior, responded, "Captain, until you are released by the medical staff you will be assigned to the research wing. It is a temporary assignment, but until further notice, you are to report to Commander Stevenson at Z-Wing."

Simon met Commander Stevenson and he was directed to participate in logistical support for the X-drive team, which meant he was in the same wing as the research, but not actually included in the research.

He still felt this was a cool assignment and went about his tasks with a positive attitude. He still mostly managed a desk between visits to physical therapy. But the coolest thing about it was that he was in the same area of the Federation as Gabby. They had been able to see each other almost every day for a year, and he couldn't wait to see her every time. It was almost November and he was starting to think about what to get her for Christmas. He tucked this thought away as he made his way to the cafeteria, where she was waiting.

"Hi Simon!"

"Hi Gabby! You look very cheerful today."

"I am, because I have a surprise for you."

Simon had no idea what she could do that would surprise him, but he knew if she put her mind to it, she could come up with something. "Okay, what is it?"

Gabby knew Simon would be surprised when she told him what had been happening in her life. She had not informed him before about her contact with Heather, because she wanted to keep this secret. Having someone she could look up to, and be close to, was a dream she had held inside for many years, and now it was happening. She vowed to herself to protect that relationship at all costs.

She had also been talking with Heather about her growing feelings for Simon. He was the first person she had ever known who made her feel like a girl. She even giggled around him. It was like she could be so free and not worry about him seeing her vulnerabilities or concerns. She trusted him. It was a strange experience for her. She had known other guys in school and had even told them she loved them, but truthfully, she didn't think she actually had. Simon was different. She had not told him she loved him, but she was sure she did.

At almost the same time as Simon asked her what the surprise was, Heather walked through the cafeteria. Stephanie had insisted Abby escort her through the cadets, commanders and marines to her table. Abby brought along several agents, and together, they provided both close in and distant security. They did not perceive a direct threat, but they were just not taking any chances.

Gabby stood as Heather approached. The two of them had a short hug, and then they sat at the table. Simon apologized for not jumping up, but he had to move a little slower than that. Heather understood.

"Hi Simon, how is your recovery going?"

"Hi, Mrs. Wilson. It is going very well. I think I will be able to actually function properly in a few months, but full recovery will still take a little longer."

"Very good. Well, I am sure you are wondering why I am here this afternoon."

"Yes ma'am, that thought is dominating my mind."

Heather and Gabby both laughed. "She is here to tell you something very important, Simon."

"Yes, well, I am here to tell you that my husband wants to meet you personally. He asked me to stop by and see if you would be available this evening to join us for dinner."

Simon had no idea what was going on. He looked at Gabby, who was nearly laughing, but reached across and held his hand. "I don't actually have any plans, ma'am. My next physical therapy session is at two and I should be done by three thirty. After that I am available."

"Very well. Gabby will collect you from therapy and bring you over. Rest assured, this is not a grilling, but a relaxed meeting. Gabby can fill you in. Now, if you will excuse me, I have some other items I need to attend to." With that she departed with her security team.

Simon looked at Gabby and said, "What is going on?"

"My dear Simon, there have been quite a few things happening around you for a while now. The biggest is a change in the relationships I have. Tonight, I want to introduce you to some very special people in my life. They are fast becoming my family."

"What do you mean? Who is becoming your family?"

Gabby got up, walked around to where he was seated, and leaning down, gave him a quick kiss on the lips, the first intimate contact between them. "Simon, I will explain everything when I pick you up at three thirty. In the meantime, you go to therapy and don't worry, everything is fine."

Simon completed his therapy wishing he had extended that kiss! His mind was running way ahead. He knew he felt for her. My god, he admitted, I know I love her. However, there was confusion as well. Had Gabby established a relationship with Mrs. Wilson? What did she mean she had a family? He was very confused by the time Gabby arrived.

"So, tell me, what's up?"

"I want you to relax and trust me."

"I do trust you Gabby. More than anyone I have ever known."

She smiled. "Good. Then just keep that thought and let's enjoy the ride."

She led him to a limousine parked in the transportation area. His eyes got big as she helped him inside. Once inside, he was amazed at how many amenities were available. But he was still confused about everything. "Are you sure you won't tell me what is going on?"

"No, you will find out soon enough, I don't want to spoil the surprise."

"You could not possibly spoil anything at this point. I am completely confused and mixed up."

"Good, then when it becomes clear, you will enjoy the surprise even more."

He was not surprised but very impressed and nervous when they passed security for the President's home. They got out of their limousine and he found himself surrounded by several security people. One of them asked if he had a cellphone. He said he did, and they took it and turned off location information.

That concerned him, as how would anyone know where he was if that was not on? But he went along.

Then they were led down a long corridor. At the end of it, one last security agent compared their documents with information on a screen he could not see, then allowed them to enter. Once inside, he found he was in a yard with a sidewalk that led to another vehicle. They climbed inside and the suburban drove them around several blocks and finally stopped in front of a beautiful huge house.

As they climbed out of the suburban and were walking up to the house, the door opened and the President of the Federation Council and his wife, plus some other people, walked outside to meet them. Gabby ran up to Heather and gave her a great big hug. She then turned to the President and gave him a hug. Simon had no clue what was going on.

"I think we have overwhelmed young Captain Jackson."

Everyone chuckled, then Gabby walked to him. "Simon, please allow me to introduce my family. Let me explain, they have adopted me. This is my mom, Heather, my dad, Jeffrey, and my sister, Tamara. This is my other sister, even though she isn't, Erica."

Simon was not sure what to think. He was part shocked, happy, just, what?

Jeffrey walked up to him. "Captain Jackson, you would do me a great honor if you could set aside any preconceived notions you may have on what your expectations were for this evening. I know Gabby has orchestrated a huge surprise for you. Trust me, we are overjoyed at welcoming her into our family. I hope you can work with it and relax."

"Thank you, sir. It's just, such a surprise. I had no idea."

Gabby walked up to him and reached out her hands and held his face in her hands. "Simon, I love the people around us. I finally feel at home. I hope you can understand I wanted to keep this very secret from everyone, until the time was right. You are the only person who knows about this, and I hope to keep it that way for some time." She leaned in and kissed him.

Simon kissed her back this time. "Gabby, I will support whatever you do. It is just a bit intimidating, that's all."

"Yes, it is!"

"Come on in, let's introduce everyone and get the evening started."

Simon learned a lot about the Wilson's on this night. Everything he learned, he liked. He had met Heather unofficially as Gabby's mom, and could understand why Gabby had fallen in love with her. He met Tamara and others, and then he spent some time with Jeffrey.

"I know, it is difficult to call me Jeffrey, but I insist, during a family, relaxed get together."

"Yes sir, I mean Jeffrey. You are right, it will take me a while to get used to it."

"I want to tell you that I read the reports from your accident and it is clear that you were not at fault for the crash on the moon."

"I know. It doesn't make it any easier, though. I was in command of that craft. No, I did not know the rotational stabilizer thrusters would fail. No, I did not know we even had a problem with mass distribution in the craft. But still, I was in command and lost eight marines."

"I know. It is tough to be in command. It always means that when someone gets hurt or dies you bear the brunt of it. But some things are just too important not to do. Take this X-drive we are calling the faster than lightspeed drive or star drive. We have lost a lot of people in the pursuit of this goal and yet we cannot stop the research. More may die. But it is too important to our species survival to stop doing the work."

Simon had not known anyone in a position like the President's before. He was impressed at the compassion he felt the President had for those doing the work, and also the ability to face the guilt that came with the need to continue towards the goal.

"Mr. President, I am glad you are in charge. You do provide all of us with the inspiration to achieve great things. I know that before I met you today, I had great respect for you. This evening, this conversation, has done nothing but strengthen that."

"Thank you, Simon."

"Also, thank you and your wife for giving Gabby something she desperately needed, a home. I love her, and I know she loves me, but this need she has is so much bigger than two people. I am very happy for her."

Jeffrey liked this young man, not only because of the things he said, but because of the way he said it, his demeanor, how he interacted with everyone. He knew Simon was a good one and hoped he and Gabby would find a way to make their relationship work.

At dinner, there was another surprise for Simon. "I have some big news. Today I applied to the Federation Council to be released from my military contract. It was accepted! I am now a civilian researcher!"

Everyone shouted for joy and was very thankful. Gabby got up and walked around and gave Jeffrey a hug, then a kiss on the cheek. Then she turned and gave Heather a big hug and big kiss as well. Lastly, she walked back to her seat beside Simon and sat down.

"Are you happy for me, dear?"

"Absolutely! My concern is selfish. Will I still get to see you as often as we were seeing each other before?"

She leaned over and gave him a kiss in front of everyone. "Yes, silly. I will be doing exactly what I was doing before. Only now, I will have security with me and will be a civilian."

"Okay, as long as I still get to see you. You know, you are kind of growing on me. I might not be able to figure out what to do without you if this keeps up."

Gabby smiled and felt she had hit the jackpot! She had found a family, and now she was growing closer to the man she thought she may have a chance with after all!

10.011.14

Erica had worked very hard and used up all the spare time she had for the past couple of years to earn her degree. She spent long weekends in London to complete coursework and thesis activities. They had allowed her to have a very flexible schedule, but still, she had put in the time and work. Today, she would graduate with her PhD.

Jeffrey brought the entire clan along for the event. He even coordinated with the Prime Minster and Chancellor of the Exchequer, as well as the Duke and Duchess of Cambridge, so everyone was there. Even the presidents of China and Russia attended, having developed working relationships with Erica and fully appreciating the hard work she put into the Federation and their relationships.

The graduation class did not consist of many graduates. This was a very small class, so the graduation was held in a large meeting room in the Regent's Conference Center on the grounds of the school. Erica was one of only five graduates, and the number of people who attended for the other four were less than half as many as attended for Erica.

On the day, she was nervous and excited. When the time came, she walked onto the stage and was hooded in the appropriate robes and tassels, completing the formality of endowing her the title of PhD. Once this was complete and the applause died down, she was asked to say a few words.

"Thank you all for coming today. This has been an incredible journey for all of us, but especially for me. I am only thirty-seven years old, a mother of two, and only in my third job. It seems incredible then, that I would be completing a PhD in Strategy and Entrepreneurship. Yet I have been blessed to have a position where this knowledge perfectly fits the needs of our organization."

"Jeffrey Wilson, the President of the Federation and JW Enterprises, selected me to be his personal assistant almost nine years ago. Over that time, I have watched as he established a vision for our species and been fortunate to help in many ways to bring that vision to life. I can't begin to tell you what I learned about strategy, entrepreneurship, ownership, followership, and yes, leadership, in that time."

"The studies here in London provided the theoretical foundation for so many things I am seeing at the practical level and has been a wonderful and challenging learning experience. I know that what I have learned here will help me grow and be the best leader I can be for the future."

"Thank you, Jeffrey, for giving me this opportunity and having faith in me; and thank you Dean Nelson, for the outstanding support the school provided me through this process. Lastly, thank you Steven, Addison, and Khloe, for supporting me on this journey."

Once the official graduation was complete, they went back to Kensington Palace for afternoon tea and a quiet celebration of her achievement. Jeffrey and Heather kept the kids for the evening, and Erica and Steven went out on the town in London and celebrated their life together. The next day, they all loaded up and flew back to Omaha, where Dr. Beckett began her next adventure.

10.014.12

The first time it happened they thought it was an accident.

"Nathaniel, quickly, come to the fields, they are dying!"

Nathaniel and several other farmers ran to the field and saw that the plants were all turning brown.

"What happened?"

"We don't know. The plants are just dying."

"We need these fields to grow or we won't have enough food to make it."

"Okay, we will have to plan to use more of our emergency supplies."

"Yes, but we don't have that much, we need to grow our own food."

"Yes, but there is nothing we can do now. Let's plant a new field."

The second time they were sure it was not.

The third they knew there was a saboteur or terrorist in their midst.

"Someone is purposely destroying our food crops. That means someone in our crew wants us to die."

"We have years of travel before we arrive at our first destination."

"Yes, and we should be making babies by now, so we have very young teenagers when we arrive, strong, healthy and ready to help work the land."

"Well that has changed. We might not have enough food to survive to the first destination."

It was bleak on pod one, but what they didn't know was that it was happening in six of the pods.

Nathaniel was adamant that they find out what was happening. "Look," he said, "let's take this apart and understand it. We know it isn't the soil, there is too much of it, and not the water, because systems clean it and inspect it constantly. It also can't be the seed, because this is also sealed and documented. The only item that is outside of control or inspection is the fertilizer."

"I agree, but what can we do?"

He got a team of his personal family members together, people he knew he could trust, and they found the tampered fertilizer and removed it. They began growing crops in sector nine, with constant surveillance. After two months growth, they knew they were right. A month later, just as the fields were nearing being ready for harvest, while he was on duty, two farm hands stopped by to offer help. He agreed, and they went to get fertilizer for the field.

What these two did not know was that they were being watched. When they opened the fertilizer container, all was well. Then they were seen to take something out of their pockets and drop it into the fertilizer container. As they were moving the fertilizer to the field, they were confronted. Once they knew they had been discovered, they fled.

The farm team did not know much about fighting, but they understood survival. They put together a group of people and surrounded these two, and with pitchforks and knives, they encircled them. These two pulled out guns and shot three people, but then everyone rushed them together. It was brutal, but the fight was over. The saboteurs were dead. Their pod would continue unscathed.

10.077.05

Gabby and Simon spent time together whenever they could. To any who knew them, they could see the love blossoming and growing between them. To any who did not know them, they only saw a couple of nerdish kids goofing with each other.

Gabby lived with Heather and Jeffrey. She and Heather spent nearly every waking moment they were free, together. Of course, Heather did not allow this to interfere with her very strong romance with Jeffrey. Today was one of those events. Heather woke Jeffrey at five in the morning. "Get up, sleepy head. We have a busy day ahead of us."

"What?"

"You heard me, let's get moving."

After a while they showered and dressed and then had breakfast. Once they were finished, Heather texted Stephanie they were ready. She had coordinated with Erica to convince Jeffrey he had work to do, but secretly clear his schedule. She had also packed their suitcases and had them on the plane. Once Stephanie arrived at the door, they left. They hopped into their suburban and the convoy left for Offutt Air Force Base. Once there, they hopped into their private Boeing 747 and departed.

Jeffrey had not asked her where they were going. He knew she would tell him when she was ready. She took him up front into their private bedroom and they made love in their king-sized bed for the flight. They laid together in the bed afterwards, touching, kissing, and just holding each other. "Wow, maybe we should just turn around now and go home."

She laughed at him. "No, silly. We have much more to do. You do know today is your sixty fifth unbirthday, don't you?"

"Hah! Yes, it certainly is. So, tell, me, my love, where are we going?"

"We are going to one of our favorite places."

"The beach?"

"Yes! We are going to the beach. We will be there for a couple of days. I want to make love with you listening to the ocean again."

"My goodness, I think your minx is showing."

She nudged him and kissed him. "I simply don't understand it."

"What's that?"

"How you just completely turn me on all the time. It doesn't make any sense."

He laughed. "I have wondered about that."

She laughed. "I mean right? You're average looking, kind of old, nothing to really get excited about."

"Yes, that's all true. Then there is you. Supple skin, soft lips with a darting tongue that only arouses me, passionate eyes, and legs that go on forever."

He gently squeezed her as she moaned with pleasure, looking deep into his eyes, saying, "I want you."

They made love again. It was only the announcement they were arriving that got them out of bed.

10.079.15

Simon was trying to take a nap. He was in his bunk when he heard two of the Chinese researchers talking. He knew they thought he was asleep, and they had no way of knowing he spoke fluent mandarin. What he heard scared the hell out of him. Once they had left, he knew he had to tell someone. The first person he got hold of was Gabby. He said for her to meet him in the cafeteria, it was urgent. Once Gabby arrived, he explained what he had heard.

Gabby was incredulous. "Simon, are you sure, I mean really sure? This is very important. Take a moment and think about it, because you have to be absolutely positive before we tell anyone else."

"I am positive. I heard what I told you I heard."

Gabby then looked over and waved to her security lead, Sofia. "We need to get out of here immediately. This is extremely urgent. We need to speak with the President immediately."

Sofia did not ask what the issue was, instead, she quickly got her team in motion and they extracted Gabby and Simon. As they were in the vehicle enroute to Omaha, Erica called.

"Gabby, I understand something has happened that caused you to request immediate extraction from the Federation. What's up?"

"Is this line secure?"

"Absolutely."

"Okay. Simon just learned something you need to know. Tell her."

"Erica, this is Simon, I don't really know you even though we met at the President's house, but Gabby said you are her un-sister and can be trusted."

"I am Jeffrey's personal assistant and have been since the project began. You can trust me with your life. Now what have you learned?"

"I was in my bunk. Two Chinese researchers came in and I know they thought I was asleep and would not know I speak fluent mandarin. Anyway, they said that Admiral Chen had been providing the best information possible so their attempt at building a faster than lightspeed drive had not experienced the fatalities the Federation had experienced. They said that given their current progress, they should achieve their goal before the Federation and be able to send their people into the galaxy well before anyone else and control who goes to the stars. They also said Admiral Chen had tightly controlled who participated in the research to prevent anyone from asking too many questions."

There was silence for a moment, then Erica asked, speaking very slowly, "Simon, are you absolutely positive that what you are telling me is exactly what they said?"

"Absolutely."

"Thank you, please report to the President's compound." The line clicked dead.

Erica knew an immediate response was necessary. If she knew, she was willing to bet someone else would find out and all hell would break loose and she had no idea if they were safe from Chen and his band of terrorists. She thought about it and developed a plan.

Stephanie and Abby were with Jeffrey and Heather in Florida. She turned to her security liaison, Richard. "Richard, implement security procedure Delta Six Two."

"Are you positive?"

"Yes."

"Right away."

She called Jeffrey. He didn't answer. She called Stephanie. "Yes, Erica."

"Implement security procedure Delta Six Two immediately."

"Repeat."

"Delta Six Two."

"Roger."

Stephanie raised the mic to her hand and provided instructions to implement the procedure. Security personnel came out of the sand dunes and helicopters were airborne. Jeffrey and Heather, who moments before had been enjoying a quiet moment in the waves of the beach, were quickly hustled into a helicopter landing in the parking lot and immediately extracted to Eglin Air Force Base to board their aircraft home.

"What the hell is going on?"

"Erica implemented security procedure Delta Six Two."

"Call her."

"This is Erica."

"Jeffrey. What is going on?"

"We have word from an extremely reliable source, that Admiral Chen has been maintaining strict secrecy about the team membership and what they are learning, stealing secrets from the X-drive team, and providing these to a secret facility in China, with the goal of getting to the stars first and controlling who gets there."

"Do you believe this is credible and actionable?"

"Yes."

"What is your plan?"

Erica explained what she thought they should do. "Erica, you are in command. Take the lead and make it happen. We will return as soon as possible, but I suspect this will all be over before we arrive. It is your time. Be the leader you were born to be."

"Yes, sir."

Erica called General Nelson. "General, how many marines do you have who you can absolutely depend on, regardless of internal conflict and possible sabotage?"

The general had no idea why he was being asked this, especially from the President's assistant, but he provided a response. "I believe I have a good several hundred who would be totally reliable."

"Good. Activate those units. Lock down the armory. Provide a go team of one hundred of your best at the entrance to Z-wing in thirty minutes."

"Should I look for orders?"

"General, you are getting your orders right now. If you can't follow them, I will find someone else who can."

"Yes ma'am, we will be there."

She said to Richard, "Get me to the Federation Z-wing in thirty minutes."

Richard immediately called the helicopter squadron at Offutt and scrambled a chopper direct to the President's compound. When it landed, he, Erica and a fully armed security complement boarded. Tamara had seen the helicopter land. She knew something was going on as this never happened. When she saw Erica and the fully armed team board the chopper, she prayed everything was alright.

The siren went off in the Federation. It was a tornado warning. Personnel were to take immediate refuge. General Nelson had implemented this as a cover for his team. He took five hundred American marines. He had two hundred of them secure the armory, two hundred provided general security, and he was marching to Z-wing with one hundred.

Erica landed with her security team and she moved quickly towards Z-wing. She met up with General Nelson as they approached it. Suddenly, shots rang out from Z-wing. General Nelson ordered his team to return fire. It was a very active fire fight for about ten minutes, but the marines were dominant and eventually breached the security doors of Z-wing. Once inside, they saw that the research labs were destroyed.

Admiral Chen stood by himself in the center of the large reception area inside Z-wing. Erica knew it could be a trap, but felt she had no choice but to show leadership. "Admiral Chen. I order you to surrender, in the name of the Federation."

General Nelson was confused, but he saw that something unusual was happening. This young lady was much tougher than he thought she was.

"No. I will never surrender to capitalist pigs. Especially not to some upstart female pig."

Erica walked ahead of the marines and her security detail, walked up to within twenty feet of the Admiral.

"You allowed people to die. You stole secrets. You never behaved honorably. You are a coward."

Admiral Chen suddenly charged her. Erica watched him approach and with a sudden graceful movement, she slipped out from under his arms to one side. He quickly kicked out at her, but she avoided his foot. He stopped, and pulling a knife out of his belt, made a quick stance to better gain solid footing and then charged her from close range. Erica shifted to one side, but he swung his arm and cut her along her upper left shoulder. She didn't make a sound.

He quickly charged her again, and this time she dropped well below his reach, tripped him so he fell on the ground, and leapt onto his back with her arms around his neck. He struck up towards her face with his knife, causing her to release her grip on his neck and catch his knife hand. She exerted all the strength she had and snapped it, breaking his wrist, which made him drop his knife. She quickly grabbed the knife and as he was turning over pulling out a gun, she rammed the knife through his neck and up into his brain. He immediately stopped moving.

Erica looked up at the general. "Secure this wing."

"Yes ma'am."

General Nelson immediately sent marines to every research lab within the Z-wing. They discovered several bodies, but also found a lot of people who had taken refuge in closets and vaults where no one could get to them. General Nelson called a medic, who quickly dressed her knife wound and let her know she would need several stitches to help this heal. She told him to bandage it for now, and she would have stitches later.

After about thirty minutes, he reported that all was secure.

"Very good. Take this body to the morgue."

"Yes ma'am. Uh, ma'am, what should we call you?"

"Nothing for now."

A few hours later Jeffrey and Heather landed at Federation headquarters. Erica met them at the plane, but before she could explain what happened, they wanted to know if she was alright.

"Erica, General Nelson briefed me on the fight you had with Admiral Chen. He told me you had been cut and required stitches. Are you alright?"

He and Heather were both worried about her, but she looked strong and confident as ever.

"Yes, I am fine. I will say the personal defense, physical fitness, and hand-to-hand combat lessons you taught me, Stephanie, made the difference. But he still managed to cut me on my left shoulder. It took about twenty-five stitches, but the doctor says the scar should be minimal."

"Wow. I never knew you were Wonder Woman!"

Erica finally had a laugh and relaxed. "Well, Heather, if this is what you have to do to get that status, then please, I don't want the job!"

They all laughed. Jeffrey and Heather were relieved that Erica was fine, Erica was glad she survived. Stephanie walked over to her and congratulated her on her first successful hand to hand combat.

Once they had made sure she was okay, she explained everything that had happened. Jeffrey directed a full investigation into the accusations and a retention, for now, of all Chinese military personnel. He also called an emergency meeting of the Federation Council.

"This is unheard of! We will not be treated in this manner!"

"Mr. Ambassador, you have heard the accusations and seen the information available. Do you deny any knowledge of the facts of the event?"

The Chinese Ambassador looked at Jeffrey. "You dare to challenge me and ask me questions like I am some kind of token representative? I am the representative of the People's Republic of China!"

Jeffrey paused after this outburst. "Thank you, Mr. Ambassador, for clearing that up. I thought maybe you were someone else." Then leaning forward looking directly at him, and speaking very quietly, he added, "You come into this chamber and would treat us like ignorant buffoons. You represent, at this moment, Admiral Chen and his associates, both here and in your country, who have no honor. You can either help us verify these claims or you can say you support this behavior, are a thief in the night and a murderer. You decide. Until you do and until we know the truth, please leave the council."

He waved for General Nelson, who walked over and accompanied the Ambassador out of the chamber. He shouted the whole time. Once he was out, it was relatively quiet. He waited until General Nelson returned.

"It has come to my attention that you here are not apprised of a significant change that is occurring at JW Enterprises. I am retiring, effective in one year. My replacement you have met. Dr. Erica Beckett, please come forward."

Erica stood up from the chair close to him she always occupied.

"I have met no one more competent, knowledgeable, passionate, or able to lead JW Enterprises, than Erica. She demonstrated superb leadership, personal courage, and tactical mastery with the late spy event we concluded today. She will be my replacement, which means she will be the President of the Federation Council until it reaches ten planets. In the meantime, I am giving her the title, President Pro-Tem."

Everyone applauded Erica, as everyone liked and respected her. General Nelson was both shocked and delighted that she was to be the new President. He completely respected her after what he had seen her deal with.

As soon as the meeting was over, Jeffrey and Erica went to his office, closed the door, and called the Chinese President. "Hello, Mr. President."

"Good day to you, Mr. President. What can I help you with, Jeffrey?"

"Cheng, I have some news for you. I will ask Erica to provide you a quick brief." Erica then told Cheng everything that had transpired, including the death of Admiral Chen. Jeffrey waited for a moment after she finished. "I am sorry to have to inform you of this, but we need your help in understanding what has happened."

"I know what you ask, did I have knowledge of this event? The answer is no. This is the first I have heard of this treachery. You must provide me with time to investigate. I will contact you directly, as soon as I gain a thorough understanding. Until then, good day." The line went dead.

"He is a good man. However, I think we should prepare for a visit to the UN and report what has happened and that we must find a way to finally defeat terrorism."

10.082.13

Three days after Admiral Chen's death President Jin called Jeffrey. "I have news for you. Based upon your information, we determined that Admiral Chen was working with General Zhiang in construction and running a secret research facility. No one in the central party knew of this activity. You may rest assured that the individuals responsible for this treachery have been dealt with in a most swift fashion. We will not stand by and support this behavior."

"I am sorry this happened, Cheng. I think the hardest issue to grasp is that we are still merely human and sometimes we crack and fail. Thank you for your continued strength and support. We will go to the United Nations and provide a report, not on your individuals, but on terrorism in general."

"We will be there."

"Thank you."

Jeffrey did not want a repeat of the last UN visit. "Stephanie, we will not go back to the United Nations blind, like we were last time. I want you to coordinate a massive security operation. I want a clear path from the LaGuardia airport to the United Nations and back. I want the ground around the airport scoured so we don't have any missile attacks. I want this to be a seamless visit. We will plan to be there in three days."

"Okay, we can do that."

"Erica, I want you to give the speech."

She looked at him like he was a lunatic. "What?"

"You heard me. I will go with you to the United Nations. I will walk inside with you. Then I am going to sit down and watch you give the talk. You are going to be the President soon, might as well get your first big one out of the way."

"Really? I mean your first big one was to a dinner party. Why can't I have that?"

He laughed. "Because you are so much better than you think you are. I am completely confident in you."

"On one condition."

"Which is?"

"We write the legal transfer of JW Enterprises kind of like they did in one of your favorite books, you know, that part where he could come back and pick up the gavel. I think we should do this in such a way that you can always come back and resume the Presidency, if you choose. That would certainly ensure I behave."

"If you want to do that, okay, your call. But right now, I need you to go out there and scold terrorists and any country that harbors them in front of the United Nations. They must be made to feel the heat for their actions."

"Oh, I can do that."

10.085.10

Security was tight. No one was even on the street when they arrived. There was a people movement lockdown from LaGuardia to the United Nations. It probably irritated a lot of people, but too bad. Stephanie was not taking any chances a second time. When they arrived, Erica and Jeffrey walked into the building. The Secretary General did not meet them, not because he didn't want to, but because Stephanie wouldn't let him. She was sure she made every person within ten miles angry, but she was not going to have another attack.

Jeffrey and Erica entered the general assembly, and everyone stood and cheered. The two of them had personally worked the phones the past two days, reminding people of all the projects being done in their country's because of JW Enterprises.

The Secretary General informed the assembly that Jeffrey would speak. He walked up to the microphone. "Ladies and gentlemen, thank you for your wonderful welcome. I know that you expect to hear from me; however, as I will be retiring in a year, you are going to hear from my successor. I am proud to present to you someone most of you already know, Dr. Erica Beckett, President Pro-Tem of JW Enterprises and the Federation Council."

There was applause, but not as much as Jeffrey got. He left the podium and Erica walked up.

"Good afternoon. Thank you for welcoming me to speak with you. My name is Erica Beckett. I am the President Pro-Tem of JW Enterprises and of the Federation Council. My words for you today center around trust and honor."

"We had a situation recently that provided a clear example of what honor looks like, and what deceit and dis-honor can do to people. Our Federation, like the United Nations, is built on and can only be sustained by trust. When you cannot trust each other, what good is the assembly? When you find someone stabbing you in the back you believed was your ally, someone harming and lying to you, what options are you left but to rid yourself of that ally?"

"This is much like discovery of a boil in your skin, a hurtful, hate filled space. The boil I refer to is any country or terrorist cell that acts in a superior manner to decency and the rule of law, and all those boils must be lanced."

"We in the Federation cannot take any action against a country on a planet, because that violates the premise that we are above planetary. Our founding Constitution, which this body approved, forbids the Federation from any active engagement in planetary affairs. Instead, we are concerned with developing rules for trade, interplanetary relationships, intellectual property rights, business transactions between planets and ownership, overall defense of our space and the free movement of people. It is for you to take action against a member state."

"However, I wear the dual hat, for now, of President Pro-Tem of JW Enterprises. As such, we can act on the planetary level. In that capacity, I am ordering the immediate termination of all projects with all countries who harbor, act in unison with or refuse to assist in finding and eliminating terrorists. We consider these governments illegitimate and we will not work with or support them. Not only do we know who you are, you know as well. Be on notice. When the people of these countries demand and get a government that supports their need for independence and honor, we will return. Until that time, these countries are considered to be pariah among us."

"Some of you here may feel this is harsh. Let me tell you why it is not. We experienced individuals in our ranks that we recently discovered had lied to all of us about the accomplishments of the X-drive research project. They manipulated the research. They caused people to die conducting the research. The results of our research were sent to a secret research facility they developed elsewhere. Their stated objective was to build the X-drive before anyone else, so they and their cronies could expand into the galaxy before the legitimate expansion of the free people of Earth. They sought complete domination of the galaxy at your expense. That is why they are a pariah."

"JW Enterprises is hard at work trying to build an X-drive. When we do, we will not keep it secret or only give it to certain countries. We will give it to anyone who can afford it, because, yes, this is an expensive research project and we expect to recoup our investment. But no ideology will get it first. No religion or nation will have first dibs."

"The Federation will get it first because this assures our safety and defense. In addition, we will build starships that can travel the galaxy, find those migration pods and help them get safely to a good planet, because these pioneers deserve that. Lastly, we will use our resources to monitor travel, and prevent any one planet from dominating the others, including Earth."

"But there is a bigger issue that confronts you today, that issue is terrorism. The time has finally come for you to make your decision, choose your side and act. You are either on the side of freedom or terror. There is no middle ground. We support freedom for all humans and exploration of the galaxy for all nations. Rogue regimes and terrorists support only their solution. You decide which side you are on. But remember that decisions have consequences. JW Enterprises will not rest until we have rooted out every terrorist cell and rogue regime and brought all of humanity into the civility and company of free nations and free people. I urge you to support this cause. Thank you."

Erica left the podium and the assembly broke out into raucous applause. They had just heard a fighter and a new generation leader set the stage for the next phase of war against terrorism. They had also heard about the future of space travel. It was exciting. Jeffrey was, as always, completely impressed with Erica.

"My goodness, you absolutely rocked that speech!"

Erica was still shaking from nerves and emotions. The speech made her remember the fight with Admiral Chen and her scar stung. "Thank you, Jeffrey. It's just that this whole episode with Admiral Chen makes me so angry. We have to stop this type of treachery and betrayal."

"Yes, I agree. But what you did in there today was set the bar very high. You clearly demonstrated to everyone on this planet that you are not a pushover, and that you will demand action. It was perfect. I could not have delivered that speech. In a nutshell, you done good, Erica."

The ride home was uneventful, the kind Stephanie liked. Jeffrey made another decision as well. After they returned to the Federation, he informed Erica and the entire staff that he would be available when needed, but that she was going to be the acting President effective immediately.

"I am not ready for this, Jeffrey."

"Yes, you are. The leadership you demonstrated at the Federation, the power of your presence and words today at the United Nations clearly demonstrate that you are, indeed, ready to lead. However, I will remain in the position and you can brief me regularly as to your decisions, and you can run things past me if you want. But I know you are ready for this and want you to take it and run with it."

Erica believed she could do this, but she was also scared of doing it. She was only thirty-seven years old and would be working with people from all walks of life who were mostly older, more experienced than her, and who had more knowledge than she had. Jeffrey's confidence in her was the real boost she needed. She believed in him completely, and she loved him. If he believed in her, she would just have to learn to believe in herself as well.

"Okay. But I might be talking to you and visiting with you a lot once this starts."

"I am sure you think that. I am equally certain that you won't, because you will naturally find your way through the obstacles, and you will need to make your own path. But I will always be here for you."

"Thank you, Jeffrey."

"We've come a long way together, you and me. Now is your time. I am so proud of you. I can finally rest easy and enjoy some peace and time at the beach, knowing you are in charge. Thank you for you, because you are fabulous, and I love you."

They embraced for a while. Finally, they parted, and Jeffrey went home, while Erica went to the President Pro-Tem's office, the office that would now be in charge of JW Enterprises and the Federation. She would have to see about improving her office as it was going to be the main office and turning the President's office into more of a ceremonial space. That would be proper, as Jeffrey was not going to come back to work, but he would come to see things at times.

10.088.10

One of the first actions Erica took as the new President Pro-Tem, was to appoint Gabby as the director of the Z-wing laboratories, and especially as project director for the X-drive project. The project had collapsed after the discovery of the treachery of Admiral Chen. It needed to be rebuilt from the ground up in a fresh and strong manner. She could not think of anyone who could do that better than Gabby.

She had Arabella schedule a meeting for them. Arabella had quickly stepped into the assistant shoes a couple of years back and was a wonderful addition to the team. She had made a good decision. On the given day and time, Gabby arrived at the Federation Council for a meeting, where she was appointed to run the research facilities.

"Thank you, ma'am. I appreciate your confidence in me and I will do everything I can to ensure the project proceeds in a positive and meaningful manner."

"I know you will, Dr. Anderson-Wilson. I expect no less from you."

Once they were in Erica's office, Erica gave her a hug. "I know you will get us where we need to go Gabby. However, I also spoke with Heather about this and she was a little irritated. No that is not correct, she was furious. She wants to talk with you as soon as you can get home to see her."

"Oh, yes, I think I understand why she would be concerned. There were a lot of accidents in this project over the years."

"Yes, and I tried to tell her they were because of the treachery and I think she wants to believe that, but she needs a little more convincing than I can give her."

"Thanks, Erica. I think I should go see her now, so we can clear the air and move forward."

"Good idea."

Gabby left the Federation and went home. She found her mom in the kitchen, working on dinner for the family.

"Hi mom."

"Oh, hi, dear," she replied, reaching out and hugging her. Gabby knew why Heather was so stressed, so she addressed it up front.

"Mom, leading the research on the X-drive is okay."

"No, it isn't. What if something happens to you? What if another accident happens? I know we want this drive, but I just can't lose you."

They were locked in a hug in the kitchen. Jeffrey walked in, saw them, and quietly backed out. He intercepted Tamara to prevent her from disturbing them.

"Mom, now that I oversee the project, we will build safe rooms in each research facility where we can engage processes from behind thick walls. I promise I will be safe."

Heather cried. "Please, please, please be safe and take care of yourself."

"I will, I promise."

They hugged for a while longer, and finally, Heather was able to let some of the negative energy go. "Okay then, I will try and not be stressed."

"Thanks, mom. I promise, this will be fine, and maybe now we can actually make some good progress in solving this puzzle. And mom, please don't be angry at Erica. She is doing the right thing."

"Very well, dear. I love you."

"I love you."

10.089.10

The next day Gabby was looking at the Z-wing research facilities. She saw that a lot needed to be repaired. When she was looking at the research teams that had been working on the X-drive, she saw that they had limited the researchers to only one group, nuclear engineers. No wonder they couldn't get it right, this would take a multi-disciplined group.

She had her work cut out for her. She gathered the appropriate personnel, from procurement to research heads, and they brain-stormed not only ideas, but equipment, safety precautions, and a better way to select personnel for the teams. Once they were complete she submitted her needs to Erica, who approved them immediately.

The work to repair the labs was achieved in a very expeditious manner. No more than three months had gone by until some of the labs were back up and running. The X-drive research lab took the longest, as it also required some additional safety measures to ensure the safety of staff. It didn't take long though, before Gabby's team was deeply engaged in re-learning everything that had happened, identifying mistakes, clarifying misunderstandings, and redoing the formulas.

"I still don't understand what they were thinking."

"They were linear. With only one set of knowledge and skills, they couldn't expand their horizons."

"No wonder they kept failing."

"I agree, but we still have that initial concern with the Special Relativity effect."

"Yes, but the changes we have already made have shifted the energy requirements well below what we have seen towards a more manageable level. If we can continue to tweak this downward, we have a chance of breaking through."

"By the way, I heard that the Chinese research facility was destroyed."

"I am sure President Beckett had something to do with that. I think she is a power house. She is the one who shut down Admiral Chen."

"Yes, she is a tough cookie. But I really like her."

"Well, so do I."

10.122.17

Simon had been assigned to various other projects in the research wing while he recovered from his accident, but in time he healed and was at one hundred percent. On the day he was given a medical release, he asked Gabby out on a date. This would truly be their first real date, as the other times they had been together was more for fun or just to hang out. This time, he wanted to let her know how he was feeling. He was scared to death.

"Mr. Wilson, I would like to take Gabby out for a really nice dinner, but I don't know where to take her. Do you have any suggestions?"

"Well, if I were you, I think I would take her to St. Jacques. That is the very best Omaha has to offer and it makes a statement."

"Thank you, Jeffrey. I will make the arrangements."

"If you have trouble getting a reservation, let me know."

"Thanks!"

He took the shuttle into Omaha and made his way to the President's compound. It still brought chills to him whenever he came here. He had met everyone a couple of times, but still, this was where they all lived. He felt he was entering a twilight zone of energy. He arrived and was passed through security and made his way to the door of their home. He knocked on the door.

"Hi, Simon."

"Hi, President Wilson."

"Please, when you are here in an unofficial capacity, call me Jeffrey."

"Thank you, sir, I will try. Is Gabby ready?"

At that moment Gabby walked around the corner and into the entryway to the house. It felt like a slow-motion movie. He could not say a word. She was breathtakingly gorgeous. He never knew she had such shapely legs, and her red hair surrounding her face was beautiful. He just stood there.

"Ahem, Simon, it is polite to say hello."

He was so embarrassed. He said, "Oh my gosh, I am so sorry, it's just… I never realized how beautiful you are."

Jeffrey laughed, patted Gabby on the shoulder and gave her a quick kiss on the cheek, then walked back into the living room.

"Are you ready to go?"

"Yes, I believe so. Where are we going?"

"I made reservations at St. Jacques."

Gabby knew how much a meal at that restaurant cost. She also knew Simon probably could only afford this one time a year, if that. She was about to say something, when she realized that this was his idea and his gift to her. She decided to simply enjoy it.

"Well, let's go then."

They were driven by security to the restaurant, who remained on scene, although discretely, and would take them home when the night was over.

"Good evening, do you have reservations?"

"Yes, Simon Jackson for two."

"Ah, very well, your table is ready, please come this way."

Simon walked behind Gabby. He could smell her perfume and see the soft pure creamy skin of her shoulders and neck. He felt overwhelmed with the whole experience.

They had a table in a quiet corner of the restaurant. A bottle of Chardonnay was in a chiller on the table. As they sat, a waiter brought over a single long-stemmed red rose and handed it to Gabby. She looked at Simon, who blushed profusely. She just smiled. The Host took his time and opened the bottle of Chardonnay, poured for them both and informed them the menu had been selected and would begin soon.

As he walked away, Gabby looked at Simon and asked him if he had ordered for her.

"No, I did not. This is a surprise for me as well as you. In any case, and regardless of what we have for dinner, I wanted to tell you something tonight."

"Oh, and what might that be?" Gabby watched him and smiled inside as she saw him trying to get up the courage to talk. Simon was a Marine. He was strong, intelligent, and completely a masculine example of a solid human being. However, Simon had a very difficult time talking about his feelings with anyone, so this was a major effort for him.

He stuttered and kind of fell over his words, trying to get started. She reached across and held his hands. "Dear Simon, please relax. Whatever you need to say you can say when you are ready. I hope we are not in a rush, ever."

"Thanks Gabby. I have never talked to anyone, let alone a girl, about feelings. It is hard. However, I want to tell you, that I really like you."

Gabby laughed in a warm manner. "Simon, dear, I like you too."

He grinned, feeling he had really accomplished something important. He had said he loved her a couple of times, but this was different. This was real. He took his glass, saying, "A toast then, to us enjoying each other's company."

After the toast, the waiter returned with a basket of different types of bread and a small plate with olive oil, parmesan cheese, and roasted garlic. They each began sampling the various breads and could not believe how delicious they were.

"Oh my, this is quite delicious. Simon, you were saying you were released by the medical team today. Does that mean you are fit for all duties, even those in space?"

"Yes, it means I am back on full duties as a Marine. I report tomorrow morning and have no idea where they will send me. Last I heard, there was a patrol leaving for Mars, so I could be on it."

"If that happens, how long will you be gone?"

"If it happens, and it probably won't, I will be gone for about a year."

"It doesn't take that long to get to Mars and return now, so why would you be gone so long?"

"Because it is a patrol. They go to Mars and practice landing and operating in a different environment. It is mostly training for now. It does provide for unit cohesion, so has great value."

An appetizer had arrived. It was the most delicately crafted small red potato shrimp appetizers. The flavor was delicious, with just the right mixture of cream cheese, thyme, red pepper, sour cream, and bacon. They were superb, but not so fancy these two didn't like them.

"Wow. I don't know who ordered these, but they are really good."

"I'll say. As to the possibility of Mars, I really don't know. I would hope to remain here, but if that is where they send me I really don't have a choice."

"Let me ask you this. You have a double masters in quantum mechanics and mathematics, right? Well, we need people from varied backgrounds and with different areas of expertise than just nuclear physics, if we are going to decipher this lightspeed issue. If I could swing it, would you like to be on the team?"

"Absolutely! I mean, not just to be able see you, although that is a huge selling point; but to be able to work on that project would be the gold standard of research and contribution to the future. I would love it."

Gabby's mind was racing. She would need to talk with Erica immediately to get anything done. She had good justification. "Let me see what I can do, although I cannot promise anything."

"I will go with that. I already trust you more than any other human I have ever met. What's one more time to trust you?"

Gabby blushed this time. She was saved by the arrival of a bowl of bisque. It was the scallop and crab bisque St. Jacques were famous for. It was just the right amount of spiceyness, just the right amount of creaminess, just the right amount of crab and scallop; it was just divine.

Once they finished this course, they discovered they had also drunk most of the wine. Neither of them was really a wine drinker, or alcohol at all for that matter, but they discovered that this was delicious. The waiter stopped by to collect dirty plates, bowls and utensils, and filled their glasses for the last time with this bottle.

They sat for a moment and discovered they were looking into each other's eyes. Finally, Simon built up the courage to speak.

"Gabby, you have the most beautiful eyes. I just love looking into them. It is like seeing into the universe, yet so real and here."

"I know your eyes are like that as well. You have such beautiful eyes, Simon. I can get lost in them anytime."

They remained for the main course, perfectly cooked Chilean Sea Bass with a spicy citrus sauce and perfectly braised asparagus. Once they had finished this they were over the top full and told the waiter to hold the dessert. Simon asked for the check.

"Masseur, there is no check. The meal this night is on the house."

"I don't understand, why would you pay for our meal?"

The Host had walked back to their table at the request of the waiter. "Mademoiselle and Masseur, your meal is complements of St. Jacques. We appreciate all that you do for us and this is an opportunity for us to pay it forward. So please, leave no funds and enjoy the remainder of your evening."

They left, and the security team joined them. Simon knew he needed to take Gabby home and get back to the Federation. He did not know when the last shuttle would depart, but he was fairly sure it was any time now. He walked Gabby up to the door of her house, but she insisted he come in.

As they were walking into the house, he said, "But Gabby, I have to get back to the Federation and need to catch a shuttle. I don't even know if I missed it, but I have to try or catch a cab back."

"Simon, you have taken me to dinner for our first real date and I had a marvelous time. I want you to come inside and say hi to my parents, so please come in with me."

They walked into the living room and found Heather, Jeffrey, Tamara, and Erica having a conversation. She brought Simon into the room and they found their way to the couch.

"Hi everyone."

"Good evening, everyone. I apologize for getting Gabby back so late. Also, I must leave, as I need to get back to the Federation to report in tomorrow morning."

Jeffrey told him to have a seat. "Now, there are many things a young man needs to learn. The first thing is this, you always yield to the desire of the lady you love."

Simon blushed. Gabby came to his rescue. "Dad, he might not really love me."

"Oh yes I do." He stopped, startled at his own words. "I do really love you, Gabby."

"I love you."

The two of them kissed a small kiss and melted into each other's arms on the couch where they sat. The adults all smiled at this turn of events.

Erica had spoken with Jeffrey before they had arrived home and had a plan. She thought that Gabby needed a little push to make this perfect. "So, Gabby, I understand you are looking to create research teams that are diverse in nature, instead of the singular knowledge of the previous research team. How is that going?"

"It is going very well. The teams seem to be better able to construct patterns of thought and are more inquisitive as a mixed group. We have already come quite some distance is surpassing what the previous teams took years to accomplish."

"Very good. Are there any additional resources you need for your team?"

Gabby nearly fell off the couch. Here was her chance. "Yes. I need a quantum mechanics and mathematics person on the X-drive team."

"Do you know where we might find such a person?"

"Yes, Simon has these qualifications. I would love to have him on the team, I am only afraid of how it will look to others if I ask for him by name."

The adults in the room all laughed. This was too good.

"Dear, the President of the Federation Council has released Simon from the Marines with an honorable discharge. He is currently unassigned but could be a civilian research scientist working on your team, if he decides to accept the position."

All eyes were on Simon. "You mean, I can do research on the X-drive and never have to worry about being deployed away from Gabby ever again?"

"Yes."

"Then absolutely!!"

The two hugged each other. Gabby turned to all of them and said thank you. She got up and walked over to Heather and gave her a really big hug.

"I don't know if you had anything to do with this or not, it's just that I am so happy right now. Thanks, mom."

"Simon, there is a shuttle waiting to take you to the Academy. When you get there, gather all your belongings and take that same shuttle back here. You will be housed on the compound a couple of doors down."

10.179.08

This was Erica's first trip as the President Pro-Tem. She was traveling to China to meet Cheng to brief him personally on the progress in research and discuss additional investments in China. She needed to make sure he knew beyond any doubt that China was trusted after the Chen fiasco. She brought her family along, so they could do some site seeing while she conducted business.

"Arabella, what time do we arrive in Beijing?"

Arabella looked at her tablet. "We should be there at seven in the morning their time. The President would like to meet you as soon as we are on the ground. He has some very good news to tell you, although he would not tell me what it is, and start the conversation over breakfast."

Erica believed she had made a wise choice in Arabella as her personal assistant. She was more relaxed than Erica, but not less competent. They complemented each other like she and Jeffrey had complemented each other. Plus, she really liked her.

Arabella had been working for JW Enterprises since right out of college but had then used their tuition program to pay for her Doctorate in International Relations from the London School of Economics and Political Science. It had taken her a few years, but she believed it was a good degree for the work she wanted to do – helping with the Federations goal of managing interplanetary relations.

She was now twenty-seven years old, married with two children, and working for the most powerful human in the galaxy. On top of that, her boss was Erica, a powerhouse leader, who was equally gentle, kind, and genuinely concerned about people. Life could not get much better than this.

"Very well, what do you think he wants to tell us?"

Erica had filled this role with Jeffrey and he often asked her questions to see if she was aware of everything. She needed Arabella to be that for her.

"I suspect he is excited about the new Jian drive they are working on. If it truly is what we believe it to be, it will further speed travel within close distances, like between planets within our Solar System."

"Yes, I suspect that is it as well. I guess we will see soon. I am going to take a nap, you should do the same. We want to be as refreshed as we can when we land."

Upon arrival the Chinese President was eagerly waiting for her. She had known Cheng for many years, but the relationship was through the formality of office, unlike the one Jeffrey had with him. This was her opportunity to establish a better personal relationship with him.

"Madam President Pro-Tem, it is delightful to meet you."

"Thank you, Mr. President. It has been a while and we have been through a lot since our last meeting."

"Yes, including the near retirement of Jeffrey. How is he?"

"He is fine and enjoying his time. I think he has spent more time at the beach relaxing in the sun in the past six months than he did for the entire time I have known him."

"That is very good to hear. I hope you are curious about the news I have for you today."

"I am very curious, Mr. President."

"Please, call be Cheng."

"Thank you, please call me Erica."

"Thank you. First, we have breakfast for you and your team, then the news."

"Very well. By the way, this is Arabella. She is my personal assistant."

"Very good to make your acquaintance Arabella. If you perform the same tasks for Erica as she performed for Jeffrey, we will be speaking with you regularly."

"Thank you, Mr. President, I look forward to it."

"I also brought my family with me for the trip. This is my husband Steven, whom you have met, and my daughter Khloe and son Michael. They are finally old enough to appreciate the wonderful rich history of China. I am hoping we can find tour guides who can show them the real China that your team showed me when I first visited."

"It is very good to meet you again Steven, and you two as well. I believe we already have the very best tour guides waiting for you. Arabella was kind enough to coordinate this before your arrival. Please join us for breakfast, then we will show you our country."

"Thank you, Cheng. That is very generous."

"Not at all."

After they snacked on congee and crullers, and even a cup of American coffee – Heather's blend, wherever did they get this – the children and Steven left. Arabella had also brought her family, and they departed as well. Then Cheng began discussing the news.

"We have taken the funds you provided for infrastructure development and achieved wonderful things for our people. It has improved the quality of life in China, and I thank you for that. However, that is not the news. The news is that our research project, which you also funded through the Federation project, has achieved a significant success. We have developed a functional Jian engine that can speed travel in near distances, such as between planets in a star system."

President Cheng and his entire staff showed the pride that should accompany such news of accomplishment. Erica knew how to respond in this situation. She stood, knowing this was a formal thank you from the Federation President.

"Mr. President, I am humbled by your accomplishment. This will indeed make space travel safer for all, and more expeditious. This is a marvelous and very necessary accomplishment. Thank you and the Chinese people very much." With that said, she bowed a formal bow of thanks.

Arabella was very pleased, as she looked around and saw the smiles on all the faces of the Chinese. She knew Erica had hit just the right tone and body language for the occasion. She learned a lot about Erica watching this. She saw the earnestness with which she went about building relations and supporting people, helping everyone move to a common goal. She felt Erica was extraordinary.

Once the formalities were over, Erica and Cheng continued discussions about other research taking place and the continuing need to monitor progress. They also discussed eradication of terrorism. Acts of terror had declined significantly over the past five years.

"I believe it is because of the global investment strategy Jeffrey had implemented, which targeted every country's most earnest basic needs. With these being met, it is harder for terrorists to recruit and justify their path."

"I agree, Chen. Still, there will always be some of them, and our task is to proactively seek them out."

Their official visit lasted all day. Once it was complete, Erica and Arabella retired for the evening to discuss the day's events. The next morning, they departed and eventually met up with their families at the Great Wall and spent several hours listening to the history of the wall and talking about Chinese history in general. Then the guides loaded them up and they moved on. They spent three days enjoying the sights, sounds, history, architecture, and food of China.

On the last day they met Cheng for a lunch before they departed. It was a very productive and relaxing trip. Erica had used the opportunity to cement her personal relationship with Cheng, Arabella had a chance to demonstrate she was on the ball, the families had a chance to see some important historical sites and enjoy a new culture.

Erica also had a conversation with Admiral Sokolov about retrofitting the new engines in the current fleet as well as designing the next ship using these engines. They agreed he would take a look and see what could be done and report back. Erica knew if they could get these new engines in the ships they had, it would help with the distance to Mars and the asteroid mining camps. JW Enterprises could make a lot of money in this deal and help reduce the time spent in transit significantly.

10.195.10

Erica also made a trip to Europe. She needed to build personal relationships with all the key players, including Russia and various European leaders. She especially wanted to visit the United Kingdom and visit the Royal Family. Jeffrey had made great friends of the family and she had met them, but this trip would allow her to extend her relationship with them into a more personal nature. She had also brought her staff with her.

Gabby was totally excited Erica had invited her and Simon on this trip. "Really, we get to go into real castles! It'll be awesome!"

Simon was not such a nerd for history, but if it made his girlfriend happy, then he was all in. "Do you think there will be any dragon's or damsels in distress?"

"Whatever. I know you are kidding, but seriously, this will be like the coolest thing ever!"

"Okay, all kidding aside, I think it will be fun to see some history."

Turns out, Simon became a sudden fan. He had never read about this history before and when he saw these castles and began to learn about it, he was even more of a nerd than Gabby! They went various castles, cathedrals, and palaces. After they spent an entire day at Blenheim Palace, they went to Warwick Castle and he had a blast climbing up the stairs in the north tower. The view was spectacular, looking out over the city and the hills surrounding the castle.

"Well, I have to admit. This is really cool."

Gabby snuggled into his arms and gave him a big kiss. "Thank you for trying to like things that I like. I love you."

"I love you, too. I hope you will always be so open with me. I am not good at reading people, but don't ever want to hurt you, especially when I am being myself and just missing something."

"I forgive you in advance, and I will always speak my feelings to you. Tell me, what would you like to do?"

"Really?"

"Yes, really."

"I would love to climb the Eifel Tower. If this view is so wonderful, imagine what the view must be from there."

"Let's go."

The two of them collected their security team and after some coordination, were on a transport for Paris. They found the history and architecture to be equally as beautiful as England. However, the view from the Eifel Tower was simply breathtaking. What a panorama! It was just beautiful to see the River Seine, the palaces, gardens, museums, cathedrals, just everything. They held each other and were in awe. Neither of them had ever actually seen anything like this before.

They went to Versailles and were left emotionally drained. They held each other as they walked the halls, through the mirrors and glass, the gardens, the entire spectacle of it all. How magnificent. Imagine what it would have been like to have lived here when it was new. They leaned against one of the marble pillars in the Grand Trianon and kissed a very long time, finally enraptured with each other in this most romantic place.

They were walking back to the palace when Sofia approached them. "Gabby, we have to leave, there has been an explosion in the Z-wing lab."

"No! Okay, let's go." She got on her phone and called Erica.

"Erica, what happened?"

"We don't know. I have wrapped up my meeting in Warsaw. We are enroute to the airport and will stop in Paris at Charles de Gaulle airport to pick you up. As soon as I hear anything I will let you know."

"Okay, thanks. Erica will stop in Paris to pick us up. Oh my gosh, I just pray all those safety features we built work."

"We will find out soon."

Once on board the Boeing 747 Gabby and Erica discussed the situation. From what they could gather the accident had not been in the X-drive area, so this appeared to be a random accident in another area. This involved the materials lab. Gabby was finally able to contact her team and discovered they were trying out a new super heat conducting alloy when the heat generator malfunctioned. She also discovered that no one had been injured, as they were all within the safe monitoring control room when the accident occurred.

After they had finished the discussion, Heather called. "Gabby, are you all right? Oh my God, I have been so worried about you."

"Mom, it's okay. The accident was due to a mechanical failure in the materials lab and everyone was safe, due to the new facilities we have built."

"You are sure? The safety construction you implemented made a difference?"

"Yes, and that feature is in all our labs now."

"Thank goodness. Well, sorry if I caught you at a bad time."

"Mom, I am so glad you called. I have to tell you something wonderful. Simon and I had the best time ever. We kissed on the Eifel tower, the castles, Versailles; I mean, we just are so right for each other. I know I am totally in love with him."

"That's wonderful! Doesn't it feel good all the way to your toes?"

"Yes! Oh my, I just feel tingles in so many places."

"By the way, have you met his family yet?"

"No, we have been waiting for that until we decide if we are going to make this permanent. His family is a little different, and he thinks they may resent me because of what I do."

"Oh, I am sorry to hear that. Well, you let Simon know he is joining our family, so he will always have a strong supportive family around him, just like you. I love you."

"I love you, mom. Okay, I have to have a conversation Erica on the research situation."

"Say hi to her for us."

"I will."

Gabby chuckled at the conversation they had. Her mom was the most worried person she had ever known, and she loved it. She loved that there was someone who always thought of her and loved her. It was one of life's true pleasures.

She talked with Erica for a while about the research progress, and then she found Simon napping in a chair. She sat down beside him and reached over and took his hand. "I love you." Simon was startled, but apparently, he had not been sleeping.

"Gabby, I have had a thought about the X-drive. We have been so focused on the Special Relativity effect I think we may have overlooked how we can fold space in front of the vehicle, so it does not truly move at lightspeed but moves through gaps in spacetime that allow us to leave point a and arrive at point b nearly simultaneously, even if they are multiple light years apart. It isn't actually moving through all that space, it is getting there in the most efficient manner possible."

"So, you see this as a loop process, or even a wormhole process where we move through defined spaces by folding space. How can we fold space?"

"That is where the work is. We do it already with gravity. It may mean using gravity in a different way to generate the fold, then thrust through the fold itself to jump to the new position. Perhaps the amount of folding we do will determine the distance we travel?"

"That is a wild idea! I love it." She leaned over and gave him a big kiss. Then she pulled out her tablet and began writing formulas and thoughts on the research. Simon was doing the same thing. Between them they created several avenues for study to see if there was potential for this. It would be a different direction, but it may work.

10.210.09

Out of the blue, Jeffrey called Erica and asked if she was available to take a short trip with him. Erica accepted, of course, because he was still the President, but she had no idea what the trip was for.

"Hi Erica, how are you this morning?"

He and Erica were on board the Boeing 747. He had told her they were on a trip to New York to talk with some inventors. Heather had remained behind, as she had one last conference for the philanthropy she chaired before she passed the torch to Tamara. This would only be a day trip, so he would be back before bed. He had asked her to join him in the front compartment, where there were only two chairs, and they could enjoy some privacy.

"I am fine. Can you provide me with some information on this inventor's meeting?"

"I could, but we are not attending that meeting today."

She looked at him, quite surprised. "We're not?"

"No. We are traveling to Rochester, Minnesota. It will still be a one-day trip, but there is something you need to know." Once they had settled into their seats, he began. "When this whole trillionaire process began, I had a conversation with a medical researcher. We talked about the potential for our migration pods and the psychological concerns involved. We talked about how tough it would be for people to only live for seventy years while they are on a ship that may take over a hundred to reach its destination."

"These people would live their life and die in a single place. They would have children that may also live their entire life in the same place. It would be hard to grasp what this may cause people to do, who had no hope of actually seeing the future they were working for, unfold."

"I asked him if it was possible to extend life, so people could live longer, even to one hundred and fifty years. He said it may be, but he would need to do some research along those lines. I asked him to take a look at every idea he could find, and I also asked him to think about the idea behind the rejuvenation process in Robert A. Heinlein's book, *Time Enough for Love*."

"Well, he has continued working on it and believes he has found some processes that we could use that extend life for a while. Some of these we should use if we ever send out new migration pods. Some we could possibly market here and on other planets to help people begin to extend their lives."

Erica was surprised, as she knew nothing about this. "I knew we were doing some limited research through universities but knew nothing about this. How did you keep it secret from me?"

Jeffrey laughed. "It was not easy. However, I have managed to do that. It is important to keep this research secret, because if word leaks out, people will think we are creating a super-human or conducting experiments on humans, and we will get shut down."

"I get that."

"All we are doing, truthfully, is researching possible cures, life extenders, and any other options to take who we are today and enable a longer life. This will probably involve changing our DNA, but we don't know yet, hence the research."

"That makes sense to me, I just hadn't thought of it that way."

"That's because you are still so young. You still see a long future ahead of you. I don't. Oh, maybe another twenty years, but that is it. Mortality comes into focus as you age, so the need for certain types of research changes as well."

Once they landed, Jeffrey introduced her to Dr. Michaelson as his number two and instructed him to share anything she asked with her. The program would continue in total secrecy, but Erica would now be in the loop on developments.

10.215.15

The research on the X-drive accelerated and shifted. Simon's new idea was thought to have very good potential. Based on this a new research lab was established, as they wanted to continue the current research but add this new dimension. This meant that Gabby and Simon were in the X-drive laboratory most of the time. They even had bunk beds installed so everyone could nap when necessary to stay focused. It was an exciting time. It was also a dangerous time.

Gabby was walking back from the cafeteria when a large explosion rocked Z-wing. She saw the explosion was from the X-drive area and rushed to the lab. When she entered she could see smoke and small fires, but the chemical flame retardants had not activated nor had the doors sealed for a hazmat incident. She paused and looked around, noticing that only some of the equipment was damaged.

She thought, where is everyone? Then she saw the door to the control room open and Simon walked out. She ran to him and asked if he was okay.

"Yes, I am fine. This was an interesting experiment."

"What was it?"

"We thought we would apply your theory to minimize the Special Relativity effect while warping the space in front of the craft."

"What craft?"

Simon smiled. "You remember that little craft we used for testing air currents that used to sit over there? Well, guess what, it isn't here anymore."

Gabby looked at him, then realized what he said. "You mean it worked?"

By now all the researchers were standing around them.

"Yes, it worked. We don't know where or when that craft is today, but it left in a hurry, blowing out some fuses and kicking up a storm."

"It means your theory worked, Dr. Anderson. Your theory combining both effects into a single potential did it!"

The group then cheered and clapped and laughed and smiled in happiness that they had finally made significant headway. Gabby was incredulous.

"Why didn't you wait until I was here to watch?"

"Because you would have been too nervous. But you can analyze all the data and reach your own conclusions. Great job, Gabby."

Gabby thanked everyone and then got them working on cleaning up the lab. She called Erica and let her know the explosion had been controlled and there was no damage and no injuries. Gabby instructed the staff that she wanted to keep the results secret until they could understand them and replicate them in a controlled manner. Later, Gabby and Simon celebrated with a glass of wine, an unusual occurrence that was becoming more regular.

10.235.09

"Arabella, we have a lot to do to coordinate this event."

"Yes, I agree, but we have time. I believe the initial plan you laid out will be very good for the occasion."

"Yes, well there are still some things to consider. I did decide on the succession plan. I am changing the succession of the Presidency of JW Enterprises to be defined as the individual selected by the current President of the company, but not blood related. Also, I am adding a clause where the previous President(s) could come in and directly interfere in the working of the company if the person in the President position strays to far from the vision and mission of the company. That way it will not just tie to Jeffrey but apply to any President, although I have written it in such a way that Jeffrey will always be the ranking president, regardless of how many are present. I also believe, as did Jeffrey, that a formal public transfer of ownership of the company is necessary, so everyone can see the new President is indeed, legitimate."

"I believe those changes only strengthen the company, Erica. It helps establish a very strong continuity."

"Thanks, Arabella. I have also decided we will hold the change of ownership ceremony here at the JW Enterprises headquarters in downtown Omaha."

Erica turned and looked out her fifteenth-floor window and realized how much this city had changed. There were multiple sky scrapers downtown now, plus more under construction. Omaha was now a global financial center, thanks to Jeffrey's vision.

On the day of the ceremony, she brought everyone who could fit into the transit hall in the sub-basements. They had closed all the transportation systems down at ten in the morning, so they could get it organized for a two o'clock ceremony. She had sound systems, video systems, and caterers going crazy trying to get everything prepared and in place. At one o'clock, the employees and guests began arriving. Everyone was scanned and checked. Richard was not going to have a problem with a party crasher. He had consulted with Stephanie and Abby on his plans and they had supported his decisions.

At one fifty, the children, spouses, and close family of the leadership team entered and took their seats. Shortly afterwards, Erica entered and took her seat on the platform. At one fifty-nine, she got up to welcome Jeffrey.

"Ladies and Gentlemen, please rise for our President, Jeffrey Wilson."

Jeffrey entered by the door at the far end of the hall to cheers. He walked, waving and shaking hands, all the way through the crowd until he arrived at the platform. He then walked over to the podium to speak, while the crowd continued a long applause.

"Thank you so very much, please, please, take a seat. Thank you. Well, the day has finally arrived, and no Erica, I did not write any notes for this speech." There was laughter from many of the people in the room, as the standing joke was he always had Erica write his speeches.

"Some of you here today have been with me since the beginning. I must say, today everything is far different from the world I woke up to on that March morning ten years ago. How it has changed. All it took was a knock on the door and poof, the world changed. It reminds me of a line in J.R.R. Tolkien's *Lord of The Rings*, 'It's a dangerous business, Frodo, going out your door. You step onto the road, and if you don't keep your feet, there's no knowing where you might be swept off to.' Well we were certainly swept away."

"It has been my great privilege to be part of history. We have changed the future of our species and, I believe, made our future even brighter. Poverty and illiteracy are down around the globe. People have healthcare who never had it before. Food is available, education is helping people set higher expectations for their livelihood. I believe we have done very well."

"But as I said, this was a team effort and there are those I must thank. Before this project began, there was one person who was keeping it real for me and helping me survive. My daughter, Tamara, who helped me through the darkest days of my life and showed me that life and love were possible once again. Thank you, dear, for your love, support, friendship, companionship, trust, and for having two of the cutest children ever, my grandchildren." He stepped back and applauded, and everyone joined him in his thanks to Tamara.

"The two people who supported Erica for all the years we worked together and made both of us look good all the time, Michelle and Janice. Thank you, ladies."

"My counselor, Miquel, and Felicity, my legislative liaison for Nebraska. I do not think we would ever have gotten this project off the ground and running the way we have without the tireless effort of the two of you."

"The newest addition to our family, Gabby, who has helped us relearn the true meaning of love, compassion, and parenting. Love you, dear."

"My security chief, Stephanie. You saved my life by sacrificing your own. No act of love could ever be greater than that. I will always love and respect you for your passion, honesty and commitment to the safety and security of our family. Thank you."

"I know I should save her for last, but today we have a different agenda, so let me say thank you to my lovely wife, Heather. There are no words for you, dear. You have loved me unconditionally and shown me that two people can find each other through the chaos of life if their hearts are true. I love you with everything I am and look forward to continuing this journey with you after this official retirement. Thank you, my love."

He stopped for a moment. Then said jokingly. "I seem to be forgetting someone. Is there anyone else?" Everyone laughed. Erica was already in tears. He turned to her.

"A long time ago, in a world far, far away, I asked this remarkable young lady, not a lot more than a girl really, a very young mother, to work with me as my assistant and help me change the world. Her enthusiasm was powerful, her passion was incredible, her spirit so infectious. Come up here, dear."

Erica got up from her chair and walked over to Jeffrey and they hugged a long time. Everyone cheered while they hugged, and when they stopped, she stayed beside him.

"This young lady has blossomed and become the most talented, competent, dynamic leader I have ever known. She has demonstrated through action, commitment, participation, and her genuinely competent manner, that she is the most qualified, and humble person in the room wherever she is. I have never been as proud of anyone. I can never thank you for making my life so easy during all the years we got this company off the ground. Because make no mistake, this project was a team effort and Erica played a major role. Thank you. And now, ladies and gentlemen, let it be known that I officially retire and designate Dr. Erica Beckett as my replacement, so I give to you your new President, Dr. Erica Beckett."

The room roared! Everyone was on their feet yelling support, whistling, shouting, it was just a wonderful chaos. Erica gave Jeffrey another long hug and thanked him for his kind words. He kissed her on the cheek and walked over to stand and applaud with Heather. Erica stood there, a young girl who grew up and found her voice, and let the celebration go on for a while. Finally, she began.

"Thank you, thank you. Please, be seated or we will never get out of here. Thank you. Let me first ask everyone to join me in thanking our founder, visionary, leader, best friend, and out-going President, Jeffrey Wilson." With that everyone roared again. It was loud and noisy for a very long time. Jeffrey waved, then stood for a moment to wave, then sat back down.

"Thank you, Jeffrey for your kind words. Let me say that I learned so much from you. You may not know it, but you are the most decent human being that I have ever known, heard about, or read about. Your leadership, decisiveness, vision, compassion, and genuine concern for all of us are reflected in how much we all love you. I learned a very important lesson from you: our people come first."

"Many of you have asked, what now? With a new President, will we change what we do? The answer is no. We will continue to manage our financial portfolio, establish and work projects around the globe, and support the development of space travel technology. We are on a clear path. We will hold that course steady and work even harder to achieve our goals."

"I can only hope that when I retire I am as loved as Jeffrey is by all of us today. I will make you this promise. I will never forget where I came from or the thousands of our employees who toil every day to achieve their life goals while helping us achieve our company goals. I am in this with you, and we are in this for the long haul. Thank you, everyone. Please enjoy the refreshments in the back of the hall."

Everyone roared again. Erica's husband and children came out to hug her and wave to the crowd. Eventually she brought everyone out on stage and had a large family hug fest. She thought, wow, I am only thirty-seven years old and I am now the most powerful woman in the history of the world. Overwhelming. I understand why Jeffrey kept us around to help him keep his feet on the ground. I need that as well. I think Arabella will be good at that.

10.275.09

"Gabby, do you want to go to the beach this weekend?"

"I'd love to, but why now?"

"Well, it's just that it's getting colder outside, and my bones hurt. I sure would love to go somewhere we could just lay in the sand and relax. Especially with all the long hours we've been putting in the past couple of months."

"Well, Mom and dad are going to Destin this weekend, do you want me to see if we can hitch a ride with them?"

"Sure, that would be a great idea."

Gabby called her mom and asked if they could tag along. Of course, she loved the idea. Jeffrey was now sixty-eight years old and having these younger kids around helped keep both of them a little younger.

On Friday, Gabby and Simon met them at the house at noon, and they departed. Erica had also decided to take a few days off, so everyone could ride in the Boeing 747. Jeffrey did not travel as much as he used to, but he still loved this plane.

They arrived in Destin at about five in the afternoon, and Jeffrey had already made reservations for himself and Heather at the Harbor Docks Restaurant. They would get there in plenty of time to see the sunset from the back pier. Simon had asked if they could tag along, and Jeffrey agreed. Oddly, Erica and her family also decided to go there. The thing that really topped it off was that when they arrived for their reservation, they were escorted into the restaurant and Tamara was there with her family. It was really interesting that there was no one else in the restaurant.

Simon waited until everyone was seated, then he stood up and clinked a knife to his glass. "May I have everyone's attention please?" Everyone stopped and looked at him. Gabby had no idea what was going on.

"I would like to thank you all for being here. It was difficult, I know, for everyone to get here at the same time. However, I wanted you all here to participate in this very special day."

"Simon, what is going on?"

Simon looked at her. "Gabby, we have known each other for four years. Aside from my parents and siblings, I don't think I have known anyone that long. In that time, we have shared some excitement, laughs, tears, and just hard work. In that time, I have come to love you more than life itself, and I know that I want to spend the rest of my life with you."

He then got down on one knee, and pulling a ring from his pocket, said, "Gabriella Anderson-Wilson, will you marry me?"

Gabby was completely surprised. You could see it in her eyes and face. However, she was very quick with her response. "YES!"

They instantly hugged and kissed while everyone shouted congratulations.

Gabby went straight to Heather to show her the ring and get a hug. Then she began circulating to show the other ladies the ring. Simon walked over to Jeffrey and thanked him for letting him have permission to marry his daughter. Jeffrey couldn't be prouder, he really liked Simon, and he truly believed he and Gabby made a super couple.

11.173.10

Heather and Jeffrey had been married for ten years. Everyone wanted to join them in celebration of the event, but this time, they decided to do something completely different. For their anniversary, they decided to rent Disney World. They planned this almost two years in advance, so all of their family, close friends, people they had met through the years and all of the employees of JW Enterprises, could spend a great week enjoying all that Disney World had to offer with no waiting.

"We cannot thank you enough for this wonderful week! Everyone is having a blast!"

"Well, it couldn't have happened without your support, Erica. We are just glad you were able to bring everyone for this celebration."

"Well I know I would not have missed it, and bringing the entire team together is wonderful for morale. Everyone will be talking about this for years."

They spent their actual anniversary day at Epcot. The President's and Prime Ministers and Royalty of countries from around the world they had met and worked with over the years arrived and participated in the event. They provided superb entertainment, food and drink reflecting the best of their countries as a way to thank them for all their work over the years.

The evening of their anniversary they had a dinner in a room above the French Restaurant, Chefs de France, with Tamara, Erica, Gabby, Michelle, Arabella, and Janice and their families, and Stephanie and Abby. It was a small, intimate evening with good conversation and laughter, reminiscing about the beginning of their love story up to the present. It was a magical night. The next day, everyone loaded up and headed home.

11.180.17

A week later, they all loaded up and headed for Wisconsin.

Gabby and Simon decided to get married in a quiet ceremony with only their closest friends and family. Simon's family had cut him off completely, because they hated everything the Federation stood for, so refused to accept Gabby as their daughter in law or acknowledge their wedding. It hurt, but the positives far outweighed that negative.

"I am sorry your family feels that way, son. I know you see that what we are trying to do is ensure people's safety from an Imperial style of government by establishing limitations on it before it happens. It saddens me there are people out there who still don't understand that."

"Thank you, Jeffrey. I have known for a decade that my family would not support my dreams and goals. They will not come into the current century, much less even think about the next one and beyond. To them, the world revolves around their few acres in the woods outside of town. Truly, I think everyone else I know in Hahira gets it, as they are very progressive and forward thinking; but not my family."

"What saddens me the most is that they will never get to see what a wonderful woman Gabby is. They are missing it. They certainly will never see any children we have, so will miss that as well. I am glad you and Heather are here, along with the rest of the family."

At that moment, the music began playing. Simon took his queue and left to go to the beginning of the aisle. He met Heather there and escorted her down the aisle to her place front left. She hugged him and took her seat.

Jeffrey, meanwhile, left and went into the portable trailer they had brought in for this occasion. Entering the trailer, he found Erica, Tamara, and Sheryl helping Gabby with finishing touches to her dress. When they heard him come in, Erica and Tamara left, as they were bridesmaids. The Maid of Honor, Sheryl, lingered a moment, then gave her a kiss and left to take her place as well.

"You are so very beautiful, my dear."

"Thanks, dad."

"I know we don't talk about it very often, but had your mom and dad lived, they would both be here hugging you and so very proud of the woman you are. I know I am."

They took a moment for a long hug. He was more of a dad than her own dad was, since he died when she was very young. Still, she missed him. Jeffrey gave her heart and hope, and she loved him for it. They heard the music change to the processional.

Jeffrey opened the door and helped her out of the trailer. She took his arm and they walked slowly through the flowers and the arch up to the platform where Simon waited. When they got there, Jeffrey gave her a kiss and a big hug, then turned and gave Simon a big hug as well.

He sat with Heather and they held hands, remembering the day they had stood in this very same place, under the old maple tree, saying their own vows. It was a perfect place for a wedding and the weather was beautiful, with the glow of the late sun shining into the tops of the trees.

The dinner and dance were in the barn. This time, Jeffrey and Heather got to sit back and enjoy the event, remembering their own night. When the time came they joined Gabby and Simon on the dance floor for the father-daughter and mother-son dance. Then they danced together, and it was still magical after all these years. It was only a week after their ten-year wedding anniversary. This was a perfect way to celebrate, watching their daughter get married.

Simon and Gabby Jackson left at ten, just like her parents had, in a horse drawn coach.

11.225.10

Gabby was ecstatic. She couldn't wait to share this news. First, she decided to stop and see Simon. "Hi dear, what are you doing?"

Simon looked at her and knew something was different. "Okay, you have changed. What's going on?"

Gabby was so happy and excited she couldn't hold it in. "We are having a baby!"

Simon was totally overjoyed and seriously happy to hear this. "That is fantastic! Oh my God! This is wonderful!"

They hugged and smiled and laughed for a while. Finally, Gabby said, "I want to tell mom. I think I will go home now so I can tell her before she hears it from someone else."

"Great idea. I think we can be out of the office for a day without any issues to the project. I'm coming too."

Heather was sitting in the living room with Jeffrey. They were having a cup of coffee and talking about their anniversary celebration. They had a wonderful book filled with all the memories.

"Hi mom."

"Hi, dear. What are you doing home so early?"

Gabby walked over and sat down beside Heather. She reached out and held her hands. "Mom, Simon and I are having a baby."

Heather nearly fell off the couch as she reached out and hugged Gabby. "Oh, my dear that is so wonderful!"

"I know, this is awesome!"

"Congratulations, you two. This is great news."

"Thanks, dad."

"Well, this gives us something entirely different to think about!"

"A new future is opening up for you, and I know you will embrace it and have a wonderful life with your children."

"Our grandchildren."

Everyone was very happy for them and the days and months went by fairly quickly.

The news that no one expected came when they were three months pregnant.

"Dr. Jackson, you are not having a baby. You are having three babies. Triplets."

Gabby was shocked. "What? How can that be?"

The doctor smiled. "Let's say it is a nature thing."

Heather was ecstatic. Why have one when you could have three? Everyone was so excited for them, it was going to be a wonderful event.

12.125.09

Six months later they were in the delivery room. Gabby asked Heather if she would assist. She was overwhelmed to be part of this and was so thankful for Gabby coming into her life. The only thing that could be better is if she was having a child of her own.

They had planned for this moment, and all three bassinettes were ready. It wasn't long before the oldest, Lakelyn, was born, followed by her sister Lanica, followed by their brother, Landon. Three happy, healthy babies and two very happy parents, one of whom was exhausted.

They were beautiful. Heather and Jeffrey were overjoyed at the new family. Jeffrey knew Heather held a small place in her heart where she hid her personal grief at never having had a child, but no one else could tell. This was just a magical moment.

12.195.10

It had been over a year since the change of leadership and Erica was truly in her element. She still called Jeffrey every now and then, but mostly it was just to say hi to a dear friend, not to talk work. He was right, she had a vision and a path and while he was there, she knew where she wanted to go.

She was excited about the discoveries they made in the research program. Her biggest challenge was how to get these discoveries turned into technology for sale. She called Jeffrey and asked if she could come over to talk about her thoughts.

"Hi Erica, thanks for coming over. It is so much easier to not have to get dressed up and go into an office. Hi Arabella." Arabella nodded, while Erica gave Jeffrey a hug and they went over to sit in the living room.

"Hi Jeffrey. Not a problem and I had wanted to visit with you anyway. How are you?"

"Well, aside from feeling every part of my body and realizing I am actually aging, I feel great!"

They were both laughing as Heather entered the room and gave her a hug, then sat beside Jeffrey. "Hi Erica, it is so good to see you, we don't get to visit with you nearly as much as we would like. Hi Arabella."

"Hi Heather, yes, I agree. But you know, Jeffrey did leave me in charge of a fairly big operation. Two operations really, the Federation and the company. It has been busy, which is why I needed to visit with you."

Erica asked Arabella for her notes. "I think the biggest problem I see right now Jeffrey, is that we are not getting enough research discoveries into the market. There have been a couple of cases where our competitors got to the market first, which cost us quite a bit in lost sales."

"Do you have a team focused on this specific process?"

"Yes, but I think the problem is we don't have a defined manufacturing business to take these discoveries and turn them into products. We rely on the team to take discoveries out and sell them to others for manufacturing. My thought is to invest in purchasing a large manufacturing business and tie it directly to the discovery process, so we eliminate the middleman and the time lag."

"That could be pricey, plus add additional cost to the company in the long term. Have you run some preliminary numbers?"

"Yes. Arabella."

"Thank you, Erica. President Wilson, we estimate the initial cost to be twenty-five billion dollars for the initial purchase and changes necessary to operationalize it to our needs. The savings we get from each new product, based on the past three years of tracking, equate to roughly two hundred and fifty million dollars per product; in other words, if we would have gotten the product to market quicker, our sales could have been higher, plus the cost of maintaining the additional overhead to manage that process. Based on our current average, which is trending upwards, of ten new products a year, we could see a two point five billion positive per year, meaning the purchase pays for itself in ten years. Thereafter it is all positive numbers."

Jeffrey was smiling ear to ear. Arabella saw this and was slightly nervous wondering if she had said something wrong. Erica was watching and smiled, knowing what Jeffrey was going to say.

"Arabella, two things. Please, when we are talking among family, which you are part of now, call me Jeffrey. Formal titles have their place, but I try hard to avoid them. Second, that was an excellent presentation and very good data. Are you looking at a specific company to purchase, or was that cost a general guide for the project?"

"Thank you, sir, I mean Jeffrey. The cost we used is based on the average acquisition cost we have tracked over the past three years as well."

"Actually, Jeffrey, I do have my eye on a specific company that is demonstrating an excellent product idea to market throughput time and low cost. I think we may go with them, and the cost should be very close to Arabella's estimates. My question though, does that drain us down or cause us to wander off our central purpose?"

"It is a good question, but I think in this case it is a solution to a real problem. JW Enterprises is first and foremost a for profit company. Oh yes, I know we manage a huge infrastructure investment project that is mostly self-sufficient. But the other side of the business must be focused on profit to maintain the level of investments we need to make in order to drive the company successfully into the twenty second century and out into the galaxy as the major business. Finding a way to reduce costs while increasing profits is exactly the type of initiative necessary to achieve that goal. I would add my congratulations to you, Erica, for seeing this and forcing a solution. That is the original thinking we discussed a few years ago. Well done."

"Thank you, Jeffrey. You always can make me feel so good about myself. I really appreciate your support."

Jeffrey was about to speak when a look of concern crossed his face. He turned towards Heather, and reached for his left arm, and simply keeled over. Heather grabbed him, so he wouldn't fall from the couch.

Erica yelled for Arabella to call 911. Stephanie saw what happened and activated emergency code Alpha Four Four. Heather held Jeffrey in her arms and did not know what to do. Erica leaped from her chair and helped her lay him on the couch. As they watched, his skin began to turn a grayish color. Almost immediately a fast response team burst through the front door and surrounded them, pushing Heather and Erica to the side. They had oxygen, defibrillators, and every other item necessary for this event.

Stephanie guided Heather and Erica aside, seeing that they were basically useless right now. She felt it too, but her training kept her focus sharp during crisis. She brought Arabella over and had her clear Erica's schedule. She called for transportation, so they could leave and follow the ambulance once it departed. Stephanie also called Tamara and informed her what had happened, and that transportation was enroute to pick her up for transport to the hospital. Other than that, she too waited.

Heather and Erica were basket cases. They held each other and cried, not knowing if Jeffrey would live or die. For separate reasons, they were both completely devastated, but also for the same reason, they loved him.

The response team loaded Jeffrey on a gurney and moved out the door as a medical evacuation helicopter landed. They loaded Jeffrey into the helicopter and it departed immediately for the hospital emergency trauma center at Offutt Air Force Base, a very short ride away. Stephanie loaded everyone into waiting suburban's and departed for the hospital.

When they arrived, Jeffrey had already been transferred into the trauma unit. Tamara arrived at the same time as everyone else. Heather and Tamara were allowed to get the closest, but even they had to wait in a separate room and wait. They could hear voices and noise and knew the team of surgeons and nurses were working feverishly, but all they could do was hold each other and cry, not knowing what to expect.

Erica was left alone in the lobby and sat crying; however, it was less than a minute before Stephanie walked over to her. "Erica, come with me. Heather was surprised you were not with her and Tamara. She wants you with her, not out here by yourself." She led Erica through the hallways to the room where Heather was waiting. All three of them held onto each other and hugged, tears rolling down their cheeks not knowing if the one man they all loved so dearly, who had made the world work so wonderfully for them, would live or die.

It was the longest few hours any of them had experienced. Occasionally they could hear shouting, then periods of silence. They saw people hurrying past the door. They couldn't help but believe something terrible was happening.

At last, Dr. Paulsen came in. He was smiling, and said, "He is going to be fine." All three of them were so relieved and started crying again. Heather maintained her composure the best and asked if she could see him. He led her back into the trauma unit and over to the area where Jeffrey was laying. Heather could see his skin color looked normal. He was awake, and she walked to him and held his hand, then leaned down and kissed him.

"I love you."

"I love you."

"What happened?"

"He had a minor heart attack that was made worse by his dehydration. We checked and there are no blockages of concern. We will be conducting some more tests in the coming days during his stay here in the hospital. We want to try and find out a specific cause, but sometimes these things happen due to outside issues, like stress. Once we know, we will work with you to create a recovery plan that helps Mr. Wilson stay healthy for many years to come."

"Thank you, doctor. Thank you for saving his life."

"You are welcome, ma'am. And you, Mr. Wilson, you need to get some rest. We will be moving you into intensive care in a little while, so we can keep a close eye on you. For now, rest easy knowing you can go to sleep without fear, we will be watching you every minute."

"Thanks doc."

After the doctor left, Heather found a stool and pulled up beside Jeffrey. "It sounds like you had a very big scare, but that we can get you healthy and keep you that way."

"Yes. I was so scared, and everything happened so fast. I felt this pain and turned to tell you, and that is all I remember."

"Well trust me, there was more than that. You collapsed into my arms and Erica and I laid you on the couch. Thankfully a response team arrived very quickly. Tamara and Erica are outside, would you like to see them for a moment? I know they are as devastated as I was."

She got up and walked over and waved to Stephanie, who brought them over. Jeffrey was glad to see them all, including Stephanie.

"I suspect that I am alive today because of you. I bet you called a fast reaction medical team on standby, didn't you?"

"Yes, we have been keeping one on standby since you turned sixty-five. It seemed prudent."

He held Tamara and Erica's hands and they all talked quietly for a moment. Heather told them what the doctor had told them. Once they knew he had an excellent chance for a full recovery, everyone relaxed slightly. It was only fifteen minutes later when the doctor came back into the room and informed everyone that Jeffrey needed rest, so could they all please say good night and let him rest.

On the ride home Heather received a call from Gabby. "Mom, what happened? I heard dad had a heart attack, is he okay?"

"Yes, dear, he is fine. He had a minor heart attack, but the doctor says he will fully recover, and we will work on a plan to keep him healthy."

"Oh my gosh, I am so sorry I was not there with you."

"It's okay. It did happen very quickly, but he is alright now."

"Okay, well, I will be home for dinner tonight to spend the night with you. I don't want you alone."

Heather teared up, and said, "Thank you Gabby. I will see you in a little while."

Over the course of the next few days everyone slowly returned to a mostly normal schedule, except for Jeffrey. He was put through stress tests, MRI's, scans and blood work so they could fully understand what was happening with his body. Eventually, he was released with a very positive bill of health and a plan for regular exercise, a few supplements, medications and water to keep him strong.

12.215.09

"We are live in Rio de Janeiro. Behind me you can see quite a large crowd protesting about their poverty. It seems they are mostly angry at the Federation and JW Enterprises, who they perceive as getting rich off the backs of everyday people."

About ten thousand of the very poorest people of the city staged the protest. They rallied and yelled; but did not destroy any buildings or cause any real harm. It was thought that someone put them up to it and there was no real concern.

12.225.09

Gabby had another meeting scheduled with Erica to discuss starship designs. The meeting was not the first, but this time there was a greater sense of urgency.

"Gabby, your reports indicate we are getting a lot closer to a drive that can take us to the stars. Have you begun designing or planning for a starship that can be ready when you make the crucial discovery?"

"Yes, Simon and I have been working with design engineers and we have completed a rough digital design we believe would accomplish all that we need. They are conducting theoretical wind-tunnel testing for possible atmosphere operations, and Simon is working vacuum simulations, evaluating mass distribution and other characteristics."

"How many people are you planning to be able to fit inside your craft?"

"This first design is for about forty people. That would include either large cargo holds or multiple staterooms for passengers. It can be more cargo/less staterooms, or more staterooms/less cargo. It depends on the needs of the ship's captain, so provides flexibility for commercial application. There is a galley, space for research labs, fitness activities, and other space as well. It is quite large, but also quite compact, using space very judiciously."

"Okay. How long can the ship operate without resupply?"

"We are tentatively planning for a one-year food/water storage capacity for twenty people, recycling all the moisture in the ship will help lower the amount of water carried on board. It is designed to be self-sufficient. The engines, we hope, will not need servicing once constructed; but we still have not gotten past some significant hurdles, so this is the major problem with any design idea."

"Alright. Is there anything more you need from me to help get this effort complete?"

"No, I believe we have all we need. We have tested the new drive a couple of times and we know it works; but it is not controllable yet. We have launched several items into the great unknown. No idea where they have ended up. We have to be able to send it and get it back before we can consider it successful."

"You are so close, Gabby. What are you going to call the drive when you finish it?"

"Simon and I have talked about it, and we want to call it the Wilson-Drive. It would be a permanent reminder of the vision Jeffrey had getting all of this started."

"I love that idea. Alright, you keep plugging away and I know we will get there soon."

12.247.10

A few weeks later, Gabby stopped by Erica's office. "Hi, Gabby. How are the plans coming for the starship?"

"I think with all the discoveries we have had in power generation, astrogation, you name it, we can start drafting some actual plans for a physical starship. We still need to answer some questions, like how it will look? Will it fly in atmosphere or be controlled by rockets and not need wings? How much cargo space? What type of computer system? I could go on, but you get the idea. It is one thing to think about the future of space flight, but once we achieve it, what kind of starship will it be?"

"Yes, and I think you should really move on this. If you believe you can, you should go ahead and manufacture some basic parts that you are positive will be used. I just think it is a good idea to start doing some actual physical work."

"I agree. The new craft the Federation is using for transit between planets might be a good place to start. I believe those engines will be part of this craft as well, and it is designed for over a hundred people, with life support systems all intertwined within the environmental system."

"Yes, well I will leave all of that to you. Please get started and keep Arabella in the loop, she will brief me."

"Okay, thanks Erica."

Gabby informed Simon of the development and he was as excited as she was. They took a look at the team and selected a small group of five, each one an expert in their own area, to begin the process of identifying specific aspects of the ship that would provide guidance on some physical parts they could build. Gabby put Simon in charge, as he was an expert at maneuvering vehicles in space and a very good team leader.

Over time the team established some basic requirements. One was that the computer supporting the starship would need to be smaller than anything they had ever built; yet have vastly more capability than current computers. This drove some serious research and development in the computing and systems team.

"So, you are telling me that this system can process ninety petaflops a second?"

"Theoretically. With the new materials we have developed we can put this into a space the size of your office. It will require environmental controls, but with the ability to generate and dissipate heat in space, we should be able to effectively manage this and use excess heat for other purposes."

"What type of storage do you need to support it?"

"Well, we would, ideally, like to have a storage capacity twice the size of the processing unit, so if we can have at least sixty petabytes of memory, I think we can do this."

Simon just looked at him. If he was right and this could be done, imagine the capability. "I will have to run this past Gabby, but I see no reason why she wouldn't support it. How long to build a prototype?"

Alexander thought a moment. "Simon, I don't think this is a prototype. When we build this, it will stay built, so we should build it to fit into the plans of the ship. That way we can build it in place and not worry about having to move it again."

"Okay, let me see what I can do."

"How fast?" Gabby was shocked that Alexander thought they could build a computer at these speeds.

"Ninety petaflops. Ridiculous, I know, but what an awesome system!"

"My God, that is way faster than human thought. How much do you think it will cost?"

"Initial estimates place it at around four billion dollars."

Gabby thought about it. That was a big number, but the computing capacity would be superb for astrogation in the changing environments this ship would travel. "Let me talk with Erica."

"How much?"

"We think it would be about two billion dollars for the computer system."

"Okay, so let me see if I have this right. With all the costs to date, we are pricing out this starship at about thirty billion dollars, right?"

"Yes, something like that. Mind you, this is the first of its kind and we are spending quite a lot of money researching ideas, materials and systems that can be part of it. I would estimate that if this was a known process and we could reproduce it, the cost would be closer to twenty billion dollars. Mass production of a run of ten of them may bring the cost down even more."

Erica took some time to think. She got up and walked over to the window she had that looked out over the Federation. It was a beautiful view, with the modern architecture that brought the feeling of infinity into a finite space. Two billion dollars for a computer. A computer the likes of which had never been built.

"Gabby, as long as you are building this computer, let's build two. Build one within the starship you are designing and build an additional one on SB1. We will need that kind of supercomputing power for our research, development, and construction efforts once we begin building serious starships. I can spread the cost over two projects, so it doesn't seem to be as high just for this one. Also, I want access to a terminal in my office at JW Enterprises, but not at the Federation. If this all goes according to plan, we might have ten planets before long and I want to begin pulling back a little."

"Understood. Thank you, Erica. We will get on it."

12.315.14

Erica had a lot to think about. The company financials were fine. The Federation project was going fine. Terrorism had declined significantly with the infusion of funds from the project in all the impoverished countries around the world. Research appeared to be getting close to producing a star drive. She always thought about getting to those six pods that departed with saboteurs on board and prayed the people in the pods were surviving and had decided a long time ago the first destination for starships would be those pods. But she just had an itch that something else needed her attention.

"Arabella, I need to go to SB1 and meet with Derek. Please coordinate a flight as soon as possible."

Arabella knew Erica was agitated. She didn't really know why, but she could sense it. Erica was only nine years older than her, but sometimes she felt Erica was a wise, older woman. She seemed to have gained so much knowledge and accomplished so much, all in such a short time. She was still in awe of her.

"Right away."

The next morning, they went to the new private hangar for JW Enterprises they built on the opposite side of the runways from the Federation. They had only built this hangar and some administrative buildings. Erica did not plan the future to be at the Federation, but with their long runways, this was the best place to use for near Earth transit, at least for now.

Once they arrived, Derek was waiting. "Hello, Erica, what brings you up here on such short notice?"

"Let's go to your office, I want to speak candidly."

Once they were settled in his office, she began.

"Derek, we need to move our operations off planet."

Derek was very surprised at this, not knowing anything about a reason for it. "Why would you want to do that? Isn't everything functioning well at the Federation?"

Erica thought for a moment. "Arabella, please read the latest research on attitudes towards JW Enterprises."

"We had several well-known research organizations conduct simultaneous surveys, each unknown to the other. The results show that the majority of the people on Earth are beginning to believe that JW Enterprises is becoming the new master. The perception is that we are manipulating prices, interest rates, technology access, and everything else, in order to make more money and suppress individual states from achieving the best for their people."

"Wow. I had no idea. It seems strange that a company with such high ideals could be perceived in such a way. What do you think caused it?"

"I think it has always been there. Jeffrey was fresh, he was an idea that was brand new. Today, after thirteen years living in the era of JW Enterprises and the Federation, people are beginning to doubt and question. The obvious target for this is JW Enterprises. Based on this, I believe we need to move our operations off planet."

"Okay, but what do you mean, specifically?"

"What I mean, is that we need to shift our research and development here. We need to shift personnel and operations for the company, here. We also, once we have an operational star drive and find the right planet, need to move all of this to that new planet."

Derek and Arabella were quiet for a while. This was a radical idea, not something either of them had considered.

"In addition, there is something you don't know. We have developed a star drive. It is just that it is not yet controllable to the point to trust putting people in it. I expect our research team to solve these concerns in the very near future. When that happens, I want us to take immediate steps to begin mass production of large starships, that when complete, can transport us to wherever we need to go. I just have a bad feeling about staying on Earth. I feel something is about to blow, but I cannot put my finger on it."

"Well, we have capacity to build nine starships simultaneously while docking and servicing another twelve. We have been bringing in raw material and are adequately stockpiled. We currently have three Federation ships in production, but they are only interplanetary, not interstellar. We can shift to that design as soon as one is available."

"You will have a team arriving soon that will be doing exactly that. I want you to work with Gabby on construction of the first starship. We will be constructing it here, along with some powerful computers. Once we get the first one built and tested, you can begin building additional designs. We will need a little bit of everything. We need cargo ships for people and material. We also need ships for research and exploration. We also need some ships with more firepower than the Federation ships you will be building. I don't want to suddenly give politicians the ability to hold a gun to our heads. This is why we need to plan now to shift everything we can off planet. If we start now, we can do it in incremental steps, so it won't be so noticeable."

"I like that plan. Okay, we can get started working on space requirements and construct anything we need. I believe Gabby and her team are scheduled to arrive tomorrow, so we will get started on that as well."

"Very good. Okay, we will get out of your hair. I just needed to get you on board and start moving this forward. Derek, you are an excellent member of our team and a super manager. You did a wonderful job managing the pod project, the re-tooling to intra-system ships, and I am sure you will be just as good at transforming SB1 to an interstellar workshop. When we finally shift our operation to another planet, you can have your choice to go or stay, but whatever you choose, you will be in charge and be very well compensated. Thank you."

"Thank you, Erica. Your support and encouragement mean a lot to me. My wife has already said she would like to see the stars, so once this happens, I would like to be the manager of the new construction facility we build, wherever it is."

Erica reach out and they shook hands.

"Deal."

13.187.10

"Mr. Wilson?"

"Yes, this is Jeffrey Wilson."

"Sir, this is Dr. Gustafson, Dr. Michaelson's replacement?"

"Oh yes, sorry, I was just taking a nap. I am seventy now, so taking naps seems to be a more important venture than it used to."

"I am sure it is."

"Can I help you with something?"

"No sir, I am calling to help you with something."

"What is that?"

"Mr. Wilson, we have succeeded through five perfect performances."

Jeffrey stopped in his tracks. "Are you telling me that you have succeeded in rejuvenation?"

"Yes. And according to Dr. Michaelson's direction, we have your clones ready."

"Oh my. When would you be ready to begin?"

"We need to begin within forty-eight hours."

"All three of us?"

"Yes."

"We will be there. Thank you."

"See you soon."

Jeffrey thought about what this would mean. Oh my, can't get too excited, must watch the blood pressure.

He walked into the living room and found his sixty-year-old wife reading a book. "Dear, we need to pack an overnight bag. I want to take you somewhere."

"Oh? Where would that be?"

"Well, not likely any place we went to ten years ago."

She smiled. "Okay dear. What kind of weather?"

"Oh, dress for warm weather, no reason to go where it is cold."

She got up and walked past him, stopping to give him a kiss on the way.

"Hi Jeffrey, how are you today?"

"Hi Erica. You know, I am quite wonderful."

"It is rare these days that you call me, so what can I help you with?"

"Can you bring up file Sierra Nine Six Three?"

"Sierra Nine Six Three, I just don't seem to remember that one. Hang on a minute, let me bring it up."

There was a pause for a moment. "Jeffrey is this true?"

"Yes, they just called. I am on the way out the door with Heather. I wanted you to know, so you can let everyone know. We will be at the site this afternoon; but will not start the process until day after tomorrow. If anyone wants to visit, tomorrow would be the best time."

"So, you really plan to go through with it?"

"Yes, dear, I do. An old body is a tough master, Erica. Wish that I were even as young as you. But alas, seventy is just old, and having had one heart attack, I think it is time to try something new."

"Does Heather know?"

"Not yet. I will tell her today."

"Okay, I will likely be bringing a whole plane load of people out tomorrow to visit before you start."

"Alright, see you tomorrow."

He hung up the phone and went to help Heather. Once they were done, he let Stephanie know of the plans. They departed by suburban and transferred to the Boeing 757 for the plane ride out. It was not a long flight. Once on the ground, they were again loaded into suburban's and taken to their building. Once there, the three of them walked into the facility and found Dr. Gustafson.

"Hi, and welcome! We have prepared your rooms through this door. We will need to run some tests this afternoon, but everything seems to be in order."

Heather looked at Jeffrey. "What is going on?"

"Dr. Gustafson, if you would be so kind as to let us take a few moments alone, that would be very helpful."

"Of course. Why don't you use this sitting room over here?"

"Thank you." Once they entered the room, he said, "Stephanie, this involves you, so please have a seat as well."

He paused for a moment, then began, "Heather and Stephanie, there is something you really need to know. Please understand, at the end of this conversation you are free to make your own decision. I could only coordinate for you to this point; the rest is up to you."

"Thirteen years ago, I was given the trillion-dollar program. When the project began I spoke with a lot of people about a lot of things. One of our major projects was the migration pods. In many conversations, one of the biggest concerns about the project was the psychological issues involved. How would people be able to handle such long periods of travel?"

"This led to the conversation of extending life. Were there ways to help people live longer? Could we truly make changes that would give people an additional fifty or more years? I asked a lot of questions. A certain Dr. Michaelson was the expert at the time, and I set him up in a research facility, which is where we are today, to study the human genome and see what could be done. I also challenged him to take a look at the rejuvenation idea you have heard me talk about."

"Well, this morning I received a call from Dr. Gustafson that they had succeeded, through five rejuvenations. They believe the process is now perfected. Based on that knowledge, we are here. Waiting for each of us is a clone of each of us, produced invitro and time compressed, for us to transfer into. Each body is roughly twenty-four years old, biologically. We would transfer all of our knowledge and experiences into a new body. As an added bonus, these bodies have been modified so the life expectancy is about 250 years. You only have to decide if you want to do it. I am. I beg you to join me."

Heather and Stephanie were near speechless. "Let me see if I get this straight, you want all three of us to take on new bodies? Why me? I can understand you and Heather, but why would you want me to join you?"

"Because I know what you sacrificed to protect me. I want you to have the opportunity to have a full life. Oh, don't get me wrong, I want you to stay with us and hopefully travel the stars with us, because we both love you. But I want you to have this chance in a brand-new body."

Heather was near tears. "Jeffrey does this mean we could have babies together?"

"Yes dear. We can have as many babies as your heart desires."

She got up and walked over to him and just hugged him, "I am in."

Stephanie walked over to them. "Heather, if it is okay with you, I want to go with you two."

Heather opened her arms and the three of them, all getting old with bodies that hurt, hugged.

13.188.10

Erica did not disappoint. She arrived with everyone; Tamara, Gabby, grandchildren, just everyone that loved them, as she said, a whole plane load. After a while, Jeffrey got everyone's attention.

"Please, let me say that we are scared as well. We have never been through this and do not truly know what to expect on the other side. If this works, you will be talking to some very young faces who have very old minds. We will have twenty-four-year-old bodies. That means we will look younger than everyone here except our grandchildren. I asked Dr. Gustafson to speak with you for a few minutes to explain the process and what you can expect."

"Hi everyone. First of all, tomorrow morning we will begin this process. Now this will involve a lot of time. It takes up to six weeks to complete the transfer process, then there is a long recovery period, followed by a physical therapy recovery process. They will have to learn to eat, dress, walk, a lot of simple tasks. The good news is that from previous success stories we know that after the first week, it goes very quickly. So, once you say goodbye tonight, please do not expect to hear anything for several months. At that point we will provide a brief to the President on the status."

Erica then stood and spoke to the group. "I need you all to hear something. This is all highly secret. We cannot put any of this on any form social or other media. You can tell no one, not a single soul. If the person is not in this room right now hearing this, do not tell them. There will come a time when we can let people know about this rejuvenation process, but today, for now, until you hear otherwise from me or Arabella, do not say a word. Anyone have a question about this? Seriously, if someone violates this secrecy a lot of people in this room, maybe everyone, could be killed. This is very serious. Okay, Jeffrey, please go ahead."

"Erica is exactly right, this is very serious. It is easy for us to laugh and talk about how wonderful this process may be; but there are a lot of people out there who would accuse us of many crimes, or just acting in a superior manner that they hate. So, please, keep this a secret between us."

Gabby had a very hard time saying goodbye to Heather, whom she had come to know and love as her mom. She and Heather were so close, she had placed so much of her life and stability in the relationship with her, that the thought of losing her was like nothing she had ever known before. It felt harder than anything she remembered when she lost her parents many years ago.

"I need you, mom. I don't want to lose you. I don't know what I would do without you."

Heather cradled Gabby in her arms. They had gone off into a private space so the two of them could be alone for a while. Heather needed this closure as much as Gabby, but she also knew her daughter needed to hear from her that it would be okay, and everything would work out right.

"I know, I feel the same as you. You have given me such life and helped me be a better stronger person for it, not to mention those grandchildren. But I am not going off to die. I am going off to extend my life, so we can have many more years together."

"Do you really believe this will work?"

"I know that Jeffrey would never do anything that he thought would cause me pain or harm. So yes, I believe this will work. That means that once we go through this, you and I will have years of time to be together. We may even have a chance to be mom's together, since my new body will only be twenty-four years old."

Gabby had not had time to process this thought. "That would be weird. I mean you being suddenly younger than me will be weird enough, but for us to be moms at the same time? That would really be different."

"Yes, it will be, all of it. But can you imagine how wonderful it will be? We two, who met through a long journey and found each other, who love each other, can be moms together. I think that would be fabulous and I just hope it happens."

"Me too!"

The two of them pushed the fear of the near future aside and embraced the joy and potential this change provided. After a while, they walked, arm in arm, back out to where everyone else was waiting.

The remainder of the evening was both happy and sad. There were goodbye's in case it did not work, and good lucks with all the hope and love they could convey. Finally, at seven thirty, the three of them were left alone.

"If this is a success, I don't want to stay your security chief. Instead, I want you both to think of me only as a friend who travels with you. I love the two of you with all my heart, and I cannot think of a better way to live life."

"Dear, when this is a success, you will be more than our friend, because you already are. You are my sister. We share so much, and you know how much I love you. You are a central part of this family. We three will travel the galaxy together, and one day, it will happen, when you find that someone to share a special bond with."

"Yes, I agree with Heather. We are family. Let's always make sure we three trust each other beyond all that life can throw at us."

13.201.10

Erica was very concerned about a news leak. If anyone found out that Jeffrey, Heather and Stephanie had received new bodies that could live 250 years, all hell would break loose. She had to keep a lid on this. As she was standing looking out a window thinking about this, there was a knock at her door. Gabby was there.

"Yes, Gabby, come in. How may I help you?"

"Hi Erica. I think you need to sit down."

"Really? What's up?"

"We did it."

Erica almost stopped breathing. "You mean you created a faster than light-speed engine?"

"Yes and no. We have not created the engine, but we have exceeded the Special Relativity effect. We can do it now. It's only a question of how we build the drive, not if we can."

"What do you need?"

"I believe we have everything we need on SB1. Derek is super and really helping us with design and engineering. The new computers we built are also fantastic in this process. This will be a tremendous buildout. We are building this starship from scratch, using the most advanced materials, around the hold where we will build the engine and the computer. Once we finish, this craft, which could depart from the surface and move effortlessly through the atmosphere, will execute the Wilson-Drive into the wide-open galaxy."

"How long will it take to build this?"

"I estimate it will take about six months, since we have already constructed some preliminary parts. But we don't want to rush too fast either, since this is the first one and we want to get it just right."

"Once we get it completed, who will crew it?"

"Me and Simon will test it. Once we test it and make sure everything works as designed, well, then I don't know, I haven't thought of that yet. There will be some skills we need, but we can work on that later."

Erica stood up and walked over to Gabby, who also stood. She reached out and hugged her. "Thank you, Gabby. I believe you have saved our species. Jeffrey will be so proud of you when he learns of this."

"Do you know what their status is?"

"No. I expect we will hear something soon. In the meantime, this news must be kept secret until we can plan a proper press conference. I will work on that and contact you for participation as soon as we figure this out."

"Okay, we will be quiet."

13.208.10

A week later, Erica called Dr. Gustafson to find out about the status of Jeffrey, Heather and Stephanie.

"Good afternoon, doctor. Any update?"

"Good afternoon, Erica. I was just going to call you. Yes, I do have some news for you. As you know, Stephanie was the youngest going in. She is also the first one to come out. She is, as we speak, being moved into a comfort room where we will begin working with her on motor skills. All indications are that this was completely successful for her. She looks incredible."

"That is wonderful news, doctor. How about Heather and Jeffrey?"

"Yes, Heather is responding very well. If all continues as it has thus far, we expect she will be out of recovery and into a comfort room within a few days. She is responding very well, and also looks incredible."

There was a momentary pause. Erica said, "What about Jeffrey?"

"This is why I was going to call you. Erica, Jeffrey was much older going in, and we knew his would be the hardest transition. Right now, he is moving forward, but his progress is only barely satisfactory. We are doing everything we can, but he appears to be fighting it. We will continue to force integration, but if he does not find a way to embrace the change, well, I cannot guarantee success."

Erica didn't have words. She felt her eyes grow wet and tears begin to run down her cheeks. She sounded composed, but she was not. "Okay. Maybe you should have Stephanie and Heather talk to him."

"They are not able to at this time."

"What about me? I have known Jeffrey for many years. Would it help if I stopped in and talked with him?"

"Erica, I believe that would be the best thing we could do. When can you be here?"

"In two hours."

She ended the call abruptly and called Arabella. "Get the jet fired up, emergency flight to Rochester, right now."

Arabella told Richard and they began a fast coordination for transport for Erica to Rochester. Arabella thought perhaps Jeffrey had died, she was in such a hurry. But she didn't question her. They landed in Rochester and a suburban was waiting to take her to the hospital.

When they arrived, Dr. Gustafson welcomed her and escorted her to Jeffrey's incubation room.

'He is mostly in his new body, his new brain. The problem is that he has not embraced the new body, and if he continues to delay this process from the inside, everything will begin to fail, and the end result will be his death."

"Can you reverse the process, so he can resume living in his old body?"

"Sadly, no. He has gone too far for that. His old body has already been processed and is no longer a viable entity."

"Oh. Okay, I don't want to know what that means. What can I do?"

"Sit down, hold his hand, and talk to him."

The doctor left the room, leaving her alone with this new Jeffrey, a young twenty-four-year-old. Erica pulled up a stool, reached out and held his hand.

"Hi Jeffrey. I am scared. I need you to be here to help me understand and create this brave new world you started us towards. Did you know we have discovered faster than light travel? We have, but things are also getting complicated."

She stopped talking as tears began running down her cheeks. "Jeffrey, I love you. I have loved you for so many years. Please come back. I don't know how I will survive without you in my world. You brought me a new life, hope, strength. You made me who I am. I miss you so much. I loved working for you and the travels and conversations we had."

Erica continued to talk about their adventures, her life, Heather, and just everything she could think of. It had been hours since she got here. She needed to take a break and go to the bathroom. Suddenly the doors opened, and Dr.

Gustafson and several nurses entered the room. She thought something bad had happened. "Doctor is everything okay?"

"Erica, you brought him back! His vitals stabilized while you were speaking to him. I believe he will make it now, thanks to you! You saved his life!"

Erica was speechless and watching, when suddenly Jeffrey opened his eyes. He didn't say anything since he had no motor skills yet. But he connected with her eyes. She felt a surge of energy and hope, and love in his look. She thought, I wonder if this is what he and Heather shared? She reached out and held his hand again and he closed his eyes.

Erica decided to wait around and see how things developed. She had Arabella clear her schedule for a couple of days; there was nothing really critical coming up. She told Arabella what had happened and asked her to call Derek and find out the status of the building project.

Doctor Gustafson finally walked into the room where she was waiting. "Thank you, Erica. Without your voice and touch, I believe we would have lost him. As it is, we have moved him to his recovery room and will soon be able to move him into his comfort room. We can understand the science, but there is still a lot we simply do not understand. How is it that a gentle emotional voice and touch of someone you love can cause such a tremendous change in biology? We don't know."

"I do love him, and I am glad this helped. However, I have a more serious need to speak with you. Can we go to your office for some privacy?"

Once there, Erica made a cup of coffee and she and Arabella sat down with him.

"Here is the deal, doctor. If this rejuvenation process becomes public knowledge, a couple of things will happen. First, you may be charged with a crime, destroying bodies, murder, or killed by a mob. Second, you may become the most sought-after person on the planet and be offered ridiculous sums of money to provide this service to people, which would infuriate the masses, leading to the first option. I simply do not see this as something we can advertise we do, at this time."

"Yes, the staff here, we are not too many people, but we have talked about this for a long time. We believe this is a process that should be kept quiet in its totality, while we roll out some parts of it, like organ replacements and such, that can help elongate life. Our problem is we don't know what to do."

"That is where we come in. We have discovered faster than lightspeed travel."

"What? Really? When?"

"We recently discovered this, and we are working now to build starships that we can use to explore the galaxy and find a new Earth. I would like to take you and your team, plus their families if they wish, and all of the equipment and knowledge you have gained and move you with us to a new planet. There is nothing that would stop anyone from going there for this treatment, but it would be a safer, more controlled process."

Doctor Gustafson thought for a moment. "I would need to talk with the staff."

"Doctor, before you do, let us get the starship fully operational. Otherwise one of your staff may say something to someone and before long everything is public knowledge and we are all trapped with no escape. I want to make this right for everyone; but need more time. For now, you have several clients that need your help. We don't anticipate doing anything for a year, so there is no rush. You might want to simply raise the conversation, once we make a public announcement that we have solved lightspeed travel, that you sure would like to go to a new planet and see what the response is."

"That is an excellent idea. Okay, I will keep this conversation secret, but be aware of the possibility and start quietly planning on my end. I hope this works. We can hone this process and improve it. It would be great if we had access to some more powerful computers, that would be a huge tool in our research."

"We are building some computers that are incredible, and you would have access to those. Okay, we will get going. I will be in touch. Let me know when your patients can receive a visitor, I would like to talk with them before chaos ensues."

13.235.10

This time the riots began in New Delhi and quickly spread to Dhaka and Jakarta. They did not believe the Federation or JW Enterprises were anything more than a sham, getting a few people rich, and establishing a new level of control over everyone. This time there was damage, as buildings were destroyed, and people were killed.

"As you can see behind me, there are several buildings on fire, cars are smashed, and riot police are using water cannon and tear gas to try and control these rioters."

"We spoke with several rioters and here is just some of the comments they made."

"These are nothing more than rich Americans still trying to run the world!"

"Ungodly! They seek to deny the Prophet!"

"A new world order led by a chosen few!"

"These people are murderers! They deny us our basic rights!"

"So, you can tell there is a lot of anger towards JW Enterprises and the Federation here. We will keep reporting as the situation changes."

Arabella turned the television off. "No employees of JW Enterprises were killed, although a few were roughed up and injured."

Erica stood and looked out the window. Then said, "Pull all contracts with these countries. Also, let's re-evaluate our project model. This type of violence cannot be allowed to continue, but if this is how people are going to thank us for our support and investment in the infrastructure in their countries, we will simply go somewhere else."

13.237.09

"You are sure this is safe?"

"Well, no, we are not positive, but it is as safe as we can make it, and somebody has to test it."

"Yes, but you have three adorable babies at home. You can't take this kind of chance."

Erica was nearly pleading with Gabby not to take the first starship on the first journey to activate the Wilson-Drive. She feared what would happen to Gabby's children. She feared losing yet another person on this journey, and she did not believe she was strong enough to handle telling Heather about this loss, if it happened.

"Okay. I tell you what. I will let Simon take the ship out. By the way, do you know what we are naming the very first starship?"

Erica was relieved. "No, I have no idea."

"We have named the very first starship, Starship Erica."

Erica broke down in tears. She dropped to her knees and sobbed. Gabby ran to her and held her tightly.

"I am sorry, Erica, we thought you would be pleased."

"Oh, dear, I am. I am overwhelmed with joy and gratitude. I feel so loved and complete right now. You have no idea how much this means to me. It means my contribution is worthwhile and has value. Thank you!"

"Of course, you are valued, Erica. We could never have achieved what we have achieved without you. I love you. You are the one that keeps us focused and motivated."

Arabella had also come to Erica's side. "Erica, you are as powerful a voice today as Jeffrey was in his time. You are wonderful and provide all the leadership, support, and guidance we all need to stay focused and succeed."

Erica was very emotional for a little while longer. Finally, she was able to stand and thank them for their love and support.

Gabby took the next shuttle back to SB1. When she arrived, she met with Simon and Derek and informed them the test flight was a go. She did not tell them she had agreed not to go.

Gabby and Simon entered Starship Erica and closed the hatch. They went to the control deck and took their seats, tightening their harnesses. They thought they mostly knew what to expect, but really, they only had a hunch. They released all the attachments to SB1 and Simon took control and eased the starship out of its moors and into space. He increased speed and they moved away from SB1. They wanted to make sure there was no collateral damage from activating the Wilson-Drive close to an object, so they moved about twenty thousand miles away from SB1, also far enough away that unwanted eyes could not see them or their, they hoped, sudden departure.

When they were in position, they unhooked their harnesses and took some time to let each other know how much they loved each other. They kissed, touched, and spoke softly about their lives, hopes, children, and their shared dreams. Eventually, they climbed back into their seats.

"Star Base One, this is Starship Erica, we are one minute from activation of the Wilson-Drive."

Derek had a very small team of people with him who knew what was taking place. "Roger Starship Erica, Star Base One copies. Good Luck and Godspeed."

"Roger, out."

Gabby and Simon counted down. They checked and double checked all the settings and systems, and upon reaching the end of their checklist, they held hands and together, they activated the Wilson-Drive.

Instant vomit. Pure seasickness. Overwhelming nausea. Both of them were hit hard by these physical impacts. But intellectually they stayed with it, watching the sudden shift in the star patterns until they streaked by. Gabby watched the astrogation computer and realized the system was maintaining real time, even while moving in some ridiculous speed through space. Simon was watching the power settings and other system monitors and verified that everything was nominal.

After exactly one hour, they deactivated the drive and re-entered regular space. Gabby evaluated the data in the astrogation computer. "We have traveled seven light years in the direction of Cygnus X. I believe we are now ahead of the migration pods. In one hour, we have traveled seven light years."

"Wow. We did it."

"Well, we can see the stars from a position no one has ever seen them before. But now, can that super-computer we built astrogate back home, that is the question."

Using the astrogation system, she took various measurements and readings, and calculated a trajectory for the return trip home. After she entered the new coordinates in the computer, Simon gently reached out and took her hand, pulling them together.

They were in zero gravity, but that did not prevent them from getting out of their space suits. After a little while, as they kissed, Simon slipped her remaining clothes off, then sat back and smiled. "My goodness, I still marvel at how sexy you look. I marvel even more that you chose me as your husband."

Gabby shifted his way and removed his clothes as well. Then she pulled him along, and they floated down the hall, kissing as they went, and entered a stateroom, where they pulled themselves into the sleep webbing, which would give them some semblance of control.

Gabby kissed him deeply as he touched her gently, causing her to moan with delight. She responded and brought him where she needed him to be. Inside the webbing, they found security to move with each other and passionately expend the rising desire they shared.

Afterwards, they held each other, talking quietly of their love and life and their children. Only after they had felt it necessary, did they go back to the control deck and activate the Wilson-Drive.

After exactly one hour, they deactivated the drive and re-entered regular space. This time, they did not experience sickness, so attributed the first wave of nausea to not knowing it would occur. After some checking, they realized they were only a parsec away from Earth, so activated their Jian engines and began to cover the distance. They decided to wait until they had arrived at SB1 before they said anything.

By their calculations, they had only been gone a few hours. This would be the test.

"Star Base One, this is Starship Erica, requesting docking instructions, over."

Derek and his team were completely overwhelmed. They had sat for a couple of hours wondering what had happened, knowing they would not hear anything for several hours. Upon hearing this radio call, they began shouting and screaming excitement.

"Starship Erica, this is Star Base One, you are cleared for docking at bay fifteen! Welcome home!!"

Gabby and Simon now knew they had achieved a lasting legacy. Their love was not only the best in regular space, but they had chosen lightspeed love as their legacy. They would always know this, maybe they would be remembered in some fashion.

They had learned a lot on this trip. Now they needed to figure out a way to manage the speed, so they could tell exactly how fast they were traveling, so they would know how far they traveled. Then they could plot a course for a star and know they would get there in a specific time or manage their speed to arrive at a designated time. This would still be difficult, but the biggest task was complete. They could now travel at speeds greater than the speed of light.

13.238.10

Gabby thought it best to brief Erica in person. She had instructed Derek to begin design of new starships, bigger than the SS Erica, that could be used to transport a lot of cargo, and with enhanced weaponry.

"Gabby come in. This is an unexpected visit. What's up?"

Gabby closed the door so there was only Erica and Arabella in the room. "We did it. The Wilson-Drive works."

"What? Oh my god! How does it work, where did it go?"

"First, Erica, Simon and I took it out. I know I told you I would let Simon take it out for the first test, but I couldn't let my husband go alone. We engaged the drive for one hour. We traveled about seven light years in the direction of Cygnus X, mostly towards the center of the galaxy. We would have either passed or been close to the distance the migration pods have traveled in almost ten years. After we calibrated the astrogation system we engaged and returned, coming out of the drive about a parsec from Earth. It was awesome!"

"That's fantastic! Congratulations! Wow, so we have a starship. That means we can begin exploring the nearby stars for habitable planets."

"Well, let's not get too far ahead. We need to figure out how to manage the speed, so we can tell how far we are traveling in real time, before we simply start jumping around. Otherwise we will waste a lot of time trying to figure out where we are and jumping around needlessly. Give us a year and we should have the system designed for seamless astrogation."

"A year? That seems like a long time right now."

"I know. But it also gives Derek time to build a few larger starships that can hold more and defend themselves."

"Alright, let's do this. You go work like crazy to get all the astrogation and speed control processes and whatever else you need to get figured out. You push to get this done as soon as you can. In the meantime, I am going to announce that we have broken the barrier. The Federation Council will want to build starships, but right now that means JW Enterprises is building them. So, it is still a controllable process. Not so once there are ten planets represented and we drop out of the council."

"We can certainly do that. We have already copied all the research from the Federation into facilities and labs on SB1. I suggest we cut back our research projects here and let the council know they can begin their own research once they begin funding it."

"Agreed."

"By the way, how are mom and dad?"

"You will be glad to know they are past the dangerous phase. It looks like it will be a one hundred percent success. I did stop by and take a look the other day, and I have to tell you, they all look young!"

"When will I be able to see them?"

"Dr. Gustafson said it will still be a couple of weeks. You should work with Derek to build a customized home for the three of them on SB1. That way when they are complete with the recovery, they will have someplace to live until they depart on the first true starship adventure into the galaxy."

"What do you mean? They are leaving?"

Erica knew Gabby would have a difficult time with this news. She herself had also been torn when Jeffrey had informed her that this is exactly what they hoped would happen. The three of them wanted to go see the universe, not continue to struggle with the same problems that existed here on Earth.

"Yes, that is their plan. Jeffrey told me before the rejuvenation that if it was successful, as soon as the star drive was ready, they wanted to travel the stars. So, since it is almost ready, we should house them close to the action. This also gets them out of the sight of any accidental siting's by the paparazzi. The last thing we need right now is for people to see Jeffrey as a twenty-four-year-old. I believe there would be serious hell to pay. We can let people know about this one day, but not right now."

Gabby knew Erica was right. Arabella walked over and put her arm around Gabby, saying, "You know this is the right thing to do. It will protect them and give you plenty of time to spend with them in the next year."

"I know, and yes, I agree. Okay, we will get right on this."

Gabby left, but in her mind's eye she was making bigger plans. When she returned to SB1, she pulled Derek aside and they had a very long conversation. They weren't going to just build a home for the three travelers. No, they were going to build a connected, multi-level accommodation for about thirty people. She did not plan to remain on Earth if her mom and dad were traveling to the stars. Her family was traveling together.

13.243.08

Jeffrey, Heather, and Stephanie were in paradise. They had young bodies! Stephanie was the first up and moving. It had been a few weeks now and she was doing physical training, calisthenics, yoga, karate, and other physical activity to get her into the best shape possible. She loved her new body. Heather was a good week behind Steph, but she too was doing some excellent workouts. She was working with Stephanie to get up to her level and learning the skills of self-defense. Jeffrey was the last one up. But even after only one week, he had nearly caught up with both of them. Together they had some awesome workouts.

Jeffrey and Heather also had something else. They had made love with their new bodies and discovered again a wonderful part of the love they shared. Now they would be able to grow together for centuries. Heather couldn't wait to have babies, but Dr. Gustafson had advised her to not take that action for at least a year, so they could make sure everything about her rejuvenation was complete. She reluctantly agreed to an implant that prevented pregnancy.

The three of them were sitting in their lounge laughing when Dr. Gustafson brought Erica into the room. They all got up and went to her and there was a lot of hugging and crying.

"My God! Look at all of you! You are younger than me and beautiful. Wow! I am in awe."

"Yes, and yet you know we have the memories and minds of those old people you knew only recently."

"Excuse me Jeffrey, but I was not 'old.'"

Jeffrey laughed. "You are right, Steph, you were not. I would say Heather probably was not. But I sure as hell was."

"Dear, you were old and grouchy. But now you are young and sweet."

They all talked and laughed for a while. Finally, Erica broke in to remind them they needed to have some serious conversations.

"Yes. Well, there have been some changes since you three decided to escape from reality for a while. For starters, we have proven the star drive."

"What? That is fantastic! How does it work, when did it run?"

"Let me explain. Gabby and Simon discovered the means. We built the ship, then they took it out and it works. There is still a lot to do to get it to be controllable and useful, but it is a working star ship. By the way, they named the star drive the Wilson-Drive, and they named the first starship ever to travel at greater than the speed of light the Starship Erica."

"Where is Gabby, are they alright?"

"Oh yes, they are fine, and Heather, I told Gabby not to be on that testing run. She agreed with me, then did it anyway."

"Sounds like something you would do, Jeffrey."

"Oh no, don't bring me into this. I think she hung around Stephanie too much."

"No, no. I had nothing to do with this."

"Oh, whatever. But I am glad she is okay. Do you know when we will see her?"

"Dr. Gustafson said in about a week, so I am planning to bring everyone as soon as the press conference on the star drive is complete. But I wanted to have this conversation with you first, so we can discuss some issues."

Jeffrey said, "We know. We need to maintain a very low profile, because if anyone sees us in these new bodies and puts it together, all hell could break loose. What is your plan?"

Erica smiled at how Jeffrey would intuitively know what was going on. "We need to move you to a safe location, out of the sight of the paparazzi, where you can continue to grow in strength and plan your travels. I believe it would be a good idea if you planned to take the first completed starship and travel the stars. That way you are living your dream, and we are free of the worry of people finding out you are so young."

"Okay. Where?"

"We have been shifting our research and support functions to SB1 for a while now. Truly, all that is in Omaha now is the financial services organization supporting the investment projects around Earth. All the remaining fund management, administrative, and more importantly, research and development labs, are on SB1. We are looking at building three very large cargo/transport starships that can transfer a significant amount of our operation off-planet, when the time comes. They also are being armed with some advanced weaponry we are not even letting the Federation know we have built."

"With these ships we are also building three Federation ships, so they will see that we are still supporting their activity. Simultaneously, we are building explorer starships. These can house about forty people for some time, plus large cargo and other capacities, also with weaponry. I propose to give you one of these as your own personal starship. I would like you to go find us a planet we can relocate too, while the Federation ships look for those migration pods and see how they are doing. We will also look at seeing if we can find a way to get them to their destinations faster, if they survived."

Jeffrey looked at Heather and Stephanie. "We would love that, all of it. However, we might end up taking a few people with us. I know we would prefer our family travels together. That includes you, Erica. You are part of our family too."

Erica began to cry. "I don't know why you make me cry. I love you all. Thank you."

Jeffrey walked over and hugged her. "Dr. Gustafson told us that you saved me. He told us you came here as fast as possible when you were told I might not make it and stayed with me and talked with me, held my hand, and that your voice and touch is probably what saved my life. I owe you my life. I love you."

Heather and Stephanie also walked over and hugged her. They were one family, after all, and they intended to show it. After a little while, Erica was composed, and after some additional discussion, they had agreed to a plan.

13.251.10

Erica had Arabella coordinate a news conference at JW Enterprises. While the news she would release was important to the Federation, this was a JW Enterprises discovery and she intended to make sure everyone knew who got the credit. She entered the hall where several hundred reporters were gathered. The news conference was also carried on all available systems.

"Good afternoon. As most of you know, I am Erica Beckett, President of JW Enterprises. Today we have a very special announcement to make that will affect every person on the planet."

"As you remember, our founder and first President, Jeffrey Wilson, established three goals for the survival of our species. First was to build an asteroid shield that would remove the fear of this extinction level event from human concern. As you know, we successfully accomplished this quite a few years ago. Second was to send out migration pods so even if something terrible happened here at home our species would have a chance to survive on other planets. Again, as you know, we successfully accomplished this several years ago as well. The third item was to discover how to travel faster than light, so we could make interstellar flight possible."

Erica paused, and looking around the room, she said, "Today, I am happy to announce, that JW Enterprises has broken through this barrier and has tested a faster than lightspeed starship. It works."

The room was astonished, and every reporter tried to ask a question at the same time. Erica held up her hand for silence.

"Please hold your questions for a few minutes, there will be time. JW Enterprises has spent trillions of dollars on research and development of this system. There are far too many products to name on the market today that are a direct result of our efforts. These new products are only a small portion of the results of our research, and now, we have a stardrive."

"I know there are those who believe we are trying to establish control over many things; but the truth is, we are trying to limit government and free the human potential to discover, live freely, and accomplish all your heart desires. Part of this goal is a facet of this discovery."

"We envision a time in the not to distant future, when people will be able to travel to new planets. I believe at first this will be those who are explorers. Then we will need homesteaders with certain survival and building skills. It will be some time before this travel will be for luxury purposes only, although I am certain it will eventually happen."

"My word today is simply this. We have discovered faster than lightspeed travel. We are calling the star drive the Wilson-Drive, named after our founder, Jeffrey Wilson, whose vision made all of this possible. The first starship was named, not by me, but by the actual builders of the craft, the Starship Erica. However, we have only very recently made the first leap at this travel. It will take time, probably at least a year, before we understand how to control our speed and effectively navigate through the stars. Because of this, we need you to please be patient."

"Most people alive today will probably never travel to another planet. That does not mean anyone is trying to prevent this, it is just a simple matter of logistics. We have not even built any starships yet, much less any that can carry large numbers of people, but we will begin that very soon."

"Once we do build larger starships, which, again, has not yet even begun, one of our first priorities is to find the migration pods and check on them. We will try and see if we can speed up their missions to get them to their designated planets. These will possibly be the first planets we settle. Once that happens, travel will begin to be more regular. Immigration to these planets will speed up. We will begin to spread out to other planets and live among the stars. But it will take time. Please be patient. Now, I will take questions."

"Amanda Freen, Chicago Tribune; Can you tell us, where is Mr. Wilson? Shouldn't he be here for this event?"

"Mr. Wilson is currently in the hospital. He has been undergoing some tests. As you know, he had a mild heart attack several years ago, and periodically spends some time in the hospital for additional tests. He does know about this event and is very happy. However, he could not be with us today."

"Ricardo Espinoza, El Pais; What was it like? Going faster than light is something we have seen in science fiction movies, but in reality, what was it like?"

"Very good question, and one that I will ask our research director to answer. Dr. Wilson-Jackson, if you would."

"Yes. There were only two of us on the first attempt at this faster than lightspeed travel. My husband, Simon, and I worked with a great team and we built a small starship with the engine we designed. We were about seventy thousand miles above the Earth when we engaged the Wilson-Drive. Let me say, the first feeling we both had was horrible, we felt like we should vomit, felt terrible nausea and seasickness. The view out the window went from a steady starfield to a movement of stars, kind of like in some of the movies you are thinking about when they went into their drive. It was very troubling and caused both of us to feel queasy and unsettled for some time. That being said, we were on a mission and watched our instruments and systems and after one hour we disengaged the drive."

"We took star readings with our astrogation computer and discovered we had traveled seven lightyears away from Earth. We programmed our system and engaged the Wilson-Drive again, for the exact same amount of time as we had on the way out and ended up back here. So yes, it works; but as President Beckett said, we have a lot of work to do to learn how to control our speed, astrogate at speed, understand how to effectively engage and disengage to get to where we want to be and not take multiple short odd jumps, and begin to plot the stars in a new way. We will get there, but we are not ready yet."

"Cynthia Gilford, The New Zealand Herald; Does this mean JW Enterprises will pull out of the Federation? We understand you got it started, but also understand you will only be part of it until there are ten planets and then they pay for it all. Won't this mean the Earth will then foot the bill?"

"As you know, the President of JW Enterprises serves as the President of the Federation Council up until there are ten planets in the Federation. Once that happens, the role of JW Enterprises in the Federation disappears. We will not fund the Federation once there are enough planets involved to do it themselves. We cannot afford to fund the cost of maintaining a star system management program. We will provide the Federation services, at cost for the interim, but eventually at the same price as everyone else. We would expect the Federation to operate a bid process to get the best purchase for the best price. But that will be for them to decide."

"Michael Newsom, Daily Mail; You sound like you have already decided to resign from the Federation. What is your plan?"

"Well, no, I am not suddenly resigning. We have a process in place for this. Once there are ten planets represented in the Federation Council, which will take some years to accomplish, they will then elect a new President. The military assets, that now are JW Enterprise employees, will transfer to them, along with the cost. Same with the assets of the Federation. Everything will transfer to the Federation, at cost. Now we understand this may take a little time, so we will be flexible, but transfer at cost they will. At that point, JW Enterprises will only be a private company like any other. We will continue to do the good work we do, but with no government participation involved."

"Su Li, China Daily; Where do you want to go? When you get to take your first starship journey, where will it be to?"

"I just don't know. I assume that when I finally get to ride in a starship it will be to wherever the ship is going, the purpose and mission. I have to tell you though, I would love to go somewhere you could see several planets in the sky at the same time. I don't mean like we see them, almost as stars in the background, but actual planets close by. We have all seen things like that in the movies. I would love to see them in real life. Thank you, ladies and gentlemen, we have a very bright future ahead of us."

When the media event was complete, Erica departed for Rochester. She brought the entire close-knit employee family, plus Tamara, Gabby, and their families. In all there were about thirty people on the trip. After the Boeing 747 landed, the family was ferried into the medical facility in three different convoys.

Erica met Dr. Gustafson and explained that she had brought everyone to see Jeffrey, Heather, and Stephanie. He was very pleased with this and thought it would do them good. Dr Gustafson had Erica meet with them first, just to get them prepared for the visit.

"Everyone is here today. Tamara, Gabby, Michelle, Janice, Arabella, the kids; everyone. I hope you are ready for this, because this is going to be a big shock for you and everyone else. It took me a couple of days to truly come to terms with it, so please be patient. Well, here goes."

She left and brought everyone back in to see them. It was a reunion to beat all reunions. Probably the most shocking aspect of the transformation was how they looked. Tamara was now twenty-five years older, biologically, than her dad.

"Wow. This is so weird. You are so young."

"I know, but it feels so good! Don't worry, dear, I am still the same person you have known your entire life. I am still your dad, just in a different container. I still have all of our memories, good and bad, and the emotions, you name it, everything is still here."

"I get that, but you are only a couple of years older than Lily."

"Is she here?"

"I left her and Michael in the waiting area. I wanted to see you first."

"Thank you. While I know this is a shock to you, I think it will be even more of a shock to them. But I sure would like to see them."

"Let me go bring them in."

Lily and Michael, Jeffrey's grandchildren, were only twenty-one and nineteen, respectively. They understood, intellectually, that their grandfather, who was seventy, had undergone a transformation; but they were not truly prepared for what they found.

"Grandfather?"

"Hi Lily, Michael. Yes, I am your grandfather, but in a much younger body."

"But you look my age. Last time I saw you, well, you were really old."

"I know. We discovered a means to conduct a full rejuvenation from an aging body to a younger body. It is still me, only a younger version."

"Cool. I mean, that is really cool. Does that mean when I get old I can do this as well?"

"Well, Michael, I don't see why not."

"Does this mean we can live forever?"

"No, it does not mean that. There will still be accidents, mistakes, risks we face regularly. But if we are being smart and keeping our heads on straight, we should be able to avoid a lot of the issues that cause people to die early, so we do have an opportunity to live longer. But forever? No, that is not the idea."

"Grandfather, what should I call you? I mean, you are almost my age, and calling you grandfather just doesn't make sense."

"Good point. Well, if your mother doesn't mind, I would just as well have you call me Jeffrey."

"I think it would be the most appropriate choice, but I have to say, it is so weird having my children address a man their age as Jeffrey, who also happens to be their grandfather. This will take some getting used to."

Heather had also found some interesting discussions with Gabby. She was now biologically younger than Gabby by about six years. That meant they were close enough in age to be sisters.

"Mom, you are younger than me. It's, hard to grasp."

"I know. Not long ago I hugged a young lady, now I get to hug someone almost my own age. But never forget, I am still Heather, the woman you love and your mom. But it feels so good to be in a young body! Oh, my goodness I had forgotten what flexibility feels like. I love it!"

"I can only imagine. But I am so happy it worked. Now we can share our life together for a very long time. I love you, mom."

"I love you. I think you will probably have to call me Heather, except when we are alone. Otherwise, it would seem really weird."

"I agree, Heather. Now that feels kind of weird as well, but I'll get used to it."

Jeffrey finally brought everyone together into a single group.

"Hi everyone. Well, as you can see, we survived the rejuvenation process. Heather, Steph, would you two come up here also? We three are new, yet we also hold all the memories and emotions, intellectual capacity and competencies, that we had in our previous bodies. Something else, Steph has been teaching us hand to hand combat and other physical training. She is also going to teach us armed combat. We want to not only be able to continue our lives as we thought of them, loving, peaceful, giving, sharing; but we also want to explore and find new things, and these new skills may come in handy.

"I do not know how much each of you knows about our status, but Erica, if you don't mind, I am going to share our plan for the future."

"Before you begin, let me reiterate something we spoke of before this process began. This is all highly secret. Do not put any of this on any kind of social media or other systems. Tell no one, not a single soul. Again, if the person is not in this room right now hearing this, do not tell them. There will come a time when we can let people know about both rejuvenation and our plans for exploration. But today, for now, until you hear otherwise from me,

Jeffrey, or Arabella, do not say a word. This is very serious. Okay, Jeffrey, please go ahead."

"Erica is exactly right, this is very serious. It's easy for us to laugh and talk about how wonderful this is, this rejuvenation of our bodies; but to a lot of people this might be seen as body-snatching, murder, or just acting in a superior manner that they hate. So, please, keep this a secret between us."

"Alright, so this is the plan. We are building a family. Through biology and legal maneuver, our family consists of people you know of: me, Heather, Tamara and her family, Gabby and her family. What you don't know, is that our family is actually bigger than that. I would like to introduce to you for the very first time ever, Heather and my sister, Stephanie Williams-Wilson."

Everyone cheered, very happy for Stephanie, who never had a family but who touched each of their lives is a positive way. They came up and hugged her and welcomed her into the family.

"Thank you, Jeffrey and Heather, for finally bringing me into a family where I can love and be loved."

"You are welcome, dear. Now, there is another group who are also members of the family. Heather, Stephanie and I are pleased to announce that as of yesterday afternoon we have a new daughter and niece. I am pleased to introduce her to you today, our newest daughter, and Stephanie's newest niece, Erica."

Again, everyone was so happy and thrilled with the news. This was truly amazing. The family was growing, but Jeffrey was not done.

"Alright. Now, this is so much fun. The reason is that Heather and I know something the rest of you don't. That is this, that Michelle and Janice are also our new daughters. Come on up ladies!"

This made it almost unanimous with the people in the room. The only person who was not standing with the group hugging and laughing as one big family, was Arabella. Jeffrey quieted everyone down. He turned and looked in her direction. Everyone else stopped and waited.

"Arabella, you are relatively new to some of us, but not all of us. Erica?"

"Arabella, we have already been through a lot together. In the time we have known each other I have come to know a powerful, compassionate, thoughtful woman. We have discussed this, and you have made your decision. Would you please tell the family what the decision is that you made?"

Arabella smiled, and then stood. "Most of you do not know my background. Like some of you in this room, I did not come from a large family. My parents are deceased, and my brother is a preacher. I miss having family close, sharing, trusting, and celebrating. For many reasons, not least of which is the love I feel for Erica as my big sister, I do want to be part of this family, and as of yesterday afternoon, was legally adopted into the Wilson clan."

Everyone celebrated the latest member of the family. This was such a huge step and an unexpected part of this journey they were part of. After a while, Jeffrey had everyone sit down, with the exception of Erica.

"We have some plans and need to move quickly. Erica?"

"Yes, there are a lot of moving parts to this. But before we get into it, I just have to smile and say how wonderful it feels to have the entire family gathered together in one room. We are the Wilson family, and must trust each other. We must be true to each other. We are all that we have as we move forward, and our movement will be in a lot of different directions. Never believe something you hear. Always verify a rumor with a family member."

"Now, we are going to the stars. Jeffrey, Heather and Stephanie will be transferring to Star Base One. We have built accommodations for them. This is to keep them safe and away from paparazzi until we can get our first real starship built, which is already underway. Once that happens, they are going to leave Earth and explore the stars."

"We will follow in a timed deployment to a new planet to begin building a new home. We will also explore, we will also see the galaxy, but we have to be careful and do this a step at a time."

"So, there you have it. Heather and Stephanie will join me in the first exploration, everyone else will follow. Any questions?"

Gabby stood up. "I do not concur."

Heather had told Jeffrey that Gabby would disagree. They were far to close and Gabby still needed her too much to be separated for so long.

"On what grounds?"

"On the grounds that we are a family and we should stay together. I do not want to lose mom, Heather. I want to travel with her. If she goes into space, I am going."

"Me too. Dad, Jeffrey, I cannot sit here on Earth knowing you are jumping around the stars. My family is going with you." "Us too," "All of us should go," and other comments were voiced in the room.

Erica and Jeffrey looked at each other and started laughing. Everyone looked at them, then began to ask what was so funny.

"It is just that we talked about this and we just knew this would be the response. It is the clearest example yet of the love that lives within this family. We are all so very close, and no, we will not separate the entire family. However, reality says that we cannot all depart at the same time. Erica is the President of JW Enterprises and Arabella is her personal assistant. Gabby, you are the Director of Research and Development. We still have a company to run. We cannot run off into an unknown direction and leave the company behind. JW Enterprises is the vehicle we built together that provides all that we have. We must find a way to do both."

"Yes, and it is for that reason that Arabella and I will not be leaving any time soon. I have also asked Janice and Michelle to stay and help us keep working towards the future. One significant change is that we will move our corporate headquarters off-planet, once we have some rule clarification about ownership and intellectual property finalized at the Federation. Which planet? That is where Jeffrey and the rest of you who do depart come in. This is not a departure to go have fun. This is a mission to find us a suitable planet for a new life on a new world, one that we can build and bring representation to the council as a true planetary entity."

"That said, we will be making plans along these lines for the next year. Once Heather, Stephanie and I are in our home on SB1, we will begin bringing you up, one family at a time. We will make final plans there and start our next big adventure."

The family stayed together, visiting, talking, sharing, and loving each other for the entire day. Eventually everyone left except the three patients. Dr. Gustafson wanted to run one more set of tests before he released them. The next day the test results were perfect.

"Well, I am very pleased to inform you that all is well. You can depart whenever you wish."

"When will you and your team be moving?"

"Erica will be sending some transports next week and we will begin moving to SB1. We should be finished moving within a month."

"Very well, we will see you there. Thank you, doctor, for giving us a new life and renewed hope."

13.311.18

Even with the public statements, airing informercials and other communication, vast numbers of people did not believe JW Enterprises was telling the truth.

"They are criminals that must be punished!"

"They are already living in the stars while we suffer in this poverty!"

"We should take away their money and share it with the people!"

This time the violence was destructive and targeted. Four JW Enterprise projects were destroyed; a new hospital, a bridge, and two port improvement projects. Not only this, but three employees were killed.

Erica watched the report with a mixture of anger and sadness. She turned to Arabella, and said, "Shut down all projects everywhere for three months and get everyone to a safe place. We will reconsider our next steps, but for now, our employee's safety comes first."

13.325.10

"Madam President, we need to know what the plan is for developing our starships. We have been kept in the dark long enough."

"Ambassador Sorenson, I am not aware of the council being kept in the dark at all. Instead, we have been working to fully understand how the new star drive, the Wilson-Drive, actually works. I am happy to report that we believe we are getting a handle on it. Because of that, I was prepared to present to the council today a plan for building three starships for the Federation. However, if you would rather we sit around and complain because we aren't already living on another planet, go ahead, I can wait."

"Forgive me, Madam President. I withdraw my criticism."

"Apology accepted. Now, these three ships, the first of their kind, will be funded by JW Enterprises, as are all other Federation assets. As such, they are company property until such time as the Federation can fund these themselves."

"These ships will be able to accommodate an operational crew of seventeen, with one hundred marines. There is ample cargo space for rescue operations, storage, and other needs. Each starship will be outfitted with the latest offensive and defensive weapons technology. We expect them to be fully operational within a year or so."

"A year or so? What does that mean? That seems like an incredibly long time."

"Well, Mr. Ambassador, before we invented the star drive it was impossible. So, I think even two years is pretty damn good."

"Yes, of course, I meant no disrespect, Madame President."

"None taken. Ladies and gentlemen, we are moving quickly. This new technology will change the entire purpose and behavior of the human race. We will be engaged in trying to manage chaos. Please, we need to be patient and stick together, or this entire program will simply unravel."

"You are correct. Yet, it will be hard to sit back and wait. We need to be doing something."

"You are. You are supporting the continued mission of the Federation. This mission will be even more important now as we truly do begin to explore our galaxy. We will be tested. If we are so weak we collapse at the first challenge, well, we are poor examples for our species. One of the most important things this council can do is reach out to your respective countries and assemblies and let everyone know we are moving forward as quickly as we can. We are building starships. We will be able to begin exploring the galaxy soon. But it will not happen overnight. It will take some time."

"Ten years from now there will probably be hundreds of starships traveling the galaxy. Twenty years from now there will likely be in the thousands. It will happen quickly, but it still takes a little time in the beginning. This is what we have been researching and investing in."

"The last thing we need is panic or old animosities to raise their heads and pull us back into the past. This seems to be what is happening in some places right now, so, I urge you to please communicate regularly, let's keep the conversation going, and get the message to your people that we are working hard to build starships for a brighter future. We will provide a monthly update on the construction project and soon, very soon, we will have starships traveling the stars."

Erica had to talk for a while to get them to finally agree that this was the best process. She feared the entire Federation idea would collapse. What then? Chaos. Everywhere, chaos. It could lead to anarchy and riots the likes of which had not been seen. She may have to act quicker than she had projected.

13.328.14

The mission to move Jeffrey, Heather and Stephanie to SB1 was shrouded in secrecy. They had a military transport land in Rochester, so the suburban could drive inside. This way they were never outside where a camera could find them. The transport flew to the Federation, and the suburban drove from inside the plane to inside the hangar with their transport. Inside, they met Erica and Gabby, who flew with them to SB1.

Once they arrived, Derek had a transport with window shrouds in place that met them so again, no one could see who was getting off the transport. Once they were inside their new accommodations, they could finally relax.

"Wow, this is wonderful!"

Derek was very happy they liked the space he and his team had created. It was modern and very functional, but with soft touches, carpets in many areas, a very large living room with a beautiful view of Earth, and a fake fireplace. There was a wonderfully equipped kitchen, bar, even a wine cellar stocked by Sierra, and a large dining area. Their bedrooms were spacious and complete with all the luxuries of home. There were several hallways that led to a nursery, exercise areas, and a lot of bedrooms. Jeffrey was puzzled.

"Erica, this looks very big for a few fugitives to hide out."

Erica was equally surprised at the shear size of the accommodations. She looked at Derek, who smiled, and pointed to Gabby.

"Well, Erica, I decided that if the family needed a space, this should be it. There are enough bedrooms for everyone with spares. We can have the whole family here without feeling crowded. Derek also built two additional levels, above and beneath, that contain additional recreational spaces, quiet reflection spaces, and some surprises. It should be a great place to live while we build starships."

"As a matter of fact, my little ones already live here. Simon is sleeping with them right now, since their schedule has changed to match our working schedule. I take over child duties in four hours, while he gets up and works for twelve hours, then we switch. Of course, it would be much better if we had someone who could watch the kids while we worked, but we are making do."

Heather laughed a wonderfully fun laugh. "My goodness, Gabby. You know I would love to watch my grandchildren, so we can adjust the schedules as we need."

"Thanks, mom. But I am not sure Erica is pleased."

Erica smiled. "Well, it really doesn't matter at this point. However, you have given me a great idea. Perhaps we should bring the entire family here to live and work. We have moved corporate headquarters here, so most people are commuting anyway. This would give us a more central location."

Over the next few weeks they brought up the entire family. They also brought up a few people who wanted to be part of the exploration. Sierra and Chef Stanly had a son, Seth, and married shortly after arriving on SB1. They were very excited about the opportunity to explore the stars. Sierra had collected some of the finest vines in the wine industry and wanted to take them to new planets and see if they could grow and make wine on them and see how that would affect the taste and quality of the wine. Chef Stanly wanted to taste new ingredients and discover new ways of cooking. They made a wonderful addition to the group. Derek's family already lived on SB1, but they moved into the new accommodations so he and his wife, Ariel, could be closer as well. Maria and Alexandra wanted desperately to be part of this group who would begin life on a new planet, so they moved in too.

This was the entire close group. Together and working hard at managing the company, preparing the starship, and taking care of the youngest children. Many of the children who had grown up over the years were now in their late teens or early twenties. The young adults began seeing each other and some new romances began popping up. Very soon, there were a lot of young people falling in love. They were also very smart.

Everyone had to have a skill, trade, or something they brought to the table. They were going to explore the stars and it would be hard work. Stephanie had everyone participate in stringent physical fitness, hand-to-hand combat, and weapons training. They were going to be an army by the time they were finished, so they could always rely on each other in a crunch.

They were scientists, farmers, computer experts, meteorologists, doctors, nurses, astrogators, climatologists, miners, the list was exhaustive. Every skill they could think of, someone had to know it. There were about thirty of them and they were capable of settling a planet, and they were warriors, capable of fighting for it.

14.027.09

Erica waited until the family was settled, then she moved her office to SB1. She video linked to the Federation Council whenever they held a meeting. "Good Afternoon everyone. Construction of the three Federation starships is underway. We laid the main structural beams this past week, so they are technically solid machines now. I did have a question for you. What should we call these three ships?"

"I assume it would be presumptuous to call one the Enterprise?"

The council had a very good chuckle with this and chatted about it for a while. Finally, the Mars representative provided an idea. "Why don't we hold a competition and ask the people to provide suggestions? We could then have Earth name one, Mars name one, and JW Enterprises name one. That way we all get to share in naming the first starships."

"That is a wonderful idea. I will notify the United Nations and we will begin a competition at once. How long do we have until they are ready?"

"It appears we have about seven months. Our test starship is very near the end of its research into effective management of the Wilson-Drive. We are very close. Let's say everyone needs to have a name back to us six months from today."

14.207.10

When they met to reveal the names selected, the media were allowed to have representatives in the room. Erica had flown back to Earth for this reveal. She opened the council meeting, so they could finalize this step.

"Good Afternoon. Well, it has been six months and today we reveal the names of the first three Federation Starships. They will all be called FSS, for Federation Star Ship. To begin, we should decide who will go first?"

"Madam President, since we suggested the idea, I would like for Mars to go first."

"Any objection? Hearing none, please go ahead."

"Thank you. The people of Mars held an open forum and after a lot of discussion and some very candid arguments, we reached a consensus on the name of one starship. We will name one of the first three starships for the Federation, the Federation Star Ship Red Planet."

Everyone politely applauded the announcement and thought the choice was very appropriate and reflective of Mars.

"Very good. Now I believe it is the Earth's turn."

"Thank you. The people of Earth held many discussions throughout the many cultures, countries, and governments of all our people, and reached the conclusion that we will name one of the first three starships for the Federation, the Federation Star Ship Mother Earth."

Everyone again politely applauded this announcement as well and thought the idea of recognizing the mother status of Earth was very fitting for Earth.

"Another excellent name. As far as JW Enterprises is concerned, our choice of the name of the first Federation starship, is the Federation Star Ship Jeffrey Wilson."

Everyone rose to their feet and applauded wholeheartedly with this announcement as well and thought the idea of recognizing the founder of the Federation, the visionary who had made if all possible, was the very best idea ever.

"Thank you, everyone. Now we will complete the construction of the FSS Red Planet, Mother Earth, and Jeffrey Wilson. We hope to have these ready for their first flights soon. The crew is already on SB1 learning the ships systems and their complement of marines are also in place. Once they are launched, the first destination is the migration pods to check on their status and help them make the best decision regarding destination. With any luck, they will be fully operational within a few months."

14.214.10

The riots exploded in Cairo, spreading to Istanbul, London and Paris. People wanted desperately to participate in the new future. There was serious anger at JW Enterprises. The anger was mis-guided or mis-placed, since JW Enterprises had done so much to improve the quality of life and was just now getting ready to launch the very first lightspeed starships.

That didn't stop people who felt anger at their politicians, their lot in life, or their inability to influence world events. They hated that these privileged people would expand to the stars and they would be left behind! They were angry at rich people and powerful people. It truly did not matter if their lives were a little better because of the investments made, they still saw themselves as pawns of the uber-rich and powerful governments and corporations.

When the employees of JW Enterprises were attacked and some of them killed in Egypt, the second time this had happened in only eight months, Erica ordered an immediate evacuation of all employees worldwide from their operating stations to either safe houses in their own countries, or back to the United States for those who were assigned there but who traveled around the world providing financial assistance. This decision effectively shut down the investment strategy for building infrastructure on Earth.

"Okay, what do we do now?"

Brian, the oldest financial expert in the room, said it best. "We bring all of our resources back into a central account and establish a new bank. This bank will function like any other bank and make loans the same way. However, we make this the First Galactic Bank, making it clear by establishing a new currency, the *jhetas,* tied, for now, to the United States dollar. We can change this in the future."

"The point being, we will begin making loans off planet with a single currency for the galaxy. Everyone who travels away from Earth will only be able to use this currency. If the Earth wants to change their currency to this, so be it. But for now, we could create this currency for all galactic trade and loans, financed by the First Galactic Bank. I think this is a good direction. It also means the bank does not have to be on Earth; but can be anywhere."

"How do you spell the name of that currency?"

"J h e t a s. Jhetas."

Erica chuckled. "Okay, I'll bite, how did you come up with that name?"

"Easy, I took the first letter of the names of the key players in this process and found a word. The names I used are Jeffrey, Heather, Erica, Tamara, Arabella, and Stephanie."

Everyone assembled had a good laugh at this logic. "Well, I have to say, I do like it. I especially like the idea of opening the First Galactic Bank. Would this be a subsidiary of JW Enterprises, or a stand-alone entity, or would JW Enterprises be a subsidiary of the new larger corporation? How about if you and the attorneys get together and figure all this out, create all the necessary charters, letters, and any other legal submissions, move our money where it needs to be and get this off the ground. Please move quickly."

After they left, Erica said to Arabella, "What are your thoughts?"

Arabella said, "I think this this would be an excellent means to shift all of our activities off-planet. Creating a separate galaxy wide banking instrument and having control of the currency should give us legitimacy everywhere, even on Earth, should they apply for a loan. Shifting all our resources into this would give us several trillion dollars of cash to start this up. Then as we wind down all the current projects, if people still pay, we can bring that in as well."

"I agree. We also own a lot of assets we should liquidate. The Federation property and assets alone should provide us with a couple of trillion dollars. We could negotiate some type of a payment plan with the Federation. Maybe we could get a lucrative one-hundred-year contract in exchange for the money, or only partial payment for some benefit."

"Some concerns though. We would have to start thinking about where to house the people to work the bank. Perhaps opening a branch on each planet would be a logical step or opening several branch offices on Earth. Something more to plan."

"Yes, more to plan. I think I want you to take the lead on the bank process, Arabella. This way you will have your feet on the ground at the very beginning of this and can provide specific focus on this project."

"Sounds good. Also, Gabby has appointed her number two, Dr. Ignatius Rambolt, as the acting Director of Research. This frees her to conduct work traveling in the galaxy, while still being involved in key decisions."

"Excellent. I think that is why she and Simon worked so hard to establish the Interstellar Communications Network, so they could communicate across vast distances in near normal time. In any case, everything does seem to be gently coming together."

14.247.14

Jeffrey and Erica discussed which starship to use for his discovery journey.

"The six JW Enterprise star ships being built should remain for the uses you had in mind, Erica."

"Yes, you are probably right. Okay, then go ahead and plan to take the SS Erica for his journey. I believe they have retrofitted it with some advanced weaponry, so it is not a defenseless ship."

Gabby and Simon were excited because they would go as well and could continue to conduct research and evaluation on some ideas they had for the next generation of Wilson-Drive, and their key focus on gravity, among other things. This would give them time for their kids as well.

In all, the family travelers on this very first search expedition included Jeffrey, Heather, Stephanie, Gabby, Simon, Lakelyn, Lanica, and Landon. In addition, Sierra, Stanley and Seth were aboard. It was a small crew, but they were not expecting any hardships, just traveling and looking. Jeffrey would not make the migration pods his primary interest, as the Federation ships that would launch soon would do that. His goal was to find a planet.

The day finally arrived. They all boarded after saying farewell to the family left behind.

"We have completed system modifications and we are able now to manage our speed and direction, as well as use a more advanced system of astrogation. We have loaded all the stores necessary for this group to survive for a year without replenishment. We have upgraded and added weaponry for protection. All those on board have been trained on all the technology of the ship. Based upon this, the Starship Erica has completed testing and is now operational."

Everyone waited for Erica to make the decision.

"Erica, you are the president of the company. You have to decide what we do."

"Thanks, Jeffrey. Well, it looks like we are a go. This first ship will be for exploration. We need to know where the good planets are, so we can send follow-up migration ships to those locations. We also need to know if we have any concerns with safety for humans out there, or if we are free to travel as we please. Jeffrey, you are the Captain of this ship. You are tasked with this mission."

"Thank you, President Dr. Erica Beckett. We will do our best to find a suitable planet as quickly as we can." He then hugged Erica for a moment, and said, "We will be safe, Erica, and we will return."

They boarded the Starship Erica and took their stations on the bridge. It was not a large space, but there was room for about seven people. As Jeffrey was the Captain, he named Simon as the pilot and Gabby as the astrogator. Heather was the chief science officer, and Stephanie was the chief security officer.

"Simon, please take us out from the station."

"Aye, Captain."

They released moorings and slowly moved away from SB1. As they pulled away they could see the ships under construction and the vacant ships docking stations. One day, these would all be filled, and the world would be chaotic; but for now, it was peaceful and safe. Once they are far enough away, Gabby asked if they were ready for a really cool ride.

"Well, I guess it is too late to turn back now."

"Yep, I agree with Heather. Steph, are you ready?"

"Let's do this."

"Very well, Gabby, let's go towards the inner core of this arm of the galaxy."

"Aye, Captain."

"Very well, engage."

Gabby reached and initiated the Wilson-Drive, and they were off.

14.274.10

Erica was right - chaos ensued as people dreamed of travel to the stars. Reports came in from all over the globe of riots in the streets as people demanded a seat on a starship. They all believed there were already starships built and traveling the stars, and that the decision to only build starships in space, and only by JW Enterprises, was a purposeful decision to stifle their hopes and keep them trapped on the Earth - with only the elites and powerful being allowed to have access.

"We're live from Cairo, and as you can see behind me, there are thousands of rioters being met with water cannon and large contingents of police. So far, they seem to be focused on destroying property and burning vehicles of JW Enterprise properties. That seems to be where they are the angriest, at JW Enterprises."

There were thousands of rioters in cities everywhere, even in the United States. The media was highly negative of events and painted a picture of JW Enterprises as the overlord. Media and the airways were filled with negative and harmful messaging.

Missionaries popped up raising the prospect of the end of days. The Servants of Riser reappeared spreading their belief that humans should not travel from Earth. Islamic radicals became even more vocal in flaming the fire of hatred between religions. All in all, it had become a difficult situation.

To top it off, the Federation Council was in an uproar. "But Madam President, we cannot simply tell people to shut up! They want answers!"

"Mr. Ambassador, what answer do you want me to give you? We are building the very first starships as fast as humanly possible. We have nine starships close to completion. Even if those nine starships began making as many flights as possible, they could not move more than a few thousand at a time. We have to be patient during this time."

"Yes, but we have riots now. How can we control this?"

"Mr. Ambassador, perhaps you misunderstand the purpose of the Federation. The argument you are making is one that should be made at the United Nations or in your home country. The Federation has no role in the politics or crowd control measures of a planet. That type of intervention is strictly forbidden by our constitution."

"Yes, but as President of JW Enterprises you have leverage, you can speak."

"Very well then, this meeting of the Federation Council is adjourned. Now then, let me take off my Federation hat and put on my JW Enterprises hat." Erica stood and walked to a spot in front of them, saying, "Listen, you have riots in your countries because someone has been selling people lies while you have been silent. Power is up for grabs right now because you are not countering those lies with truth. I honestly believe that if you don't go to your countries and act, you will lose them."

"As for my company, I have already been forced to end our multi-trillion-dollar investment program on Earth, because the employees of my company continue to be put in danger. That means the infrastructure we were building to help make life better here for so many people will effectively begin to deteriorate once again. I fear this will lead to a re-emergence of the downward spiral we were on for so long, but we cannot endanger people simply because those who should act, do not."

"What do you recommend?"

"That's simple. Get your media machines running and counter this ignorance. Put the word out that we are moving as fast as we can. Show footage of the nine ships nearly completed but undergoing final inspections before they launch. Tell people that as soon as they launch we will begin building nine more, and then nine more, and then we will keep building for years to come. Start processes to select people for new exploration. Stop rioters because they are only hurting good people and infrastructure needed here to improve the lives of people. Take charge. Find the leaders of these groups and arrest them."

"We are going to the stars, ladies and gentlemen, but not everyone will make it. That is the truth. You may or may not want to speak this, but it is the truth. However, right now, if you don't act to regain the initiative in your countries, you will lose everything you have built, and you can forget your ideas of establishing a peaceful planet or your dreams of living in the stars."

The council mumbled but agreed that this was their responsibility. Once the meeting ended, Erica and Arabella, her personal assistant, went to her office.

"Arabella, I believe things will get out of hand. I want us to move up the departure of our remaining key staff and get them up to SB1 as soon as we can. I don't feel safe here anymore, even with a few thousand marines to defend us. I certainly don't want to leave any of our staff here. I would feel much safer for all our team if everyone was operating and living on SB1."

"Sadly, I agree with you. It seems we humans are still a little more emotional than rational or logical. Jeffrey seemed to hit the right note, I am not sure what that right note is today."

"Jeffrey was new. He arrived on the scene before people really saw and heard about daily space travel, much less, faster than light starships, and he brought a grand vision and a new idea. He did things that everyone saw as a benefit. Today people are so used to hearing about and seeing space travel they think it is more advanced than it is and more pervasive. I don't think even Jeffrey could change the tide down here now. I think the pressure is just going to keep building until it blows."

"Agreed. We leave for SB1 in one hour."

"I'm ready."

14.301.10

It took a few months, but eventually the nine ships were finished. Three of them were for the Federation and six were for JW Enterprises. Erica made a very big deal of these ships on the day they were declared ready. She held a live press conference from SB1.

"Good morning! I'm Erica Beckett, President of JW Enterprises. Today we have some very special news I believe everyone will want to hear. But first, I want to tell you the interesting thing about working in space, which we do. It's that we perceive time, or the clock, differently. We go by ships time, so to speak, so the days are a little different from a regular pattern on Earth's surface. Right now, it is mid-morning for me, but for many of you listening it is afternoon, evening, or night. We see this as we orbit the Earth, yet it is the same time, really."

"We also base all our measurement of time in a different manner than on Earth. Our time is based upon three hundred and sixty-five days of exactly twenty-four hours each. This is the space clock all starships and the Federation use to coordinate in real time and will use to log activities throughout the galaxy, once we begin exploration. The beginning was set for January 1 of the year Jeffrey Wilson received his trillions of dollars. So today, by our time reckoning, it is fourteen point three zero one point one zero. That is ten in the morning on the three hundred and first day of the fourteenth year since the beginning date. Our world has been changing at a tremendous rate during this time, which brings us to today."

"The reason I called this press conference is because I wanted to let you know of the recent accomplishments we have made building starships. As you can see behind me, there is a starship floating in space just off the SB1 dock. It is about two hundred yards long, so not too big. This is one of the very first nine ships we have just completed, whose main purpose is to explore to find new planets, and to find the pods we launched several years ago and see how those people are faring on their journey."

"It is important for you all to know that these explorer ships are the first ones we have built, and therefore the first ones heading out into the galaxy to see what is out there. They will be cataloging planets and helping to find places where humans might live. We need to know that before we just load up a bunch of people and go."

"The mission of these ships, and their launch, will begin in a few minutes." She turned to Derek, and said, "Please have all nine ships move to their launch positions."

"Yes, ma'am."

Turning back to the camera, she continued, "The next nine ships we build will be bigger. They will be about four hundred yards long and capable of taking passengers and cargo to those new planets. We hope to get the pods to good planets and match them with new people from Earth. That way a lot of the material needed to start a new life will be readily available. The pods, while a means to save our species, were also a means to transport a lot of heavy products outward so we could have it available for new planets, if needed."

"By the time we get the next nine ships built, we should have word back on which planets to go too. Then we keep building. We will build ships forever, because we need them for exploration, defense, trade, logistics, commercial travel, even recreation. We are on the verge of changing what we see when we look up at the sky at night. It will take time, but within a few years there should be ships leaving to take pioneers to new worlds."

She paused for a moment, the said, "There has been a lot of anger recently that we are somehow keeping this all secret and for only certain people. Well that is a lie. Our founder, Jeffrey Wilson, laid the foundation for this journey and explained our path to the future. We have remained consistent to his word and vision and have told you what we were doing and what we intend to do every step of the way. Three of these first nine ships will go to the Federation so they can begin searching for the pods and be available should we meet someone or something we need to fight. The others will be strictly exploration."

"Of the next nine ships, three will be for the Federation and six for commercial use, the same for the following nine. At some point in time, someone is going to build a new location to build starships. When that happens, we will not be building nine ships a year, but hundreds. That, ladies and gentlemen, is when space travel will really go crazy. I am looking forward to that day."

"President Beckett, the ships are in position."

"Very well. Ladies and gentlemen, people of Earth, please watch your monitor closely. Now, everyone please count with me, in ten, nine, eight, seven, six, five, four, three, two, one, engage!"

On the monitors, people had watched nine ships. Suddenly, without any reason, each one seemed to simply blink out, although it wasn't that, but it was so fast it was. Empty space was left.

"And that, is how quickly it is to engage a stardrive. I would be happy to take any questions."

"Elizabeth Diego, Los Angeles Times; Whatever happened to Jeffrey Wilson? He founded your company and set this in motion, but we have not seen or heard from him in many years. Where is he?"

Erica smiled, and said, "Jeffrey is old, but he is alive and well. Actually, I can share with you that he has already traveled at lightspeed. The very first craft we built for experimentation, the research craft that actually tested the Wilson Drive and then spent time mapping the stars, building the astrogation system, the Starship Erica, departed a few months ago with him on it. They are traveling the stars to allow him to see the wonders he had dreamed of, while they, too, search for viable planets."

"Alexander Stephanopoulos, The Athen News; There have been riots, and there is much anger at your company. The perception is that you have created an ownership of the means to get off this planet and you control who can leave. How do you respond to this situation amid the reality that you do have a monopoly on building starships?"

"It is true, we do have a monopoly on building starships." There were rumblings among the media at this response, but she continued. "However, I would point out that this is not unexpected. Remember, this is all brand new. We only discovered the means to travel at speeds faster than the speed of light in the past two years. We only discovered this because we spent trillions of dollars on research. We spent money to build the Federation because we believed we would achieve this milestone at some point."

"I would remind you of the vision of Jeffrey Wilson, our founder, whom you just mentioned. His vision was to eliminate the extinction level events we could control. Through his efforts, we eliminated the potential for an asteroid to destroy us and we eliminated our possible extinction by sending out pods in various directions to ensure our species would continue even if something we had not envisioned occurred."

"Today we have reached the point he dreamed of where we have starships that can begin the exploration of our galaxy and set us on the path of expanding into the galaxy and settling many different planets around many different stars. So, it amuses me that people would be upset that we are where we are. We have talked about this and have followed this path for many years. There is no secret, there is no deception. We are building starships! We are going to the stars!"

"Amanda Holcomb, Atlanta Constitution; How many people will be able to take advantage of this opportunity and leave Earth?"

"A good question without a good answer. Today, no one, except the people assigned to these nine starships, will be able to depart the Earth. The reality is, most of us, people alive today, will likely never get off planet Earth, because there are too many people to take everyone somewhere else. That is not meant to be mean, just a statement of fact. Realistically, it would take hundreds of starships departing the Earth every day just to keep up with population growth, much less give everyone a chance."

"However, one day I believe there will be multiple companies building starships and it will no longer be a monopoly that we hold with our limited production. One day there will be hundreds or thousands of starships, possibly huge commercial passenger starships, traveling to hundreds of planets. I look forward to that day. But until then, we will continue to do what we do and continue to move forward."

15.101.10

Erica was beginning to understand more of what Jeffrey had meant, when he had said ten years was enough for anybody to lead this company. JW Enterprises had so many moving parts, was going in so many directions, and through the Federation project was engaged both as a business and a political entity. It was a lot and she knew it would wear her down. She realized that she needed to start seriously thinking about her own retirement, which meant she needed to bring Arabella into the conversation in a stronger manner and let her know she intended to follow Jeffrey's lead.

"Arabella, can you come in for a moment?"

"Of course, what's up?"

"Please take a seat, I need to speak with you about something."

Arabella was a little nervous at the way Erica had said this, but she sat down to listen.

"About ten years ago or so, when I had been with the company for about five or six years, Jeffrey informed me he was retiring, and that he was going to name me as his replacement. He also informed me I should begin looking for someone to be my personal assistant, someone who could be for me who I was for him. Through that process, I found you."

Erica paused and then sat down beside Arabella.

"Well, it is my intention to retire after ten years as President of JW Enterprises and the Federation Council. One other thing I intend to do is to announce you as my replacement. If you accept, you should begin looking for a personal assistant who can be for you, who you are for me."

Arabella was shocked. She had never expected this or thought about it. "Seriously? I had not even considered that idea. Why would you want me to run this company?"

"Because you have become the most qualified person in the room and the only one I can imagine taking control and running this business."

"Is this the way it always goes? After ten years your assistant becomes the President?"

"No, it isn't an automatic promotion. Jeffrey had said that he could only run this business for ten years and believed we should establish a pattern of ten-year leadership terms, but it is not a requirement. However, after being both his assistant and now the owner of the company, I can tell you, I also believe ten years at the top is enough. But maybe your personal assistant will not be as qualified as you are and will not be able to replace you, or maybe the business will change and morph into something one person can manage, but that is for you to find out and decide."

Arabella chuckled, saying, "You mean to tell me that you and Jeffrey knew you would be his replacement for four years before he retired?"

Erica chuckled as well. "Oh, yes. And he made sure I was challenged with everything possible to help me grow into the leader I needed to become in order to do just that. Should you accept, I will challenge you as well, for the same reasons."

Arabella thought for a moment. "You are really sure this is the right decision?"

Erica smiled, and said, "If I had any doubt, I would never have informed you."

Arabella smiled, and said, "Thank you. Okay then, I accept, Erica. I am scared and excited, and I am a little nervous about the challenge, but I accept."

15.127.12

Tamara was totally excited. Her son, Michael, had graduated from the Academy a few weeks earlier, and after a vacation with friends, was coming home. She soon heard the knock on the door and almost ran to it to open it up. She wrapped her arms around him, saying, "Hi Michael! Oh, I have missed you! I love you!"

Michael hugged his mom. "I love you, mom! It is great to be back home. I wish grandpa was here."

"I know. He is so proud of you, but for now he is traveling the stars looking for our new home."

"Yeah. Is Lily here?"

"She is out shopping but will join us for dinner. We are eating with Erica's family tonight."

"Great! Finish the Academy and then have dinner with the Federation President! Wow, mom, are you sure about this? Couldn't we just have a quiet dinner at home?"

Tamara laughed. "It will be fine. Just like your grandfather, she is only Erica when we are in private, so no pressure."

About that time the door opened, and Lily came in, saw her little brother and jumped into his arms. "Hey little brother! I have missed you! Glad you are home finally!"

"You know sis, it's not like we have not seen each other for three years. After all, I did come home for holidays."

"I know, but now you are home for good!"

It wasn't long before Steve arrived, so they had a true family reunion.

"Hi dad!"

"Hi Mike! Good to see you!"

"Mom says we are having dinner with Erica tonight, but can't we have a small family dinner here?"

Steve looked at his wife, and smiling, said, "There are many lessons in life you need to learn Michael. One of the most important lessons is to keep your wife, or in this case, your mother, happy. So tonight, we eat at Erica's."

At point one eight they walked down the hall to Erica's apartment. Erica met them at the door and invited them in. She was also excited because her daughter, Khloe, was home from completing nursing school.

"Please come in! Dinner will be ready in a few minutes. In the meantime, Steven can fix whatever you would like to drink. Addison, please take their jackets. Khloe, would you help your father serve drinks and place the hors d'oeuvres on the coffee table?"

Everyone was in motion, until Michael and Khloe saw each other. These two had grown up together, only two years apart. But now, in this instant, something was different. They made eye contact and Khloe blushed. Michael stumbled over his hello. Erica and Tamara exchanged a knowing glance, and both smiled, believing these two made a perfect couple.

"Hi Michael. I am glad you are complete with the Academy. Do you know what you plan to do now?"

"Hi Khloe. No, I don't have plans yet, but it will probably involve space exploration. How about you? You just completed your nursing program, didn't you?"

"Yes, and I also want to do something that involves space exploration."

The two of them sat together at dinner, and even though their parents were overjoyed at having them home and looked forward to conversations with them, they basically ignored everyone else.

"How was the Academy?"

"It was hard, but there were times it was super! I learned a new game there, Space Tetramax, ever heard of it?"

"No, you know me, I was never into the tech game stuff."

"Yes, I remember, you were always the one who would help people or give them the shirt off your back. You know, Khloe, you are the kindest person I have ever met."

Khloe blushed again, saying, "Thank you, Mike. I think you are the only one who ever tried to understand me. Your heart is also very big, just hidden behind that tough guy image."

Michael smiled, and said, "You know, Khloe, we are older now, and I have to say how sorry I am that I never even asked you out on a date. So, to make it up, would you go out with me?"

Khloe beamed, and whispered, "I would love that."

Over the next few days they left no doubt that a love was growing between them.

15.137.09

Arabella was determined to find the right candidate for her assistant position. She worked with the human resources staff to identify personal characteristics, communication styles and other needs. Once they completed these base criteria, they selected three individuals to interview. She reviewed the documentation on all of them and then flew them up the SB1 one at a time for a conversation. Once she was finished, she stopped in to discuss the candidates with Erica.

"Erica, do you have a minute to discuss a staffing issue?"

"Sure, come in. What's the problem?"

"Well, I am working on hiring my assistant, and it is difficult. Of the three we identified, and I interviewed, well, each one brings a set of strengths to the table, but I am not sure how to truly define which one stands out above the others."

"I understand. I had a similar problem, and as you remember, I brought you to Jeffrey, so he could ask a few questions to validate my decision. However, in your case, you must decide on your choice before I can validate it. Otherwise, if I interview them, it is my hire, not yours. Perhaps you should start fresh and see where it leads you? Also, Jeffrey said I should look for someone who complemented my own personality and skills, so I spent a lot of time pondering that, and eventually it led me to you."

"Thanks, Erica. I think perhaps you are right."

She thought about all that they had said and the candidates she had interviewed, and finally realized the reason she could not decide on one of them was that they were all just like her. In reality, she needed someone who was not like her, but complemented her.

She took a couple of days to do some soul searching, and then she revised the skills and characteristics she was seeking. This led to a different set of individuals available to interview. One in particular stood out, and she brought her up for a conversation.

"Arabella, this is Danielle McPherson."

"Hi Danielle, please come in and have a seat."

Danielle entered the room and after shaking hands, sat on the couch. "Thank you for seeing me Dr. Roberts."

"Please, call me Arabella. Can I get you anything to drink?"

"No thank you."

"Okay, so tell me about yourself."

"Well, I grew up in a military family. My father was in the Air Force and we traveled extensively throughout my years until I graduated high school. He retired in Omaha, so I went to the University of Nebraska in Lincoln. While there my parents were killed in a vehicle crash – a drunk driver hit them head-on."

"I am so sorry about your parents."

"Thank you. I continued to study and recently completed my MBA. I have been working full time at the Federation in administrative support for several years and hope to be accepted for a position on SB1 soon. My brother basically disowned me, because he said I was turning against Earth by supporting JW Enterprises, but he's always been an idiot. Anyway, I decided it was time to up my game. I am not married and have no children. I love sports, teams, reading, exploring, understanding, and volunteer as much time as I can to Big Sisters."

"Why do you want this position?"

"This position would allow me to work closely with you and learn even more about international and even galactic events, learn how strong females lead and compete in today's environment, and be on the cutting edge of our exploration of the galaxy. This is more than a dream job, it is a superb opportunity."

Arabella had reviewed her background check, security information, notes from people who knew her, transcripts, and anything that could be found to define her. She looked at her and said, "Follow me."

They walked down the hall and Arabella knocked on Erica's open door. Erica said, "Come in."

"Erica, this is Danielle. Would you please ask her some questions?"

Erica smiled, remembering when she had done this with Jeffrey. "Of course. Good morning, Danielle."

Danielle could hardly breathe, she had not expected to be brought in to see the President of the Federation and JW Enterprises. She stumbled a good morning in return.

"Okay, so tell me, what do you see as the toughest challenges we face, and what are your thoughts on overcoming them?"

Danielle was taken aback for a moment, then responded, "President Beckett, it appears to me one of the toughest challenges ahead is how the people of Earth adapt to the reality of outward migration. In time, this will begin to remove the best and brightest, leaving a continuously shrinking pool of brain power. It may not be felt for some time, but it will not be too many generations out before this loss may become evident. The problem is the Earth retains significant weaponry, animosities, divisions, and influence in human affairs. Absent a means to assist in resolution of these issues, it could get very ugly in the future."

"As to how to overcome it, I can only think that the support JW Enterprises has provided in infrastructure buildout and the establishment of a Federation where the rights of all planets are protected, are the best efforts to mitigate this. There will come a time when the Earth will need to sort itself out, and that is beyond anyone's ability to mitigate, so the strength of the new planets and the Federation may be the only thing that prevents the Earth from destroying itself and others."

"Very good. Thank you, Danielle."

Erica looked at Danielle and nodded.

Arabella said, "So, Danielle, when can you start?"

Danielle looked from Arabella to Erica and back. She had a huge smile on her face. "Really? Seriously? Oh, my God, I can start right now!"

Arabella laughed, "Okay, how about if you close up your activities in the administrative section at the Federation and start up here on Monday at eight in the morning. Also, pack for a long stay. You will be assigned quarters on SB1, so you will not be commuting, but living here."

"Oh, my gosh, yes! Okay, I am so thankful for this opportunity. I promise you will not be disappointed."

After she left, Arabella said, "That was me when you offered me this job."

"Yes, and that was me when Jeffrey offered me this job. I think you made a very good choice."

15.148.8

The first galactic explorers were deep into their exploration. Erica had sent Jeffrey, Heather and Stephanie away from SB1 to avoid the possibility they may be seen. There would be too many questions if people saw Jeffrey as a twenty-four-year-old instead of the seventy something they believed he was.

They had launched this first starship, the SS Erica, before the nine ships being built at SB1 were finished. This had been the very first starship to achieve travel at greater than the speed of light, and one day it would end up in a museum, if it survived.

Gabby was ecstatic. She and Simon raced into the control deck with the news.

"Jeffrey, I believe we have found a way to overcome gravity!"

Everyone on the deck was shocked.

"Really? You mean we can finally land our starships directly on the surface without all that heat shield and turbulence re-entry stuff?"

"Yes! Once we outfit our ship with this new technology we can go as slow as we want through the atmosphere and land, without worrying about our ship being damaged or harmed by gravity. Same for launch, we can simply fly straight up into space without the speed required to break free from gravity."

"That is wonderful!"

Heather thought this would be something to name after these two. "Tell me, Gabby, what do you propose to call this gravity solution?"

"Simon and I would like to call it the Wilson-Jackson Gravity Management System, or WJGMS for short."

Heather smiled, knowing this would be a wonderful legacy for her daughter.

"Wonderful!" Jeffrey was delighted, he hated turbulence, and re-entry was the worst. "When can we use it?"

Simon said, "Well, we thought we would provide the technical details to Derek on SB1 and let them test it on a vehicle there. That reduces our risk and puts the testing where it belongs – where we are building new starships."

"Good plan, Simon. Please make it so; and well done, you two."

Gabby and Simon beamed with joy and turned and ran to their lab to prepare to transmit the details of their discovery.

"It is hard, sometimes, to remember those two are geniuses and parents, since they act like such kids at the same time."

Heather laughed. Stephanie smiled, and said, "Yes, they do seem immature. But they are having the time of their lives and yes, they are definitely geniuses."

Everyone, not just the geniuses, were having a blast. They had stopped in so many places and simply marveled at the beauty of the galaxy. The nebulas, stars, everything was so beautiful. They had stopped at numerous planets and explored a couple as possible sites for settlement. They could look up into the sky sometimes and see where Sol was, just a speck of a star in the sky, knowing that the Earth was by that star. It was humbling and exciting.

The last planet they had visited had spectacular views of the heavens.

"My God, Stephanie, just look at that sky!"

"I know, it is so colorful and rich."

"I think it has every color of the rainbow in the clouds. It is so deep and pure. Startling."

"Yes. By the way, does it seem the plants are moving?"

They all stopped and watched for a moment.

"Yes, those big leafy ones are definitely stretching in our direction. We should take samples and see what their chemistry is."

They had avoided touching it, but once they had a sample and observed it under a spectrometer, it did not provide any hope these plants would be something humans would want to live beside. They seemed to be what they were, some form of carnivorous vegetation to be avoided at all costs.

So far, of the fifty planets they had physically visited, they had found ten planets where humans could survive, and three planets they believed were highly suitable for human habitation. They were interesting percentages, but they were not looking for perfection, just something that fit in the ballpark.

"You know Simon, it seems the planets we are rejecting are much more interesting than the ones we can live on."

"Yeah, I noticed that too. They are harsher, brighter, and tougher looking."

"It seems that the thin bandwidth of planets where we can relax and thrive is even narrower than those we could live on, even if uncomfortably."

"You know Gabby, I wonder if there is some algorithm we could put together that would help in the survey process?"

"Let's take a look at the data and see what we can come up with."

They also enjoyed life on a starship. Heather enjoyed watching Gabby and Simon's toddlers more than the others, but they all enjoyed the camaraderie of the close quarters. Stephanie insisted they all participate in strength training and physical combat training. They were all tough and worked hard at maintaining it. They ate wonderfully, because Chef Stanley could create magic with limited resources. They studied and learned about various subjects. They had a lively debate on what they were doing.

Heather loved being out here among the stars. Going from star to star, searching for planets. It was not just work, it was fun.

"I think the prettiest planet we have seen was that ice planet. Those blue-green colors were like emeralds sparking in the night."

"Well, dear, I can't argue with that since it was beautiful, but really, that red planet, with all the colors of red you could imagine, from bright fire truck red to deep crimson and how they flowed like rivers of color – to me that was the prettiest."

"Can't argue with either of you about that. But you have to agree the triple planet group we saw was gorgeous. I mean their colors may not have been that outrageous, but the combination of the three of them turning together around their sun so close together, that was wonderful."

"We are truly blessed."

15.160.17

"Where are we this time?"

"Not sure. It is a time/distance trip. We are going to come out about three parsecs from the star, a white dwarf. Simon and I want to test our new algorithm on planet identification in a new star system to see if it works, so our exploration can go quicker."

"Very well, let's see what's out here."

BOOM!

"Look out!! Meteor!!"

"I see it, trying to avoid!!"

BOOM, BOOM!

"Hull breach, port storage!!"

To be continued…

Made in the USA
Middletown, DE
17 April 2019